IMPERIAL
BO

HAMMER
and
CRUCIBLE

CAMERON COOPER

STORIES RULE
EDMONTON • ALBERTA

This is an original publication of Cameron Cooper

Copyright © 2020 by Stories Rule Press
Text design by Tracy Cooper-Posey

Edited by Mr. Intensity, Mark Posey

Cover design by Dar Albert
http://WickedSmartDesigns.com

FIRST EDITION: March 2020

Cooper, Cameron
Hammer and Crucible/Cameron Cooper—2nd Ed.

Science Fiction—Fiction

IngramSpark ISBN: 9781774382448
Amazon KDP Print ISBN: 9781774380062

Praise for Cameron's Space Opera

This is epic science fiction at its finest. Realistic far future worlds. Incredible characters and scenarios.

Cameron knows how to tell a story, regardless of whether we are going back in history or forward in time.

Until this book I had forgotten just how much I love good science fiction and Cameron's is not just good, it's exceptional.

The concepts are staggering and intensely interesting.

The Umb Judeste, *Beyond The Inner Elbow.*

STELLAR BARGES ARE GENERALLY RUN by family corporations. Mine, *The Umb Judeste,* belongs to Carranoak Inc. I hold a razor-thin majority of shares, so technically, the barge is mine. The irony of that struck me as I laid on steel decking, staring up at dazzling daylights, my jaw on fire. I had been slugged right on the corner of the jaw, in a near-perfect roundhouse swing, by the only member of the Carranoak family who could claim a second degree relationship to me.

Until that moment, I hadn't known she was on the barge. Perfect fucking greeting.

I had come down to the main concourse when I heard a supply frigate had emerged through the gate and was coupled to the *Judeste*. Supply ships provide a break from the routine. There's always something interesting on them, even if it was only the communications squirt which comes along for the ride when a ship used the gate. Current gossip is addictive, especially when you haven't got much else to do.

I stood at the edge of the swirl of new people carrying sacks or briefcases, or nothing. Some stared at the signposts for directions. *Judeste* personnel plucked travelers out of the stream and took them away. Others were regular visitors who strode off, confident of their direction.

I got startled looks and second glances as the arrivals

passed by. I was used to it and ignored it.

One of the junior pursers, Jimmy, spoke to a tall woman with wheat colored hair which matched mine—or, I should say, mine as it used to be. She was tall, had a small sack over one shoulder, a military bearing and civilian clothes. Jimmy turned and pointed at me.

That got me curious. I waited as the woman wound her way through the milling arrivals. As she drew closer, I realized it wasn't just the hair which was similar. She came right up to me with a fast, long-legged stride, her face working. At the last second, I realized who she was.

Before I could open my mouth, she swung her fist. "Double-timing *broad!*" she ground out as her punch landed. I dropped heavily. Of course I did. I figure it's been sixty years since I'd last taken one in the face. The old bones have turned brittle since then.

As everyone lingering in the arrival area formed a loose circle around us, muttering to each other with delighted horror, I pressed my fingers against the tender spot and wondered if my jaw had dislocated. These days, tripping over my own feet could be fatal. My heart staggered, righted itself and decided to keep ticking for now. The sour taste of adrenaline made me swallow. Swallowing hurt, too.

"Hello, granddaughter," I croaked.

Juliyana bent and peered at me. Was she waiting for me to get up so she could take another swing? She'd have to live with disappointment.

Her face worked with the fury driving her. The anger checked as she watched me gasping. Her gaze measured me—properly, this time. Her mouth opened. Horror painted her face. "Shit on a shovel...you...you're *old!*"

"Not too fucking old to hit, though, right?"

Juliyana propped her hands on her knees, bellowing hard.

She was still a Ranger, last I'd heard, so it wasn't unaccustomed exercise shorting her breath. I'd seen guilt rip the guts of people before, though.

I held up a hand. "Help me up," I demanded. "Then you can explain to me what the fuck is going on."

* * *

"I thought you were way over on the other side of the empire," I said to Juliyana as the elevator pod rose up through the levels. We had the pod to ourselves because I'd shooed off everyone who tried to get on it. If I own the joint, I'd use the privileges which came with it. I wanted to be alone for a moment while I put myself back together. An old woman already looks vulnerable. No need to add to the impression.

Juliyana was an exception. Her, I wanted right next to me until I sorted this out.

"You were in the war with the Quintino Rim folk," I added. Talking was not fun.

"The Quintino offensive ended ten years ago," Juliyana said stiffly.

I shrugged and pressed my fingers against my jaw once more. I'd ask Andrain to scope the bone, just in case. I was his most consistent patient, these days.

As we passed through the greenhouse levels, Juliyana squeezed the strap of her sack, her throat working. I noticed and stayed silent. The anger would push it out of her. No need to tax myself going after it.

She held onto her tongue until we got off the elevator at my level.

"You're not at the top?" she asked, surprise lifting her voice, as she peered up and down the blank corridor. Unlike most strangers to the barge, she had correctly named the ori-

7

entation. Arriving ships always emerged through the gate with the bulk of the barge to their right. The wharf was at the bottom, down by the reaction engines. Ships cruised the length of the barge, all two kilometers of it, to reach their berth. Newts erroneously assumed the irregular, ugly triangular barge was lying down, despite internal gravity running across the ship.

If Juliyana had been a typical newt, she would have asked why I wasn't at the end of the ship, not the top of it. But then, if she had been a typical newt, she wouldn't have known the top of the ship was where the senior members of the family lived, and corporate headquarters were located right beneath where the gate attached to the ship like an astronomically sized hook-eye.

Because Juliyana was a Ranger, she was used to quickly orienting herself according to the local gravitational pull, even in strange places. "Up" was always against the pull of gravity. The convention saved officers from handing confusing orders to subordinates.

I stopped myself from being impressed by her grasp of local conventions. "Why should I be at the top?" I asked, as I headed down the corridor. "I'm not the CEO." I palmed open the door to my apartment and let her in.

I followed, moving stiffly. I went straight over to the printer, clicked though to analgesics, and selected the biggest dose of the strongest meds the terminal would issue me. In response, it demanded my finger. I put my forefinger against the pad, let it draw a drop of blood. That would have Andrain demanding I attend his clinic, for sure. I'd deal with it later. For now, I just wanted to numb my jaw. I guessed there was a lot of talking ahead.

The printer pinched the end of my finger and injected the painkiller.

Juliyana parked herself on the only comfortable chair in the sitting room and stared at the wall. I had it set for a tropical beach. The waves were crystalline clear and made a pleasant background murmur. The sun was hot, and the sand came right up to the edge of the floor.

"Get out of my chair."

She picked up her sack and stood. I sat down.

Juliyana looked around for another perch. Then she shrugged, put the sack at her feet and straightened.

"Start talking," I told her.

She stared at me, instead.

"Ten seconds, then I'm paying you back for the punch."

She blinked. "It's just...you're different from how I remember you."

"I got old. It happens."

"I've never seen it before. Does it...hurt?"

I scowled. "Your ten seconds are up."

She put a hand on her hip. The hip was just above where the butt of her pistol would normally be. A furrow dug between her brows. I wondered if she was aware of how much she projected her thoughts. She said quickly, "You set up my father. You handed him over to the Imperial Shield." Her expression darkened and her jaw grew hard. "You got him killed."

Then, damn it, she wept.

While Juliyana got her shit together, hunched up in my chair, I printed a second armchair. I could afford that much. While it was growing to full size, I printed two random meals, five hundred calories each, and hot. We both needed it.

Juliyana didn't allow herself more than a moment or two

of self-indulgent pity. While I ate, she picked at the contents of the steaming bowl in her lap and gave me an incoherent story about conspiracies and bad intentions and wars and shoddy business practices…it sounded to me like just another day in the empire.

I finished my bowl, surprising myself. Getting knocked to the floor was good for the appetite, apparently. I put the bowl aside and held up my hand. "Stop, *stop*. Back up and start again." I drew in a breath and added in my best military tone; "Report, Lieutenant."

Juliyana colored to her hairline. "It's Private now, remember?"

I *had* forgotten.

Yet my command got her turned around properly. She put the bowl on the floor beside the chair and pressed her hands together. "I found a report, don't ask me where, but I verified the serial number, it's legit…." Her wrists paled as she pressed harder. Her fingers slid between each other and gripped. "When Noam died, he wasn't with the Rangers. He was doing something mysterious for the Imperial Shield. And *you* approved the transfer. You never told me that. You never told anyone."

I weighed that closely. "That's because I never approved such a transfer."

"Or you did, and you've forgotten about it since?" she asked. "It was forty-three years ago…and you didn't remember I was a private, just now."

"Fair point. Only, being busted back to private is minor — "

"Not to me." She scowled.

" — while giving up a single Ranger to the Imperial Shield is a blow any colonel would remember. Son, or not," I added. Work with good soldiers long enough and they all become difficult to transfer out. "Basic cross checking would tell you

I wasn't his CO at the time. It wouldn't have been me who approved the order."

"L. Andela, Colonel…it was your chop, Danny."

"Signatures can be faked."

She dug in her sack, pulled out a pad and tapped it on, turned it around and shoved it at me.

I peered at the screen. The text was blurry. I waited for my focus to properly kick in and scanned the document. It looked authentic. Only, fakes weren't useful unless they *did* look authentic. "What can I say? Someone is jerking you around." I handed the pad back.

"Doesn't *that* bother you, either?" she asked. She scrolled through the pad.

"Truth? No, it doesn't," I said tiredly. "What else have you got?"

Juliyana lifted a brow. "Isn't that enough? Dad was Imperial Shield, on special assignment, when he died —"

"When he went mad, shot up a ship, rammed it into another, and fired nukes at all the others," I amended. "Then he killed himself. Precision, Private."

Juliyana swallowed, the furrow returning to her brow. "What if he didn't go mad at all?"

"I saw the footage," I told her gently.

That made her pause. She rallied. "What if he was doing exactly what he was supposed to do? What if he was following orders?"

I was too tired to laugh. The poor girl was grasping because living with the stain Noam left behind was hard. So I gave her a bit more rope to tug on. "Why would anyone give such orders?"

She sat forward. "The Imperial fleet was facing down Cygnus Intergenera. No one ever stops to consider that fact when they talk about what Dad did. Cygnus never accepted the

Emperor taking control of the gates array at the end of the Crazy Years. The Drakas suit is *still* in the courts."

"So?" Although I could already see where she was going with this — the earlier babble had primed me.

"So, by ordering Dad to make it seem like he'd gone mad, the Emperor dealt with Cygnus in a way that didn't point at him. They *had* to appeal to the Imperial court after that — they'd been defeated in battle, and the Emperor wasn't to blame. He made it look good by stripping Dad of all his medals and honors and removing his name from the Ranger roll." Her voice grew strained.

I cleared my throat. I'd been there for that, after all. "And you think I set my own son up for something like that?" I asked mildly.

Her gaze was steady. "He *was* working for the Shield," she insisted. "And you were…well, you weren't yourself, toward the end. Everyone says so."

"I didn't handle Noam's death very well," I said in agreement. Now I was the one with the croaky voice. "That was *after* he died, though." I rubbed at my temples. Another headache was setting in. "I don't know why someone would prime you this way, Juli. It doesn't matter, because *I* won't take the bait. I didn't sign that order. And it was forty-three years ago."

"And I've been stuck in the bowels of drone ships and barges, doing shitwork, ever since!" she cried, leaping to her feet. "When do I get my life back, Danny? When do people forget what he did?"

She was crying again.

I got to my feet. Everything ached. I moved over to the bedshelf and opened it. "It's late," I told her. "You need to adjust to local time. Take the bed." The sun was setting over the sea, turning it pink, while birds dove for their supper.

Juliyana got to her feet, a good soldier obeying orders, although I could see she wanted to argue the point. As she moved past me, I held out my hand. "Give me the pad. I'll take a look."

Her face lit up.

So bad at hiding what she was thinking!

She shoved the pad into my hand, rolled onto the cot and sealed it.

I sighed and got to work. I built a table and two chairs, which took up most of the space left in the sitting room. Then I settled at it with a full jug of blue tea. I was going to need it, for the pad was stuffed full of documents and Juli's notes.

I scanned them, building a rough outline in my mind of what was there. I girded myself and returned to the one document which would dismantle this entire conspiracy she had built in her mind; The orders over my signature.

And yeah, there was a part of me which wondered if I really had forgotten signing those orders. In the last ten years I've overlooked and plain missed a lot of things, more of them each year. Andrain says it's part of the aging process — according to the documentation. For him, I'm a walking experiment. Geriatrics is an almost forgotten realm of medicine.

For me, it's no experiment. So I put off checking the orders until I thought I was ready to face them. Half a jug of tea was gone by then.

I'm not an archivist. I worked in the combat battalions, not support, but I've picked up tricks over the years. I cracked open the underbelly of the document and worked my way through the coding.

Clean and clear. Not a digit or line out of place. It had all the hallmarks of an Imperial document — heavy on code, with shielding, redundancies and fallbacks to preserve the integrity.

I sat back and stared at the moon rising over the sea, sending a white path toward the beach, and considered. I would remember something of this magnitude, surely? Or had I conveniently wiped that section of my memory, too?

There is only one bit of my personal history I can't remember, and it had nothing to do with Noam, dead or alive. The stuff I forget these days was recent. Events from forty years ago and even further back were clear. Whole. Except for that one dark patch—and I had everyone else's accounts to cover that.

There was one other thing I could do before I gave in to Juliyana's paranoia. I dug out a screen emitter and set it up on the table and went through the dozen steps to log into my backdoor on the Rangers archives.

I'm not the only high-ranking officer of the Imperial Rangers Corps to build a backdoor safety net for themselves. I know that, because a senior officer taught *me* how to do it. There were a thousand reasons why it was a good idea, even though it was against regulations—*all* of them, for the very first regulation was the declaration that no Ranger ever put himself before the Corps and his fellow Rangers. All other regulations spilled down from that tenet.

Only, I don't like the idea of an enemy locking me out of my own data. Wars are won or lost by the quality of the information used to build strategies. And if ever the archives were to fall into enemy hands, being able to sneak in where they weren't looking and wipe the archives was the equivalent of keeping a backup gun and two spare blades under your uniform.

So I used a door I hadn't cracked open in over fifty years.

The serial number on the document was as genuine as Juliyana had insisted it was. Without that serial number I would never have found the document on the archives. It was buried in strange files in an out-of-the-way corner of the archives. The location made no sense at all. No one would think to look there if they were searching organically or logically.

I opened the document. It looked exactly the same as Juliyana's copy except for the chop.

G. Dalton, Major.

Gabriel Dalton. Noam's commanding officer. Which made perfect sense.

I sat back, weak with relief. I hadn't forgotten, after all.

But shit, damn, fuck it. That meant Juliyana was right: Noam had been working for the Imperial Shield when he died.

What the fuck had he been up to?

2

THE DREAMS WERE BAD. I should have expected that, given what was on my mind when I fell asleep in the chair not long after finishing the last of the blue tea. I woke up early, aching still, and not even close to rested.

Andrain's message was waiting for me, as expected. I thought about breakfast, decided it was too much bother, and headed for the hospital. Juliyana was still in the sealed cot when I left.

Andrain grinned when he saw me. "I heard about last night. On your back in one blow."

"You heard before my terminal pimped me, or after?"

He lifted my chin, turned it, and gazed at the corner of my jaw. "Some swelling. I'll scan, just to be sure. Did she apologize?" He dropped my chin and started setting up the scan controls.

"She wanted to know if growing old hurts."

"What did you tell her?"

"That it was none of her fucking business."

He spared a glance. He wasn't fooled. "How are the head-aches?"

"I'm looking at one."

He tilted his head and raised a brow.

"Still having them," I growled.

"Severity?"

"About seven," I lied.

"It was about six, last time," he said.

Damn, I'd forgotten.

"They're getting worse, then," he concluded.

"I need one of those shots to snap in my sight," I said. "It's getting blurry again."

"I'll check to see when the last one was. You can't have them too frequently. They'll impact your cognition."

"Because getting old isn't doing that already."

"Lie down and stay still," he replied, his tone serene. Damn him.

He scanned, frowned at the results, then coordinated three different shots and smiled at me. "There. Feeling better?"

The ache was receding. I sat up cautiously and blinked. I could read the text on the pad in his hands. I managed to scare up a smile for him. "Yes, thank you."

Andrain rolled his eyes. "Much better," he agreed. "The jawbone is whole and sound. The local swelling will subside by the end of the day. If you need more analgesics, I've primed your printer for something a little stronger. It will make you sleep, so don't take it if you want to stay alert."

"Noted." I got to my feet. Slowly. "Anything else?"

Andrain's smile faded. I knew what was coming, but it had been a while since the last time, so I braced myself to be polite and nod.

"You know you could avoid all this if you underwent rejuvenation," he said.

"Damn, why didn't I think of that?"

"You're only in your fourth century...there's so much more you can do—"

I held up my hand. "I've had my time, doc. Discussion ended."

"You're being selfish."

That got my attention. "You think?"

"I do. Longevity was the singlemost critical technology and medical breakthrough of this millennium. It allowed humans to set up very long-term projects. A single human, a single vision, could direct projects which required generations to be completed without losing focus or drive. The original vision was held intact over the lifetime of the project. Because of longevity, we can travel to distant stars and set up gates for the others. Before then, we were boxed into a single solar system and doomed, because life goes on and population pressure was killing us."

"Is that why you accepted a contract on a family barge, Andrain? The romantic notion of finding new worlds, blah, blah, blah?"

Only he wouldn't be distracted. He shook his head. "The human diaspora which brought us to where we are today could not have happened without longevity. It makes astonishing achievements possible. By refusing rejuvenation, you're denying humanity your unique contributions."

"I think I've contributed more than enough to humanity's future," I replied. "So does everyone else."

"That's not true," he said quickly.

"No? Then why isn't the empire beating on my door, shoving regen contracts at me, and begging me to return?"

"Now who's being romantic?" he shot back. "It's only been forty years. Give 'em time."

"Forty-three," I told him. "If they wait any longer, it'll be too late."

Andrain didn't argue with that, which didn't make me any happier.

***

Juliyana had made breakfast and was eating it at the little table, her pad in front of her.

I'd dropped a copy of the genuine orders onto her pad for her to find it, before sleeping last night. Why I had done it, I couldn't say. I could have lied and said I'd forgotten about the orders. Shoved her out the door and got on with growing old.

She snapped up straight when I entered. "There's oat-meal."

"No, thank you."

Juliyana nudged the edge of the pad with her spoon. "He *was* working for the Shield, then."

"Don't let it get into your head," I warned her. I sniffed cinnamon and my stomach rumbled. Irritated, I went over to the printer and hit the preset for my breakfast.

"Something is wrong about the whole Drakas disaster," she said. "There's more going on than anyone ever admitted to."

"This is what I meant by letting it get into your head." I sat and wolfed two forkfuls of eggs quickly, then added, "Even as a lieutenant, you were working with less than complete information."

"Sure, some of it was above my rank." She shrugged. "This is *completely* different. The Imperial Shield are a black hole, they never share anything—"

"They're called a Shield for a reason."

"They're called a Shield because they guard the Emperor. Only that's just one section. They do all sorts of mysterious things, *and* they build the array gates, even before the Emperor federalized the array. They've never let anyone see the real process that goes into building them."

"Because they're grown, not built."

"They're bio-mechanical, which means they're built *and* grown." Juliyana looked irritated.

19

I ate two more quick mouthfuls, to get my stomach to shut up. I put the fork down. "Look, Juli, you can't dig into this. You understand that, don't you?"

She sat back. "Why not? Something's not right and I think it goes right up to the Emperor—"

"Which is exactly why you can't dig into it. Of *course* it reaches to the Emperor, in theory at least. The Shield is his to command." I rested my hand on hers, as gently as I could. "Your father was doing something mysterious for the Shield. Granted. If you want to choose to believe he was just following orders when he died, if it helps, then you should hold on to that. Don't try to hunt this down. You won't like where it takes you. Other people won't like where it takes you. Those orders were buried very deep for a reason."

Her jaw flexed. No tears this morning. "*You* could hunt it down. You're the Imperial Hammer. They'd listen to you."

I sighed. "I *was* that woman, once," I agreed. "I have no military authority anymore. I had none left, even before I resigned my commission. I was the soul survivor of a war that wiped out four battalions and half the Imperial fleet. It destroyed any credibility I had as an effective officer. I did far more to end my career than your father managed." I smiled to take the sting out of it and borrowed shamelessly from Andrain. "Give it time. They'll ease off on you, eventually."

"How long?" Juliyana asked, her tone reasonable. "Fifty years? A hundred? No one will care after that."

"And neither will you," I assured her. "Time will take the sting out of it. I promise."

"Then you won't help me…"

"I think I was just saying that I *can't* help you…and that you shouldn't dig into this, either."

Juliyana shook her head, her jaw still tight. "You're making excuses."

I quashed the irritation that was trying to build. I wasn't used to junior officers arguing back. "Very well. Dispute this, then: My last crush shot was forty years ago. I'd have to use commercial passenger crawlers to get anywhere, which would take *months*. And commercial lines don't go where I would need to get, to even begin to look into this."

She opened her mouth again.

"Besides, I don't have the money to use the cargo lanes, *or* a crush shot," I added.

Juliyana closed her mouth. She got to her feet. "Got it."

"I'm sorry."

She shook her head as she shoved the pad into her sack and closed the sack. "I don't think you're sorry at all." She slung the sack over her shoulder. "I *am* sorry about hitting you. I'll be on my way." She moved to the door.

"Leave it alone, Juliyana," I urged her.

She paused with the door open. "He's *your son*. I thought you, of all people…" She pummeled the door frame with the side of her fist. "Forget it," she said bleakly.

The door closed behind her.

I finished my breakfast, even though I didn't want it anymore.

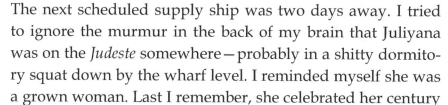

The next scheduled supply ship was two days away. I tried to ignore the murmur in the back of my brain that Juliyana was on the *Judeste* somewhere—probably in a shitty dormitory squat down by the wharf level. I reminded myself she was a grown woman. Last I remember, she celebrated her century a while ago.

I got on with my life. Such as it is. I have no official role in the family corporation. Although if I wanted to, I could send

Farhan, the current CEO, a request and have an official title, even an office, before lunch. That razor-thin majority shareholder position gave me leverage. I just didn't care to use it.

I had come back to the barge to live as far outside the mainstream fuss as was possible. I could have *really* dropped out by applying for a homesteading license on some still-fertile ball. Built a cabin and slept in the rocking chair each day. Only, who would give *me* a license?

At least the *Judeste* had to give me room and board. Farhan had been reluctant, though. Forty years ago, I had been a white-hot magnet for all the ills of the empire, and all the bad graces, too. And I was claiming my right to live on *his* barge.

The last forty years of letting the world pass by should have made up for that. Last night had been an aberration.

I visited the park level and stressed my hips with walking too far in summer-level heat. Was there a single joint anywhere in my body which *hadn't* noticed the impact with the deck? It kept me from admiring the roses and the willows as I usually did.

That just made me cranky.

I went back to my apartment and scowled at the table and two chairs and the second armchair. I broke them down and fed them back into the recycle chute. Shoved my armchair back into its usual position, facing the beach, and sat.

My battered old pad was tucked between the cushion and the arm. There was years' worth of distraction on that thing, but I stared at the waves instead, until the headache was too bad to focus.

Andrain's knock-out painkiller sounded really good, by then. I pushed my finger into the printer, got the shot and rolled onto the refreshed cot and sealed it tight.

Deep twilight, cool air, white noise. The perfect conditions for sleep.

So, of course, I didn't. For two hours.

Until I did, and then I dreamed.

And I'd been hoping the analgesic would shove me into the deep sleep phase and by-pass all the crud in my sub-conscious.

Yeah, wishful thinking. More fool me.

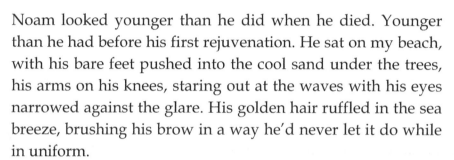

Noam looked younger than he did when he died. Younger than he had before his first rejuvenation. He sat on my beach, with his bare feet pushed into the cool sand under the trees, his arms on his knees, staring out at the waves with his eyes narrowed against the glare. His golden hair ruffled in the sea breeze, brushing his brow in a way he'd never let it do while in uniform.

"Tide will turn soon," he said.

How the fuck he knew that beat me. He'd never stepped foot on a planet that wasn't a war zone.

"We're good, this far up the beach," I told him.

He considered and shook his head. I wanted him to look at me, only he wasn't reading my mind, right then. "Nope," he said simply.

Look at me! I tried to shout, but my throat wouldn't cooper-ate.

"You'll stay here, though, right?" he added.

I looked at the flat ocean, my heart screaming, my pulse thready. It was the same ocean. It never changed its essential nature, even though it could have moods. Only, what was that on the horizon?

My focus wouldn't kick in, yet my pulse jumped another notch or two. What was going on out there? Was that...a wave?

23

The horizon threshed and shifted. I couldn't *see* properly, damn it. And the pain in my head was building, the harder I tried to make my eyes cooperate and focus properly.

Something was coming.

Something was *coming*.

Something was coming.

I blasted out of the cot like a silk-skinned smart bullet, to sprawl on the cold floor, sweat-soaked and breathing way too fucking fast.

The fear from the dream had followed me into wakefulness. I propped myself up, shivering, trying to off-load the sensation of doom heading in my direction with a loaded shriver and bad intentions.

I didn't need an analyst to interpret the dreams—they were nearly all the same theme these days. I was sick of the repetition. I get it, okay? Clock's ticking. Message received. Dismissed.

The concierge was flashing.

Grateful for the distraction, I got to my feet in slow stages, taking my time, then moved over—okay, I shuffled. Over to the panel, pressed my finger against the pad.

The screen cleared and wrote the message.

You spent a year digging into the Drakas thing after Dad died. What if your breakdown was their way of getting you out of there, where you were digging too deep?

J.

Damn stubborn. Relentless. Irritating…

A storm brewed over the ocean. Dark clouds on the horizon. I shivered and switched off the wall and left it smooth obsidian black.

Then I went back to the park. At least there, the sun was shining and birds were singing, even if it was too fucking hot to walk. I could sit on a bench.

I walked, instead. Sitting let me think too much.

I'd learned not to probe the blank spot in my memory, or anywhere near its borders. The year after Noam died was too damn close to the event horizon. It didn't stop me from juggling the meta-question in Juliyana's message, though.

Discounting any hidden agendas, one came down to the fact that the blank spot was damned convenient. It pushed me away from examining anything in that time period too closely.

I shivered despite the heat and kept walking. The turbines were running, so the leaves rustled overhead, sending leaf-shaped shadows skittering over the path, dancing like motes.

That was the last thought I had.

It wasn't like waking, this time.

Things came together very slowly. For a while, I didn't feel the need to make sense of anything. I drifted.

I listened to sounds with childlike wonder, none of them familiar to me.

Sense does return, eventually. With it comes dismay. A sinking sensation.

"Oh, your pulse just jumped. You're back with us. Hold on—I've sent for the doctor."

The AI nurse's voice was pleasantly professional, caring, and horribly familiar.

I made my eyes open and forced them to focus. The railings were up on both sides of the bed, of course. I was on my side, a hand under my cheek. The classic therapeutic recovery position.

I didn't bother trying to move. I knew I didn't have the strength. It would take a while to come back.

"Water," I told the nurse, my voice croaky.

The tube extended, touched my lips.

"Just a sip or two," the nurse said.

A sip or two was all I could manage, anyway. I had to hold the water in my mouth, and let it soak the parched flesh, until my throat was moistened enough to swallow.

Footsteps. Andrain bent to peer at my face. He was serene, still, although the humor had gone. "There you are."

"Wanna sit."

He considered. "If you can get yourself into a sitting position, go ahead."

I scowled. He and I both knew that wasn't possible right now. I tried, anyway. Best I could do was turn onto my back.

Andrain relented and lifted the head of the bed, so we were more or less at eye level with each other. Then he did something he'd never done before. He lowered the bar and sat on the edge of the bed.

Shit…

I braced myself.

He nodded. I'd given myself away. "Yes, it's bad." He paused. "Yet it's what you've been expecting all along, in a way."

"Facts, doc," I croaked.

"You're dying, Danny."

I rolled my eyes. "*New* facts."

He shook his head. "With proper management of your aging, you might have lived for another thirty or fifty years. But…not now."

That *was* news. I stared at him. "How long?"

"The scan I did this morning bothered me, so I spent some

26

time digging into the data. I've got forty years of research data, after all." His smile was barely there. "These seizures, Danny...they're killing you."

Something is coming...

I shivered violently. "That explains the bad dreams," I whispered.

He nodded. "Actually, you're more right than you know. It's not unusual for terminal patients to recognize when death is close by. Bad dreams, dark thoughts...it's a preparation of a kind. There's a great deal of documentation on it."

I repeated, with false patience, "How long?"

He hesitated. "Possibly weeks. It's determined by the seizures themselves. If you don't have another seizure, no further disintegration will take place."

"But the next one could kill me."

He shook his head. "It's very likely the next one *will* kill you."

I let that sink in. "And you still have no idea what is causing them?"

"My best guess is your implants are malfunctioning," he said. "As you refuse to let me examine them, or have them upgraded—"

"The only way for a civilian like me to upgrade is to go through rejuvenation," I said sharply. And the implants would not be military grade, either.

"Yes." His tone was flat.

We both knew my opinion about that option.

"As it isn't your brain generating the seizures, but an outside agency, the standard epilepsy inoculation won't work." Andrain got to his feet. "The seizures are several weeks apart, yet the rate is increasing. Slowly, though. So..."

"I have from several to a few weeks," I finished. "Thanks, doc."

He smoothed out a wrinkle on the blanket by my foot. Nodded. Turned and left.

I sat for a long while, letting thoughts chase each other around, not straining for coherence or logic. I was drained and I knew Andrain wouldn't let me out of here for at least a day. It would take that long for me to get my shit together, anyway.

After a while I slept.

And after that, I *did* think.

Finally.

Talk about the last minute.

By the time I got to the loading ramp, the passengers were boarding. I scanned down the ragged line, breathing way too hard for a short walk from the elevator bank. The frigate's payload manager scanned wrists for serial numbers, checking against his cargo manifest.

A secondary scan by his assistant confirmed crush status, before the passengers were allowed onboard. It spelled quick death to a freight hauler's business if their customers were squashed to red jelly when they jumped through the gates.

The double-check saved me. Juliyana was just stepping up with her wrist held out.

I beckoned.

She narrowed her eyes. She pulled her wrist away from the manager's handheld and said something to him.

He scowled and growled something back. Cargo freighters aren't commercial cruisers. They make their money from freight haulage, so keeping the customer happy isn't a factor for them.

Juliyana came over to me. "He won't hold the ship up, so

make it fast."

"I'm dying."

"I know."

"I mean, sooner, not later. There's a thing…and it doesn't matter." I started again. "Thing is, I thought I had years. Decades. Now I don't."

Her eyes were still narrowed, although the impatience faded. "And that makes a difference."

"All the difference in the world." I shifted on my feet. "I don't want to step out with things not finished."

Juliyana waited. I used to do that to sub-officers. Stare 'em into an untimely confession. It works too fucking well, alas.

"After Drakas…before the Blackout…" I paused, for the date of the empire's Blackout was neatly in the middle of my personal black hole. I only knew of the chaos and disasters the Blackout caused from reading other people's accounts. "Back then, I should have gone out the proper way, you know? A meal, sex, then a bullet or a blade or a pill. Maybe a note. Only I didn't."

"Too stubborn?" Her tone was dry.

"I *think* I was holding out still. Waiting. Thing is, if I'd done it then, the world and I would have been square. Now, though…there's this thing of yours."

The cargo manager put his fingers to his mouth and whistled. Hard. There were no more passengers lined up.

Juliyana glanced at him and gave a gesture which might have meant "I'm coming" or "fuck you."

Either way, the manager didn't like it. He waved, a flick of his fingers. *Move it.*

Juliyana turned back to me. "You're going to dig."

"I don't know how far I'll get," I warned her. "My resources aren't what they used to be. Shit, *I'm* not what I used to be." And Andrain would have a *lot* to say about me taking off right now, too. Only, that was a different bridge.

Behind us, the warning alarm sounded as the frigate lifted from the deck and floated toward the external lock. The gusts from the hover engines blew our hair back and ruffled our clothing.

"Seems I'm coming with you," Juliyana said. "You knew that. It's why you're here."

"You might thank me, at least."

"You just wasted my ticket on that hulk." She jerked her thumb over her shoulder, at the frigate as it eased out of the lock. "It's non-returnable."

I smiled. "Oh, you're going to burn a lot more than a ticket on this venture," I assured her. "I'm broke. You're a Ranger. You're buying my fare out of here, too."

3

THE VERY TOP DECK OF the *Judeste* is a real observation deck. Glasseen steel windows — *small* ones — let you see outside the ship. No screens, no avatars or representations. As close to seeing with your naked eye the glory of deep space, short of stepping out there in a suit.

The view isn't unobstructed, though. The jump gate attached to the front end of the barge blocks most of it. Only, watching a ship emerge from the suddenly violet shimmer into normal space can take your breath away. When a ship was due, folk squeezed in the cramped space, craning to peer through the windows.

It didn't surprise me to find the family CEO, Farhan, there. There were no ships due for three days — I'd checked. The ship Juliyana and I waited for — the *Aurora Queen* — was four days out. The *Queen*, which did not live up to her name, was one of the Hakim Hext Cruiselines' commercial crawlers. Hakim Hext was the only spaceline company serving outrigger barges, and it operated on a shoestring, jamming passengers into cramped shells which should have been upgraded a few decades ago.

Nevertheless, Juliyana and I had tickets for its return. As Juliyana had booked them, complaining loudly about the scalper prices, it occurred to me that as a majority shareholder, I should probably inform the CEO I was leaving the barge. There would be proxies to sign before I left.

Farhan grimaced when he saw me and turned his head back to the view. He had his share of the family genes—tall and rangy. His skin was a lot darker, though. "Líadan," he acknowledged. "What can I do for you?"

"This is a formality," I said. "I'm letting you know I'm leaving the barge for a while."

He glanced at me again, genuinely startled. "You?" He rolled his eyes. "*Of course* you're leaving." He laughed. It was a soft sound, devoid of humor.

I waited, puzzled.

He finally pulled himself together. With a jerk, he yanked his jacket back into place. "It's not due to be released yet. How did you get hold of it? Or shouldn't I ask?"

"About what?"

He narrowed his eyes. "The annual report..." he said slowly. "You don't have it?"

"It's bad news, then?" I surmised. I barely managed to say "then", instead of "again". I tried to think back to when the last report came out, only it wasn't a highlight in my memory. The timing seemed about right, was the best I could guess.

He turned back to the view. *That* was why he was here. He was brooding. "We haven't found a viable planet in over a hundred years."

"The ore belts are lucrative," I pointed out. The mining of ores was the bread and butter of the family. There were *always* more satellites and asteroids to suck the guts out of. Opening new planets, establishing gates, and selling the rights for them was cream. Very rich, very lucrative cream, but still just cream. No one gambled upon finding viable planets as their sole source of income. The Carranoak family certainly did not.

"Ore pays," he agreed. "Just not enough—not in the long

term, not for us. The hits we've taken lately...finding a planet would solve all of it." He stirred. "What do you care, anyway? You've never shown up for a single board meeting."

"I've grown aware of money and costs, lately." I recalled Juliyana's bellyaching.

He turned to face me properly, his expression alert. "If you're not leaving because of the report, then why *are* you leaving? Is this something to do with Juliyana?"

Of course he'd heard about her arrival. Whenever a family member set foot upon the *Judeste*, he would be informed.

"Indirectly. She's coming with me. I don't know how long I'll be away."

"Just long enough to avoid the fallout." His tone was withering. "Typical."

"I'm not following."

He turned back to the view again. "You brought all the bad luck with you. Now the cumulative effects are catching up with the family, you're leaving again."

"Bad luck is a myth."

"Is it? A disgraced Ranger with a criminal son settles upon the barge, with voting rights on the Board." He held up a finger. "Our insurance rates have risen steadily every year since you arrived. The insurance companies are now holding out for indemnity clauses and say they won't renew without them."

I winced. "Expensive?"

"Unbelievably." He held up another finger. "In the last ten years, three of our major mining rights contracts have come up for renewal, and I've had to negotiate hard just to *keep* them. Asking for better terms was out of the question. In two cases, I had to lower the royalties, slash docking fees, give away storage and more. The mining companies are wary — to them, rising insurance must mean higher risk."

He held up another finger. "The restraints on cash flow means I can't service longer term liquid arrangements. Interest on short term is horrendous. So, the cost of commodities, including food and air and water have gone up three hundred percent."

He dropped his hand. "People are leaving the barge, finding work and accommodation elsewhere. Exit interviews show a trend—they're heading to other barges, where the conditions are cheaper and up to date. We haven't renewed the dormitories in twenty years. Fewer people mean less cash flow." He shrugged. "And around it goes." He turned back to the window. "You asked," he added, his tone bitter.

"It's not all on me." I wasn't surprised when my voice came out hoarse.

"Noam carries a lot of it," he said bleakly.

I only remembered then that he and Noam used to be friends. "You have a bad seed on board. So what? Every barge, every ship…hell, half my basic recruits were criminals on redemption passes."

He nodded. "Yeah, that's how it's supposed to work. Screw up, fix it and work your ass off for twenty years to make amends." His glance was sideways. "Not a single contract negotiation, the insurance renewals, not one adjudicator breathed your name. Not one. But our universal credit rating is down fifteen thousand points. Tell me again your reputation doesn't impact this family."

I recalled Juliyana's note. What if your breakdown was their way of getting you out of there, where you were digging too deep?

What if my reputation wasn't all on me? What if they had arranged that, too?

"Maybe I'll have good news for you when I get back," I told Farhan.

"The good news is that you're leaving."

There was nothing I could say in response, so I did what he wanted. I left.

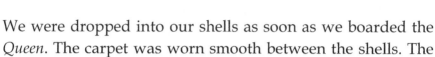

We were dropped into our shells as soon as we boarded the *Queen*. The carpet was worn smooth between the shells. The soft lining of the fuselage was dented. The shells looked newer—just.

I sank into the liquid beneath the impermeable surface and wriggled as instructed so it settled around my back, ass, head and legs, reflecting that military shells were far easier to use. Juliyana clearly agreed with me, for her jaw was set as she fought to arrange the gel around her properly.

The gel came right up to the level of my shoulder. As I held my breath, expecting to be submerged, it settled.

So did my heart.

"We're right *there* at the gate, already," Juliyana fumed. "None of this is necessary." Her voice was muffled, for the shells rose twenty centimeters above the gel itself, while they were open. The pilot, if he deemed it necessary, could snap the shells completely closed, containing us inside if he was forced to high-gee maneuvers.

That had never happened in my lifetime, though.

"They're just being cautious," I ventured from my own shell. There were two dozen other passengers in the cramped cabin, and the crewman moved along the lanes, checking to ensure we were all settled properly, before heading for his own shell. He paused by my shell, gave me a startled look, then double and triple checked I was properly inserted into the shell.

I stared right back.

He gave me a stiff smile and moved on. I heard him flirting with Juliyana, who shut him down fast.

I watched the screen attached to the ceiling of the cabin, while Farhan's withering observations about insurance came back to me. I coupled it with the crewman's extra precautions over me. "Cautious for insurance reasons," I added.

Juliyana's snort was a fair comment.

The *Aurora Queen* lifted gently from the deck of the *Judeste*, then moved ahead slowly.

Gentle and *slow* were a commercial crawler's *raison d'être*.

I dialed with my finger, switching the screen above me to an external view. It had been a long time since I had seen the *Umb Judeste* from a far perspective, although five kilometers out wasn't that far at all. It was enough to see the entire ship at one glance, though.

Only a commercial craft drifted out so far, before coming around in a *slow, gentle* curve to line up with the gate at the end of the ship, then pick up speed — still at a pace which put us at just over one gee.

As we approached the gate, the view cut to an advertisement spouting the joys of shopping with Cygnus Commercial. *All transactions bonded and warranteed!* Hakim Hext Cruiselines was mostly owned by Cygnus Intergenera. I sighed and switched off the screen.

I had also forgotten that commercial flights killed brain cells with boredom.

The transition through the gate was seamless. Our first stop was Melenia Station, the biggest commercial hub on this side of the empire. At just over one hundred and fifty parsecs away, it was only a hop, skip and a jump from the *Judeste's* current position, which meant time in the hole was correspondingly longer. *Hours* longer.

And none of us could move around the cabin in that

time — a luxury I had forgotten about.

I think I slept. I'd been short on sleep lately. No dreams. I couldn't sink deep enough to dream, which was a good thing. Thrashing about would scare the other passengers.

The screen switched on when we emerged from the other end of the hole, showing an orange-red globe in crescent view. Also sparkling in the red sunlight was Melenia Station, a sprawling, former donut-shaped construction in geo-synchronous orbit around Melenia IV, below.

The sun glinted off a dozen other craft, all heading to or from the gate which laid behind us.

It took another six hours to reach the station itself at crawling speed — which was what gave commercial craft their name.

By then, I was seething. As we were checked off-board and handed our sacks, I said to Juliyana, "Change of plans."

She raised her brow as we walked through the shield doors into the station proper, and into the stream of humanity moving along the concourse. I got startled looks. I ignored them, but I tried to pick up my pace, aware of the people behind us making irritated noises.

"See if you can change our tickets to head to Zillah's World."

She pursed her lips. "It's way over by the Rim."

"Exactly. Another long haul like this one will kill me…or I'll kill someone instead. Zillah's World is far enough away that time in the hole will be reduced to an hour or so. And if I remember properly, the gates are close to the station, there." I raised my brow at her.

She nodded. "They are. Only, you wanted military grade crush juice. Zillah's World is purely a civilian hospice."

"It will have to do."

Juliyana looked as though she wanted to protest. Probably

something about cancelation fees and going off-plan. Instead, she looked around. "There's a lunch bar there. Park yourself. I'll sort out the tickets."

I moved over to the long counter and sat on a stool, suddenly grateful for the respite. Moving fast had taken the pith out of me.

The menu wanted me to order. I ordered water. It defaulted to the same welcome message and cheerfully and politely insisted I order something. So I moved through the river of people finding their landing bays, over to the outer wall of the station, which was white and pristine tensor graphide, put my back to it, and slid down until my ass was on the deck.

Had interstellar travel always been so exhausting?

Juliyana, when she returned, merely slid down the wall and settled beside me. "Done." She rested her head back against the wall. "I had to pay a second set of gate fees. The taxes were raised last week."

I had forgotten about taxes and gate fees. In the military, we didn't pay them, of course. "You're a well-paid Ranger," I said. "And this is the only way."

"It's extortion."

"You're always free to refuse to pay it."

"And get to where I want to go, how?"

"You could buy a long-haul ship, point it in the right direction and wait."

She rolled her eyes at the infeasibility of that idea.

"You could build your own gates." I said, keeping my tone reasonable. "That's all the Imperial family did."

"Then they *charge* everyone to use them."

"That's because they spent seven generations developing the technology."

"And now they keep it a big, dark secret."

"Of course they do. They have to earn back their original research investment. There's nothing stopping you from doing the same thing. Not even the Imperial Family will try to stop you."

"Because they know no one can replicate the work. And why would they? It's already been done. Anyone who tries would be repeating all that time and effort."

There had been attempts over the years to deconstruct the gates and figure out what made them work, only the franchise holders for the gates didn't put up with tinkering which might damage their investment. Nor would the people living in that sector appreciate losing their access to the greater Empire.

"If you don't want to do the work, then shut up and smile when you pay your gate tax," I told Juliyana.

She sighed. "I *hate* commercial travel."

I could only agree with her on that one.

Our departure was hours away. It could have been worse, for the Zillah's World connection was once-weekly. After a while, my ass and back started to hurt, pressed against the wall. Juliyana helped me up. I hobbled over to the café, and this time pleased the menu by ordering a sandwich.

Juliyana ordered pastrami on rye, with a pickle, salad, soup *and* a chocolate cake to finish. When I raised my brow, she tapped the corner of the menu, where the simple Cygnus logo sat. "The pickle the Cygnus files print is mild except for the end, where the bump is. The chocolate cake has a gooey center." She shrugged. "I'm at least eating a salad, too."

"It's your metabolism." I peeled open my own sandwich and frowned. Only now I remembered the Cygnus bread did not settle well in my stomach. Instead, I rolled up the deli meat and ate it with my fingers.

"I've been thinking about what you told me, about Cygnus and the gates." I chewed. "The Emperor took control of the array, because Cygnus was handling it badly." I still remember the official memo that went round, when gate control, manufacturing and administration were all turned over to the Emperor. "That was the only way to end the Crazy Years."

Juliyana nodded enthusiastically as she swallowed. "The Crazy Years was his excuse. Of course the Imperial family wanted the array back in their control."

"They already had control," I pointed out. "The actual manufacturing of the gates, the construction of them, has always been a family operation."

"Only the manufacture of the parts making up the gate, the mechanical parts, at least, was parceled out. Centuries ago, there were a dozen companies making their fortune providing the Imperial Family and the Imperial Shield with parts for the gate. Then, Cygnus Intergenera convinced the Emperor they could do it all as a one-stop contract, *and* they could do it cheaper and better." She pointed at the menu, with the logo on the corner. "Now Cygnus has a stranglehold on the galaxy. They're the most powerful corporate state in the Empire, and the Emperor didn't like it." She paused. "The Crazy Years is how he took the array back out of their hands."

"That was in 245 or 6 or something. Drakas was years later."

"It was 247, and Drakas was 251," Juliyana replied. "I didn't say the connection was direct or obvious, because everyone would have noticed. There *is* a connection there, though. The Emperor took back the array and a few years later, Noam apparently goes mad and destroys Cygnus Intergenera's premier battalion."

"Who were lined up in protest against the Emperor taking

the array back," I concluded. "You realize how crazy you sound?"

"It sounds absolutely insane," she said. "Only you have a memo with your signature faked at the bottom of it, and that shifts the crazy."

"Who benefits from something like this being bought into the open? That's what I can't figure out. The Emperor wouldn't like it. Cygnus wouldn't appreciate having shareholders and the buying public reminded of their military troubles and the Emperor's disapproval. After that, the list grows very short."

"That isn't the point," Juliyana said, with a touch of impatience. "I have the information, you've verified there is something screwy about it, now we follow up."

For the first time it occurred to me to ask, "Where, exactly, did you get the information? You never did explain that."

Her face hardened. "It hardly matters. We've verified the data—one document, which puts the others in an interesting light. If the Emperor has arranged things to suit himself, and if he did put my father out there as his scapegoat, it's a short step to considering if he needed Noam to be out of the way. Just like you were pushed out of the way."

I scowled at that. "I was not under any influence when I resigned my commission."

"Except for the influence of an entire Empire screaming for your head as a coward," Juliyana shot back. "There is at least a possibility that the Emperor manufactured the Crazy Years, just so he could take back the array. I think that is what we are both thinking, yes?"

"The information you have suggests that general direction," I said cautiously.

She rolled her eyes. "Presume that everything the data suggests is true, just for a moment. The Emperor arranged the Crazy Years, so he could take back the array. Then he covered up everything and misdirected."

"Misdirected how?"

Juliyana shook her head. She wasn't going to be derailed. "What if my father was involved in the Emperor's schemes to arrange the Crazy Years? Then, him going mad and shooting out the Cygnus military forces and dying right after that was a very neat way of getting my father off the board. He was dead and unable to blow the whistle on the Emperor."

I stared at her, my heart doing little flattery things. We were talking in the privacy bubble, yet I still had the need to check over my shoulder to see if anyone was listening. "That really isn't something you should suggest out loud," I said.

"No one can hear us." She was calm. But then, she had spent weeks contemplating the data I was still trying to wrap my head around. She had adjusted to the enormity of the concepts.

"Or maybe Noam just went mad," I said.

"He was transferred to the Imperial Shield," Juliyana said, as if that discounted my suggestions completely.

"Where he did the work he was assigned, and then he went mad." My throat was aching. "No conspiracy, no power -hungry Emperor."

Juliyana scowled and picked up her pickle. She turned it to show me the knobby outgrowth at the end. "There. It's like all the vinegar collects in that bump." She took a bite and winced as she chewed.

I returned to my sandwich.

We reached Zillah's World eighteen hours later. Fourteen of those hours had been spent waiting on Melenia. Zillah's world has extra screening which most stations don't bother with. All of them were bio scans, designed to find anyone with high risk viruses or parasites. Such people were isolated and put on the nearest shuttle away from the station.

Only the harvest teams and a select few biochemists were allowed upon the surface of the planet. They collected and sampled the plants in the equatorial jungle belting the planet. Even though the quarantine prevented just anyone from landing on the ball, the scientists who administered Zillah's World were still highly cautious about introducing diseases and bacteria amongst the residents of the sprawling hospice and research station floating overhead. Those bugs might be transmitted down to the surface by the research team and the harvesters. Xeno-bugs amongst the natural pharmacy down there would be a disaster for more than Zillah's World's single-themed economy.

Once our skin was sterilized and our internal biome classified as safe, we were permitted to move around the public areas of the station. I asked the directory to give me the nearest hospice outlets, while scratching at my arm. The scanning process was supposed to remove all the seared skin cells, but there were always some left behind. They would itch and irritate until they flaked away.

The directory showed me the layout of the station, then tracked a path for me to a clinic about a kilometer away.

Juliyana lifted her brow. "Do you want me to come with you?"

"I'm a big girl. I think I can ask for a crush shot all by myself. Why don't you find a hilton and get some shut eye?" It was one of the basic axioms of a Ranger. Get sleep when the opportunity presented itself.

Juliyana nodded and hitched her sack back into place. She glanced at the directory, probably committing to memory the location of the clinic I was heading for. Then she turned on her heel and moved down the corridor. There was no public concourse on this station. It wasn't a major traffic hub, but a destination. The people who actually got off a ship were here for a purpose. Either they were patients, professionals or laborers, here for therapy or work.

I turned in the opposite direction to Juliyana and made my way through the pristine white corridors. I found subdued steel glass walls and a negative pressure door, with a discreet sign bearing the name of the clinic. *Zillah Garden Advanced Medical Clinic and Services Inc.* I went inside.

There was an actual human at the front desk. He looked me over and tapped on his pad. "Rejuvenation, yes?"

I snorted. "I'm here for crush juice, that's all."

He lowered the pad. "Oh, I don't think so."

"Why not? You sell crush juice, don't you?" It was a rhetorical question. Everyone offered crush juice.

He gave me a strained, polite smile. "We would have to do a scan to establish a baseline, but I can tell just by looking at you that your bio markers would not fit the profile range for the safe administration of crush juice."

I stared at him, my heart thudding. "So, basically, you're saying I'm too fucking old?"

He grimaced. "I suppose that would be one way to state it, yes."

4

THINGS GOT HEATED AFTER THAT. At least, on my side.

The core of the ZW station was a research and hospice. Surrounding that core were dozens of for-profit clinics and therapy centers, plus all the support services — food, accommodation — who provided the station with its economy. Given the weird and wonderful chemicals available via the bio-cocktail on the surface, people came here for alternative therapies available nowhere else. The station also provided the straightforward therapies, too.

Including crush juice.

If Zillah Garden Advanced Medical Clinic and Services Inc. did not intend to give me the crush shot I wanted, I was sure the next clinic along would be happy to take my money. I headed for the door, intending to turn left and walk until I came across that clinic.

Before I could reach the door, though, the assistant got a hand around my elbow, while talking fast. He was sweating. It was his job to add to the clinic's revenue stream. Turning customers away would not look good.

He managed to get me into one of the consultation room, seated in a comfortable chair, while I fumed.

Then he requested my serial number, his hand waving toward my wrist. "It's a simple procedure." Desperation shaded his tone.

I figured he would get his ass chewed out, possibly his pay docked, if he didn't complete the formalities. Reluctantly, I held out my wrist.

He waved the pad over it and nodded. "Thank you." He went away.

Far more quickly than I suspected was normal, the medico appeared. She smoothed down her white shift nervously and indicated the other man who had come into the room with her. He did not wear white. "This is Harvey Blankenburg, the director for the clinic."

They *really* didn't like a paying customer walking on them. I nodded at him. I didn't bother smiling.

"Do you mind if I sit?" Blankenburg's smile was full of white teeth, the epitome of good health. He didn't wait for me to say yes. He settled on the chair opposite me and gave me another blinding smile. "I must admit we've never had anyone of your caliber in our clinic before."

"You mean you've never had anyone so old before."

"I'm quite sure we've had people far older than you. I myself am in my fifth century."

"Then what the fuck are you doing in a place like this?" I asked him. "Most people get over the need to shill for a living in their first century." I wasn't bothering to spare him, as I had no advantage to gain by sitting here. I wasn't even sure why I was cooperating this far. "Time is ticking. I have things to do, places to go. Are you going to sell me a crush shot, or not?"

He wove his fingers together and placed them on the table in front of him. It was supposed to be a friendly, let's-be-frank gesture, yet he had barricaded his hands in front of me. I was only in my fourth century, but I knew what that meant.

"I think we can find an arrangement which suits you *and* us. I'm not here to tell you 'no'."

The doctor cleared her throat nervously.

I didn't look at her. She had no power in this room. I kept my gaze on Blankenburg.

"We have a range of half-life mortgages available, all of them with minimal bondage—"

"How much does crush juice *cost* these days?" I asked in amazement. I have never paid for crush juice in my life. The Rangers took care of that for us. I had learned from conversations with private carriers and freighter grunts that commercial crush juice was a month or two's worth of wages and bonuses. By scrimping and saving across the approximate five years a crush shot lasts, civvies could buy their next dose and therefore continue to work in space.

A half-life mortgage to pay for the juice said inflation had exploded in this section of the Empire.

Blankenburg paused, while his jaw worked. "Mortgages are not available for crush juice. Why would they? Most people can afford an inertia inoculation. I presume that you can, too. That is a secondary arrangement we can deal with later."

My jaw sagged as I realized what he was not saying. "You're pitching me on rejuvenation?"

"Well…yes. I mean, that is clearly your first priority."

I sat back. Caution mixed with the anger I was feeling. "I'm not shopping for rejuvenation."

His jaw dropped.

The doctor gave a strangled sound. "Biologically, you're in your last decades. Of course you must rejuvenate and, I judge, within the next few years, before your telomeres have shortened beyond the point of regeneration."

I looked her in the eye. "I'm already dying." I looked back at Blankenburg. "Rejuvenation is not on the table here. Move on."

"It doesn't matter," the doctor insisted. "Rejuvenation addresses a vast array of medical conditions and resets them out of existence."

"Next?" I asked Blankenburg, my jaw tight.

He shook his head. "There is no next. If you want crush juice, you must rejuvenate."

Cards up.

I was breathing too hard. Hyperventilating myself into an oxygen-deprived panic attack wouldn't help me here. I controlled my breath, waiting for calm to return.

Rejuvenation was out of the question. Juliyana was a Ranger, but her pocketbook wasn't endless. She could not afford to pay for my rejuvenation. Neither could I. I had lived aboard the family barge without income for decades. There, they had to feed me.

Blankenburg must have guessed some of my thoughts, for he said, "You're a former Ranger, yes?"

"You looked up my serial number. Congratulations."

He shook his head. "You have a military bearing about you."

"So has half the Empire."

"I've never been in the Rangers. Neither has anyone I know," Blankenburg replied. "I believe the current recruitment rate is eighteen percent of the statistically surveyed population of the Empire."

"So I was a Ranger, so what?"

"Then you have never negotiated for rejuvenation before. Half-life mortgages are the normal way of arranging them."

"Not where I come from." Enslave myself for thirty years to pay off the medical debt? "Anyway, you said your mortgages were bonded."

Bonded mortgages were even worse. Not only did I have to work for someone else for thirty years, but I didn't get a choice about who I worked with. True, I wouldn't have to pay interest on the mortgage, but whoever held my mortgage bond got to tell me what to do, where to go and how to breathe. I would be a slave in all but name, so that at the end of the thirty years, I would get another twenty or twenty-five years of free life, before having to go through the rigmarole all over again.

No, thank you.

"The rejuvenation process the Rangers provide is not a form of bondage?" Blankenburg asked me. "After all, you work for the Emperor, for more than thirty years. If you stop working as a Ranger, no more rejuvenation. The difference is?" He cocked a brow.

He had a point, but I didn't like it. "That's completely fucking different."

He pressed his palms to the table. "It is not my intention to get into semantics. I am only here to find a solution for you."

I rubbed my temple. "No offence, Blankenburg, because you give the appearance of having good intentions, but your offer sucks like a vacuum."

The medico leaned forward. "Do you have a headache?" Her voice was sharp.

"Only all the fucking time," I told her. "Especially when I have to deal with assholes like you." I looked at Blankenburg. "Are we done? Do you have any other offer to make?"

"I don't think we could make you an offer you would consider." He was smart. He knew when to give up.

I got my feet.

"At least let me scan you before you go. I might be able to relieve your headache," the doctor said, her tone concerned.

"I already know how to relieve the headache," I told her, and demonstrated that by turning and leaving.

I lied. My headache did not go away. It got worse.

Juliyana had found a two-berth room. I parked myself on the other bunk, as she sat and listened to the shortened version of my clinic visit.

Her response was pragmatic. "Where does that leave us, then? Should I go on alone?"

"Gabriel Dalton won't talk to you. Not about this. Hell, the chances he'll talk to me are slim. He hates my guts. But he knew me. He doesn't know you."

She nodded. "Then you're probably not going to like this. Gabriel Dalton's military record is sealed. I can't get into it, not officially." She considered me. "You have a different way of reaching him?"

"Not from here. Any communications goes through the array. The array is controlled by the Emperor." I considered. "All I need is Dalton's location. A face-to-face is the only way to handle this."

"Now who's being paranoid?"

"Basic security precautions," I told her. "Why do you think senior officers still hand orders over personally?"

"Without the crush shot, you can't get anywhere near a military base," Juliyana said. "He will just have to talk to me, instead."

"Suck up a breath and hold still for a while," I told her irritably. "I'll figure this out."

"When? No offence, Danny, but your head could implode at any time. If you drop dead, then it's on me. I can't be a supernumerary on this. I need to be up the sharp end with you, so I can take over, if that time comes."

"A few days will not kill me."

"They *might*." Her voice was tight. "I'm not in this to make sure you get your closure."

"You want your career back," I said heavily. "I am aware."

She lifted a brow. "So how do you intend to fix this?"

"I don't know yet. But in the meantime, there are things we can do."

"Like what?"

"I think a conversation with Dancy is in order. I can do that from here."

"*Dancy.*" Her voice was flat. She didn't like Dancy any more than I did. He had replaced her mother in Noam's heart. "The man is so self-centered, I'd be surprised he's even registered that Noam is dead."

I upped her dislike to a few notches above mine. "He made Noam happy," I reminded her. "He was the closest person to Noam when he died. A few questions about Noam's state of mind at that time might generate some interesting answers." I reached for my pad.

It took three hours for a channel to become available.

And within a few seconds of hooking up to Dancy's private code, I realized the conversation would be of no help. Dancy glared at me through the screen, his jaw working. So did his throat. "That was forty years ago. Why are you trying to dig that up now?"

"He was my son," I reminded him. "I have reason to ask questions right now. I'm sorry if they distress you." I was mortally aware of the time counting down in the top left corner of the screen. The direct live feed to Dancy would only remain open for as long as the gates did. That would last only a few minutes.

"Distress me?" His voice rose. "You have no idea..." He got himself back under control. "It took me years to offload the damage he left behind. People are only just starting to trust me again. For years they figured I was as nuts as he was, and likely to take down the nearest military establishment in some sort of crazy suicide run, to complete his work."

Behind the screen of my pad and well out of sight of Dancy, Juliyana raised her brow. I could hear her *wow* without her needing to say it aloud.

I wouldn't break through Dancy's bitterness with a simple appeal to his better nature. I braced myself and said, "I'm dying, Dancy. The doctors tell me I have weeks, maybe only days. As a favor to me, before that happens, would you answer a few questions about Noam for me?"

He blinked at me, his intense dark-eyed gaze seeing me properly for the first time. "Damn, Danny, I'm sorry."

I nodded.

Dancy rubbed the back of his neck. "I don't know if I can give you any answers you will find satisfying. Noam and I… Noam left me, weeks before he died."

Juliyana sat up.

I hesitated. "I guess I'm sorry, too, then. I didn't know that."

He grimaced.

"Exactly how long before he died did he leave?" I added. "I'm sorry to prod, but…"

Dancy sighed. "Six weeks? I'm not entirely sure. Not anymore. It's not something I documented."

Dancy was a researcher—an archival archeologist. For him to forgo documenting anything was significant. I nodded sympathetically. "What was Noam like before he left?"

"About what you'd expect from a man winding himself up to leave. He was moody. He picked arguments. That is, when he was actually home."

"Well, he *was* a Ranger."

"Was he?" Dancy asked. The bitterness was back in his voice. "For nearly a year before he left, his uniform stayed in the closet. He didn't wear it, not once. When I asked him about it, he snarled at me. I never asked again."

I didn't ask him what Noam was doing all the time the uniform stayed in the closet, because I already knew. It was something to do with the Imperial Shield. Only, I couldn't tell Dancy that. "So, when he was home, he was argumentative?"

"Why do you need to know this? Really?" Dancy demanded.

"I'm trying to figure out what Noam was doing before he died," I said carefully. Dancy already knew Noam had been up to something mysterious, so there was no harm in referring to it.

"He was diving into the deep end of crazy," Dancy said. "You won't make sense of it."

"Actually, craziness usually has a coherent logic in it—at least to those who own the construct."

"What does it matter?" he said tiredly. "It doesn't change anything. And it won't bring him back."

"No, but it might let you feel a little more kindly about him," I said gently.

"I feel nothing about him at all, anymore. Don't bother bringing me up to date, even if you find something out. Is there anything else, Danny?"

"I have to ask. Did Noam leave behind anything which might give clues about what was on his mind around them? Journal entries? Personal funds?"

Dancy's jaw worked. His eyes glittered. "If he did, I wouldn't know. I deleted his personal archive." He stared at me, daring me to berate him for this.

Instead, I said, "I'm sorry, Dancy. I won't bother you again. Thank you for your time."

He didn't nod or speak. He merely broke the connection.

The timer in the corner of the screen disappeared, to be

replaced with a dialog box telling me the cost of the call, and a button to accept the charges. That single conversation had cost me the equivalent of a month's rent.

"I think this is the last phone call we'll be making," I said dryly, handing the pad back to Juliyana.

Her face paled as she saw the cost flashing on the screen. She prodded the pay box and put the pad aside. "And such a helpful conversation, too."

"Actually, it was. Noam's behavior before he left confirms he was with the Imperial Shield. It is proof the transfer orders are legitimate."

"We already knew that," she pointed out.

"And now we have independent corroboration. We also know there are no personal files or journals to help us figure out what's going on. That cuts off a great many avenues of investigation. If he was away from home a lot, and even Dancy didn't know what was going on, it's likely any other of Noam's friends would also draw a blank. So, we must concentrate on his commanding officer, who can point us toward his next CO."

"First, we have to find him." She glanced at the pad beside her hip. "And we are *not* phoning him." She got to her feet. "Let's go and get some real food, while I can still afford it. I could murder a steak right now."

It sounded like a fine idea to me. But then, I forget things.

5

JULIYANA GOT HER STEAK. ONCE upon a time I enjoyed a good steak, too, but these days my appetite lasts as long as the sizzle does. A full steak was wasted on me. I settled for another sandwich, printed. I had too much on my mind to worry about the size of the bill, too.

"When do you have to report back for duty?" I asked Juliyana as she chewed with a blissful expression. We had even snagged a table and two chairs. Considering the bottom line of the bill we would get for this meal, the table and two chairs didn't seem like too much to ask for. At least we weren't at the bar, where the stools were placed so close together it was impossible to eat without ramming your elbow into the next person's ribs.

"I took a leave of absence." She swallowed. "They didn't even argue, which shows you how much I was needed around there."

A leave of absence could negatively impact one's military records. Juliyana was risking much to deal with her father's history. "How long do you think this will take?" she added, her voice inflecting upward.

"I have no idea. Nothing seems to be straightforward about this, so I figured a time limit would be one more problem to deal with. I'm glad to hear there isn't one."

"I can't stay away forever," she pointed out. Her eyes narrowed. She was looking at something over my shoulder.

"Man on your six, coming your way," she murmured, then shifted her gaze to her dinner plate.

I didn't turn around to look. "Armed?"

She smiled as if she was saying something funny. "No, but he looks useful."

I braced myself, although the last time I had been in any physical altercation, I had ended up on my back, with my jaw close to dislocated. I wasn't sure how useful I would be.

Juliyana made a great show of cutting her next forkful of steak, which kept the knife in her hand. She didn't take the bite.

"Danny Andela?" came the question.

Juliyana looked up as if she was surprised at the interruption. I jerked as if I had been just as surprised and swiveled on the chair to look up at him.

Tall, heavy shoulders, not-puny wrists. A potbelly from too many carbs and no muscle definition. Juliyana could take him. I wasn't certain I could, not anymore.

"Who wants to know?" I said.

"I'm Billy." He crouched so his head was level with ours. It stopped me from straining my neck, which I appreciated.

Juliyana put down her fork. The knife had disappeared.

Billy gave her a wide smile. "You can put the knife down, too, Juliyana. I'm not here with violence in mind."

"Okay, so you know who we are. Talk fast, or you lose a finger," I told him.

"Or two," Juliyana added.

His smile didn't slip, although he took his hand off the edge of the table, where he had rested it to maintain balance.

He glanced around, spotted a spare chair, snagged it and brought it over to the table and sat down.

I tried not to let it bother me that he hadn't asked if it was okay for him to join us. My gaze shifted to Juliyana. Her face was smooth, her eyes blank. She was pissed, too.

He didn't seem to notice. Instead he looked at my plate. "A bowl of soup and a salad would go well with that sandwich. Can I get you some?"

"I have zero appetite," I said, my voice flat.

"Another steak, Juliyana?"

"Ten seconds and counting," she replied.

He held out his wrist. "Feel free."

Juliyana waved her pad over his wrist. It pinged as she read it. Her face still did not twitch. She passed the pad over to me.

Instead of the usual serial number ID read out, a white square sat in the center of the screen. Five words.

Billy Kurzel. Agent at large.

"It doesn't tell me a fucking thing," I said, putting the pad down. It was another lie.

"Who do you work for?" Juliyana pressed.

"Various different parties," he said airily.

"You're not getting any closer to the point," I said.

He nodded calmly, as if he didn't know Juliyana could break his neck and go back to her steak without raising her pulse.

"Appearances can be so deceiving, can't they?" he said. "When I heard the Imperial Hammer was on the station, it made me sit up. I'm sure everyone who looks at you discounts your history." His gaze upon me was steady.

"Let me guess. *You* don't discount me?"

"Precisely. I have spent an instructive few hours going over your history. It is a pleasure to meet you, Danny Andela."

I didn't let down my guard. "The clinic sent you, didn't they?"

Juliyana rolled her eyes and made an impatient noise.

"Whatever happened to patient confidentiality around here?"

"I wasn't a patient," I reminded her. I recalled the quick scan the boy at the front of the clinic had taken of my wrist. "The clinic and I chose not to complete any business arrangements. They sold the information to this barracuda, instead."

Billy's smile shifted a little. "Blankenburg thought I could help you. As it happens, I can almost guarantee I can."

I looked at Juliyana. "He's a recruiter for paramilitary outfits."

Billy's smile disappeared altogether. He glanced over his shoulder, for we were not sitting inside a privacy bubble right now. "I didn't say that," he said quickly.

"You have access to tech which can divert a serial number inquiry. You hotfooted it here as soon as you heard I was on the station." I smiled at him. "And you know who the Imperial Hammer is. There are not too many people outside the Rangers who know the name. The paramilitary outfits we used to fight certainly did." I smiled at him. "You realize you're sitting beside a Ranger right now?"

His glance flickered toward Juliyana. "You're not in uniform. You can't arrest me if you're not officially on duty."

"Oh, I'd much rather hear you hang yourself a bit higher, before my grandmother drops a heavy load on you," she said, her tone bright and cheery.

Billy's eyes narrowed. "I think we've got off on the wrong foot."

Juliyana snorted.

He turned to me. "You have spent your adult life enjoying the privileges of military life, which includes regeneration and the very best and most advanced medical care available in the Empire. You didn't pay a cent for it. What if I could make that happen for you again?"

I gotta admit that for a fraction of a heartbeat, I entertained the possibility. Then, like cards rifling from one hand to the other, the sequence of decisions and logic reasserted themselves: My time was done. My reputation was gone. Let it go.

I shook my head, regretfully. "All I'm looking for is crush juice. I have no time left to sign up for even a short-term contract."

Billy rubbed his jaw thoughtfully. "You don't seem to understand. You can very nearly write your own terms. The people I represent understand your value." He paused. "If you have something to do, somewhere to go, and clearly you do, because you want crush juice, then there may even be a way for us to delay the contract activation long enough for you to deal with your personal issues first."

"Wow, they really want you, don't they?" Juliyana said.

"You understand I was kicked out of the Rangers, don't you?" I asked Billy.

His eyes sparkled. "You formally resigned. It's of no concern to us. You were a senior colonel in the combat battalions. Your expertise cannot be bottled or turned into an algorithm. People will pay for your experience and wisdom." He leaned forward to emphasize his point. "Do you know how many wars are running in the Empire right now?"

"I'm sure you're about to tell me."

"Official, declared wars; thirty-seven. Those are wars between acknowledged states, including corporate and ballbound. Undeclared wars, skirmishes, infiltrations and other paramilitary activities, documented and undocumented, well... I could sit here a long time listing those. The people I work for have an interest in many of those arenas and could use someone with your skills."

"But first I have to rejuvenate," I said, my voice dry.

"With us, the rejuvenation therapy you would receive

would be the most advanced that is currently available. As good as military grade."

"Of course it would be," I replied. "You would want your performing monkey to be at her best."

Billy did not seem to be offended by the analogy. The corner of his mouth lifted a little. "I *can* tell you that if we don't find a mutually agreeable arrangement, the only option you have left is a civilian therapy." All amusement faded in his face. "There is a reason most people choose bonded mortgages for their rejuvenation. The civilian rejuvenation therapy is not worth the price. Besides, thirty years out of the hundreds we all get to live, now, is nothing."

"Thirty years out of every fifty or sixty is fucking bullshit," I replied. "And besides," I added, my anger kicking in, "I'm not interested in rejuvenation. I keep repeating this, and no one hears me. If I have to repeat myself to you once more, Juliyana will shove the point of her steak knife into whatever organ she is currently pointing it at."

"His left testicle," she said calmly.

Billy looked down and licked his lips. He frowned. "I don't understand—"

"Clearly," I replied. "Let me make this simple enough so you get it. I am not looking for rejuvenation. I want crush juice. Period."

He swallowed. "Your cells are too old for crush juice." His voice was strained.

"In that case, we have no common ground upon which to do business. I suggest you leave. Quickly."

He rose to his feet, scraping the chair across the floor. He straightened his shoulders. "You will be back," he told me. "You will come back when you have figured out that mine is the only way. And then, the people I work for will not be as understanding as they would have been now. Think on that."

He turned and moved away.

Juliyana watched him go, then dropped the steak knife on the table with a grimace. "As much as I hate to say it, he may have a point, there at the end."

I didn't answer her. I understood both their perspectives and I didn't like either of them. The idea of selling half my life to gain the other half made me feel sick. Slavery has always offended me, despite the fact that in tens of thousands of years of human history, we have never managed to fully eradicate the disease. It keeps returning—a new name, a new strain, each time with restored virulence and persistence.

What was worse about this modern version was that people sold themselves into their own slavery to gain long life. They seem to feel it was worth the trade.

I did not. I looked at Juliyana. "There is a reason I look the way I do right now," I pointed out to her. "Our family has a long history of military service, for the same reason."

Juliyana rubbed her temples, frowning. "I don't understand," she said. "You formally resigned. You should have got back pay, hospital bonuses, vacation pay, decoration and honors bonuses, time served... It should have been more than enough for rejuvenation, even if you ate algae pseudo food for a decade."

I cleared my throat. "Are you done with your steak?"

Juliyana's eyes narrowed. "You did have the money, then..." She looked up at me as I stood up. "What did you *do* with it all?"

"I'm tired," I said, making my voice waver querulously. "I want to lie down."

Juliyana considered me for a moment, her fingers tapping the handle of the steak knife. Then she got to her feet. "Is there *anyone* mixed up in this who isn't holding back a fuckton?" She stalked off.

The dreams were bad, right from the beginning. They gripped my head and my heart and squeezed. Noam refused to look at me properly, no matter how much I strained to see his face in the full.

The sensation of something coming, some nameless and formless dread, was more intense, more certain than it had ever been. I felt that if I could peer over my shoulder, I might see it right behind me, its teeth bared.

Only, I couldn't look. All I could do was hold my breath, while my old, thin heart tried to cope.

The worst of it was that even though he would not look at me, Noam was not just asking me to stay, this time. He was trying to warn me. In the wordless way of dreams, he was trying to make me see the menace behind me.

Also in the way of dreams, I was helpless to turn around.

When I woke, I found I had sweated through my clothes and the sheets beneath me.

It was almost a relief to haul my exhausted body into an upright position. I reached for my pad, under the pillow. I knew I was reaching for distraction but didn't care.

At least one ship must have come through the gates while I was sleeping, for communications and newsfeeds had been updated. I had dozens of messages. Even for an old woman hiding away in an apartment on her family barge, I always received a ton of mail. Most of it was to do with family administration. As a major shareholder, I was legally entitled to copies of any communications to the Board from the CEO or anyone with family related business.

Most of the mail I read once, then deleted. I was still going through them, when Juliyana stirred and pushed herself up on one elbow.

"It's the middle of the night," she pointed out.

"Yep."

She sat up properly and scrubbed at her hair, then wound it up and tied it into a knot at the back of her head. "Now I'm wide awake, too." She moved to the edge of the bed and stretched. "Most people use their implants for messages," she pointed out, looking at my pad.

"Uh-huh."

She studied me. "Using your implants gives you headaches, too?"

"Something like that."

I thought I had shunted her aside, for the silence stretched while I opened and discarded two more messages.

"How can you stand it?" Juliyana asked softly.

"Stand what?"

"Having your body break down like it is? Watching it happen. Feeling it."

I looked up at her. "I should take Billy up on his offer, then?"

"No, that's not what I'm saying. There have to be alternatives. There has to be a way. Anything is better than just giving up."

"I'm not giving up. I'm here with you, aren't I?"

"Only you're obsessed with *not* rejuvenating. It's like you're punishing yourself for something..." She grew still. "Really? Is that what you're doing? Do you think dying will make up for what Noam did?"

"Back off, Ranger. Right now."

Juliyana stiffened. "Yes sir." She grabbed her sack. "I'm going for a shower." Her voice was tight.

I let her go. I might've argued, or even tried to apologize, except my attention was suddenly and sharply grabbed by the message I had just opened.

It was from the Carranoak accounting department, sent directly to me, with no copies to anyone else. It was a request for me to approve the dispersal of this year's dividends for the Board and the major shareholders. All I had to do was add my chop and indicate which of the holding accounts should be used for dispersal.

It had to be a mistake. Farhan, as the CEO, got to approve the dividend payout. Only, technically, as the majority share-holder, I outranked him. Had some AI failed to take into account the family dynamics, and instead followed formal procedures?

I looked at the amount glowing on the screen. Farhan had been depressed about the miserable financial situation of the family. The dividend payout for each of us was, I admit, a lot smaller than previous years. Only, I was looking at the bottom line. The sum total of *all* dividends.

The amount made me tremble.

I looked at the screen for a long time, my heart thudding.

Then I pushed the board back under my pillow, as far away from me as possible, thrust on my boots and went out for fresh coffee. Sleeping wasn't helping me.

Being awake wasn't fun, either.

6

JULIYANA WASN'T WRONG ABOUT IT being the middle of the night. The corridors were deserted and the lights turned down to just enough to see my way.

It was disconcerting. I have rarely been on a station which wasn't permanently awake. Hell, most of the bars and stores didn't have doors or locks, for they never shut. They just rotated through staff in endless shifts, while the concourse lights blazed, the noise spiraled, and passengers came and went in tidal waves.

Even the *Umb Judeste* was alive at all hours on the lower decks, although the higher family levels could reach this level of stillness. Sometimes.

My chances of finding fresh coffee in these ghostly corridors were not good, although I pressed on toward the wider passage where the landing bays were located. That wide lane was as close to a concourse the station had to offer. I could perhaps find a public printer I could coax into handing over a cup.

Hunting for one was something to do, other than sleeping. Or reading messages on my pad.

The main corridor was as empty of people as any other corridor I had already passed through. I didn't mind being alone, though.

The passage differed from the functional corridors which ran off it, not just because it was wider, but because it was irregularly shaped. Bays carved regular spaces out of the sides. Each bay was a storefront. There was even a bar — with shutters over the windows and zero light showing anywhere. No advertisements pocked the façade, either.

I couldn't imagine any spacer gravitating toward this bar, except it was the only one I found as I moved up and down the corridor. Most stations had a bar, a more-or-less discreet brothel, a day-hilton, longer term accommodation and at least one food outlet in between landing bays and official services and administration. Unregulated and unofficial merchants plied up and down the concourse, selling goods and services which ranged from unusual to illegal. I was offered a three-humped camel, once. I had to look up what a camel was.

They came for me out of the narrowest of service trenches just as I passed by, my irritation growing, along with my need for caffeine.

I spotted them from the corner of my eye, and my arm came up instinctively. My right hand reached for the shriver, which was no longer on my hip.

They wore reflective masks and muted clothing, which blocked all telling details. I couldn't base gender upon height, either. The only thing I knew for certain was that they were not friendly. That was all I needed to know.

The arm of the first slapped up against my forearm, making my arm and shoulder creak heavily with the impact. The second and third stepped around him and came for me from the flanks.

Not good.

It occurred to me with the sensation of the last piece of a puzzle dropping into place, that they were utterly silent in their approach. They were not raising their voices with threats or demands.

They wanted this to be soft and invisible.

So I opened my mouth, filled my lungs, and bellowed as hard as I could. "Help! Help me! They're attacking me!"

"Shut her up, will you?" the leader breathed. Male.

The two on my flanks were trying to get their hands on me. Inevitably they would, for I was outnumbered, but I had no intention of making it easy for them. I kicked and punched and twisted. I kept my feet moving. It had been decades since I had taken on three at a time. Once, it would have barely raised my pulse.

The most shocking aspect of the struggle was how truly weak I had become. Women recruited in the Rangers were taught early in their careers how to offset their gender disadvantages, with moves and blocks and defenses which didn't require huge amounts of upper body strength or muscle. Yet now, even those tricks, when I applied them, didn't send my attackers staggering back or drop them to the ground. They grunted. I was handing out pain, certainly, but it didn't slow them down.

Even though I put my full body weight behind my fist, it landed with the impact of a pillow.

"Duck, Danny," Juliyana said, from behind me.

I was really glad she had not directed me to leap to the side. I was exhausted. Gratefully, I dropped to the ground, thrusting out my hand so I could stay squatting and not lose my balance. It was not out of the question that I might have to move fast in a moment. I needed to keep my feet under me.

Juliyana leapt over me, using her impetus to drive the heel of her hand against the middle guy's face. I suspect she was aiming for where she thought his jaw might be, underneath the reflecting mask.

A metallic crunch sounded, as her fist drove through the

mask. This time, the man staggered back in an uncontrolled manner I found highly satisfying. Even more comforting was the thud of his landing.

Juliyana swung to tackle the one who had been reaching for me from my right. He had shifted to come at me from behind. All his attention was on Juliyana, for she held her standard issue serrated blade.

So I hooked my elbow around his ankle and yanked with all my might. It was delightful to feel the floor vibrate as he dropped.

Juliyana spun again. Her hair, still wet from the shower, sprayed droplets around her as she took on the third man.

I crept-walked my way out of the range of action, then carefully got to my feet. I didn't need to watch the outcome of the bout. Juliyana was a trained Ranger.

By the time I turned to see how it was going, the third man also laid on the floor. A puddle of blood spread from beneath him. Juliyana sucked the tip of her finger, looking vexed. "He hurried me."

I glanced up and down the corridor. Despite this being the most central and busiest corridor, the shut down station meant not a single other soul had been stirred by either my shouting, or the sounds of the fight. Although, like most knife fights, it had been eerily silent.

I tugged on Juliyana's arm. "Put your knife away," I ordered her. "Leave them."

"We should report to the station authorities." The good Ranger, following procedure.

"They'll have paid off station security at least. No one came running," I pointed out.

"*Who* paid off security, though?"

I pulled on her arm again. It barely moved her, because I was weak and shaking with adrenaline aftermath. I tugged again. This time she stirred and followed me along the corridor. After a few steps, she put the knife away.

Walking was the best thing I could have done. By the time we reached our rented room, my shaking had subsided and my brain was working things through.

Juliyana sat on the edge of her bunk, her hands on her knees, squeezing them. "What was that all about?" she asked, sounding deeply confused. "We haven't been spending money here. You don't dress rich. What did they want from you?"

"They didn't want something from me. They wanted *me*."

Juliyana put it together with an almost audible click. Her mouth dropped open. "Billy's employers..."

I nodded. "Apparently, telling them no wasn't enough."

Juliyana's face grew stormy. "I should have punctured his balls for him."

"He's just a go-between. He passed on my 'no.' and whoever they are decided negotiations were not quite done yet."

"Could they do that? Abduct you, force you to take rejuvenation and *make* you work for them?"

Her naivete was understandable. Like me, she served in the combat battalions. I had no direct experience with civilian law enforcement, although I had a number of friends who had dedicated their Ranger careers to law enforcement. Some of the conversations around the table, late at night when they were relaxed, had been brow raising.

"These people have methods to force their recruits to behave themselves. The most popular one is the introduction of a drug tailored to their DNA, which makes the recruit dependent upon the father organization for their steady supply." I drew a breath, let it out. "That's what they were doing forty years ago. I'm sure they have far more creative ways to bind their soldiers to them, these days."

Juliyana shuddered. "I've heard rumors, over the years. I'm combat, so I never saw any evidence of it. I figured it was exaggeration, at best."

I glanced around the room. "We can't stay here. We'll need another room, under a different name." Although how I was to manage that, I would have to figure out later. Getting around the serial number in one's wrist required funds, time and some dubious connections.

Money did not have to be a problem anymore, though. I pulled the pad out from under the pillow and turned it on. The message glowed up at me.

"Danny?" Juliyana asked quietly, as if she thought she was interrupting me mid-thought.

She *was* interrupting, only I had been around and around this thought track more than once already. I looked up at her. "I can get us out of this, in a way that will let us follow Noam down his rabbit hole. But…"

"Do it," Juliyana said, her voice flat.

"No questions?"

Juliyana slapped her damp hair back over her shoulder and straightened her back. "I know they were just paramilitary thugs, yet it feels like things are moving. We picked up a twig and prodded, and something stirred and hit back. So now, I *really* don't care what it takes. I have to follow this to the end." She raised her brow and looked at me. "You?"

I smoothed my thumb over the corner of the pad, feeling the softness and thinness of the skin on the ball, thinking.

I could return to my apartment on the family barge and wait for the next seizure which would kill me. Or I could follow this trail as far as it went and see where it led me.

I thought of Juliyana's first reaction after the fight out there in the corridor. She had reached for procedure, for what was right.

"Like father, like daughter," I murmured.

That was the crux of it, right there. The Noam I knew didn't match with the Noam the rest of the world thought they knew. And now I had evidence that they were wrong, all of them. Every single person in the Empire.

Except for the two women sitting in this room. Oh, and whoever had goosed Juliyana into this chase in the first place. Somewhere along the line, I knew we would find who that was. I had been in such chases before and recognized the shape of the track forming ahead of us.

That was when I realized I had made up my mind. I was already forming strategies for moving ahead.

So I pressed my thumb with its thin skin over the glowing green button on the screen, entered my personal account information, then shut down the pad.

I looked at Juliyana. "Okay, then."

7

ZILLAH'S WORLD WAS TOO LIMITED for what we had to do next, although we stayed there for another twenty-four hours while we planned and did some necessary research.

At the end of that time, at the very last minute, Juliyana brought us a pair of tickets upon a five-star cruiser to New Phoenicia.

I had given up any hope that travel would become less of a strain. Even a smooth, cushioned five-star line jump left me half-crippled and forced to move slowly.

Juliyana did not make me feel guilty about slowing her down. She trod steadily alongside me and sometimes wordlessly propped me up, especially when we reached steps.

New Phoenicia is one of the busiest travel hubs in the Empire. It was also one of the oldest. That was not what drew me to choose it as our destination, though. It was the often-overlooked fact that New Phoenicia also had a suburb in its floating city devoted to medicine and human therapy. Unlike Zillah's World, it was not a research organization with tacked -on shopfronts. New Phoenicia was purely about profit—and they made a handsome one because their services were as good as any the military could provide.

In fact, the military often used New Phoenicia for medical services when they were at full capacity themselves. It was how I knew about the therapy complex in the first place. The hospice attached to my battalion had reached out to New

Phoenicia more than once, when engaged in long, hard wars where they needed the extra capacity.

I had even suffered through being a patient there once, myself. That was long before I rose through the ranks. I was a green grunt still learning how to duck properly and keep her head down.

Amongst the hundreds of thousands of visitors per day station saw, we were two anonymous women. Well, not so anonymous in my case, for I drew the eye. Yet we could disappear in this crowd and not draw *too* much attention.

We took the shuttle to the therapy complex. We could have walked there, for air tubes and walkways ran all around the city. We didn't, because I had the money, now, and I just didn't have the energy, anymore. It had been a long few days.

Unlike the clinic on Zillah's World, there were no human attendants in the foyer. There were discrete inquiry terminals, soft lighting and a pleasant murmur of industry from behind the doors lining the foyer.

I pulled Juliyana to one side. "I will fast-track this, but it could still be two months or more."

"I have my orders. It will take me all that time to deal with them, anyway."

"You'll have to find a way of disappearing, while you find us new IDs," I pointed out to her. It was one of the points I had not specifically discussed with her, but now I was nervous.

"I'll be fine. I'll find some poor sucker just emerged from his rejuvenation, and shack up with him in his hilton, while he vents all his newfound energies upon me."

I stared at her.

"What? It keeps my name off any registration role."

I decided she was joking. I also decided she was good

enough to not have me direct her every single step.

Juliyana smiled grimly. "I can be resourceful, too, Danny."

"I have no doubt of that, or I would not be leaving you alone out there."

She looked surprised. "Okay, then."

We both smiled.

Then Juliyana left. I turned to one of the terminals. After a round of introductions, which included me baring my wrist and having my serial number scanned, then the terminal welcoming me back, I told the AI what I wanted. "Express rejuvenation and inertia inoculation."

One of the internal doors opened with a soft swish. "Right this way, please," the terminal told me.

My nerves shrieking, I stepped through the door.

A medical aid in casual clothes, which likely would be recycled after every shift, settled into an armchair next to mine, in front of a crackling fire which was completely fake, but looked real enough to make me relax.

She asked many questions, some of them bewildering in their irrelevance. What did my preference in olives tell them?

She took no notes, so I presumed the conversation was being recorded. Or perhaps she had the new advanced implants which allowed her to take notes mentally. For all I knew, she was accessing my personal file directly and adding notations even as she sat with her hands around her crossed knee, with her foot swinging casually.

"Our records indicate you have some non-organics. One of ours, in fact. The left arm," She frowned. "And your large toe, not ours."

"Ever tried walking without your toes?" I asked her.

"We could regenerate the toe for you, if you want."

I raised my brow. "Really?" Then, "Why not?"

Her foot stopped swinging. "Your implants are quite old."

"As I'm very old, that's hardly a surprise,"

Her smile was ghostly. "I meant they seem to be malfunctioning. Have you been getting headaches lately?"

"The better question would be how often I *don't* get headaches. It would be a shorter answer."

She nodded. "Implant replacement is part of basic rejuvenation. The only question remains, what type of implants you prefer. We have a range—"

"The best," I said.

She hesitated.

"What implants are the Rangers using, these days?" I added.

"Those are a proprietary, limited issue licenses."

"You have a civilian version which is as good, if not better, right? For those willing to pay for it, I mean." I fixed her with a steady gaze.

She gazed into the middle distance for a moment. Then she nodded. "We can arrange that."

I wondered if her implants were letting her speak directly with someone outside the room. Another version of Blankenburg, perhaps. One with the sense to let his empathetic staff deal with the patients.

Selecting a rejuvenation package is not a simple affair. By the time she worked her way through the options and variations, discussed them with me and I made my selections, a meal was served and three rounds of coffee. Decaf, of course. The staff were discrete and pleasant, leaving us strictly alone at all other times.

A pad was presented to me, displaying a long contract with all the options I had chosen, including priority service,

CAMERON COOPER

advanced muscle development and my preferred cosmetic age. A table spread over several screens, listing gene expression choices. It was that table which made rejuvenation shopping so detailed and exhausting. Every package was tailored to one's own DNA. There was no such thing as a default package.

The aid got to her feet. "I'll give you some time to go through it. Take however long you need. If you have any questions, you can ask the pad. It is hooked to an AI who will explain most of the basics to you. If it cannot answer your queries properly, it will send for someone who can. There is no rush." Her smile was warm.

There was certainly a rush from my end, although I didn't bother her with that detail. Express service was in the contract—I spotted it in my first pass through the initial pages. As I was paying for preferred treatment, they would make sure it happened. The advantage of for-profit organizations is that they rely upon their reputation. A few whispers that they failed to meet their contractual obligations would damage their reputation and their revenue would dry up. I trusted them as far as the contract extended.

I read through the contract, every clause. There were a lot of them. I asked the AI, via the pad, to adjust some of the causes. I'd had more than a few years practice dealing with contracts. Directing a battalion was as much an administrative function as it was a battle commander's role.

When I was ready to sign, the medical aid magically returned. She witnessed my chop, I directed payment to the financial account she gave me, then she took the pad away. Business was concluded.

I was escorted to a suite with a bedroom larger than my entire apartment on the *Judeste*. When I was here several decades ago to rebuild my left arm, I shared a larger room with

76

other Rangers. It stopped us from going mad with boredom. Now, though, I wanted the privacy that came with the upgraded price.

I sat on the feather soft sofa and waited for the treatment to begin.

No one really remembers rejuvenation. Even the classic, long-term processes still leave the patient unaware for long periods of time. During those times, unpleasant things were done to the body, including the brain. At least, that was how I remember my last rejuvenation—a mostly blank period of time, bereft of thought, interrupted by a few moments of strained coherency.

That was not my experience this time. I sat on the sofa for an hour or so before the strain of the day's traveling caught up with me. I went to bed and snuggled into a mattress that was cloud soft and wondered if I would sleep at all…and if I did sleep, would I dream, as usual?

It was the last thought I had before I woke to morning sunshine and even a damn bird singing, nearby. I was refreshed and was not at all tired. I stretched.

The medical aid who had taken me through the contract stepped into the room. She was smiling again.

"Well hello," I told her. "Are we finally getting started, then?"

She surprised me by sitting on the bed. She gave a soft laugh. "You are already ten days into your treatment."

I stared at her.

"Look at your hand," she told me.

I lifted my hand up. The back of it, which had been covered in liver spots the last time I looked at it, was now free of all of them. The veins which had ridged so heavily were still distinct, but far less protruding than they had been. I was looking at the hand of a middle-aged woman, not one on the brink of dying.

"You started while I was sleeping..."

"It seems like sleep to you, of course. That is intentional. Patients are far less stressed if they are unaware of the impending processes."

"Only now you have tipped your hand. I know that more processes are impending."

"Only because the therapy has not finished. Are you hungry?"

"Is that why you woke me up? To have me eat something?"

"We could feed you nutritional yeast but having you awake and aware and moving around the room will help us assess progress so far. Feel free to get up and order a meal from the terminal."

"It isn't a printer?"

"We have a chef on staff." She got to her feet.

"You have a name I can use?"

"Dominica," she told me and went away.

I eased carefully out of bed and paused to stare at my knees. There were no longer wrinkles around the bones. The skin looked, and felt, firm.

It was only then I realized there were no mirrors in the room. The omission was deliberate, of course. They didn't want patients scaring themselves halfway through the process.

I went over to the small, efficient terminal and ordered my usual eggs. My stomach rumbled heavily and panged. I added bacon and toast. I upgraded the cup of coffee to a jug of coffee and cream, too. My mouth watered as I ordered it.

I sat on the sofa and found my sack placed at the other end. I dug out my pad and went through messages.

There were ten messages from Juliyana, one for each day

passed. All of them were cryptic, noncommittal. They consisted of "I'm fine, everything is proceeding," in one form or another.

Three days ago, I had received a message from Farhan. My spirits dropped when I saw it. Because I was expecting it, I made myself open the message.

The content of the message was no more or less than I expected, either. Farhan demanded I reroute the money back to the family account. He preferred to presume that I had diverted the dividends because of a simple misunderstanding. Although he did not fail to add the veiled threat of bringing Rangers down upon me.

The longer the delay before you respond to my request, the more certain I will become that your intentions are not those of a good family member, which will force me to proceed accordingly. It was nice corporate doublespeak. I deleted the message.

When the meal arrived, I wondered if I could eat any of it. Farhan's disapproval lingered, making my stomach roil. Then I caught a whiff of bacon.

I ate every single morsel, licked my fingers and wished there was more. I was on the verge of ordering a desert. Why the hell not? Then the jug of coffee registered, forcing me to my feet and into the *en suite*.

By the time I reemerged, I was exhausted. Sleep was tugging at me as if I had not slept for days. I barely stayed awake long enough to stumble over to the bed and climbed beneath the covers.

So soft… So warm…

My very last thought was that perhaps I would not dream this time, either, which made me very happy.

The next time I woke, I spotted an exercise leotard folded and sitting on the sofa.

I wanted to eat, but Dominica assured me my meal would taste far better once I exercised.

I was escorted to a gymnasium that included a full-sized swimming pool. The entire gym was completely empty. I had asked for privacy and they were abiding by the expensive agreement.

Dominica put me through a series of exercises which would have been impossible for the old woman who shuffled into the hospice, however many days ago it had been.

I wanted to laugh out loud as I felt my body respond to the demands with energy and strength. Just being able to touch my toes was enough to make me giggle.

I punched bags, and high kicked. Chin ups were no effort at all. I ran around the half-track, while Dominica timed me. It wasn't quite my personal best but if I had really wanted to, I had the sensation I could have burned that old record easily.

On that same awakening, they put me through the inertia inoculation. Patients had to be awake for crush juice shots. The flex of muscles, a moving body, and a higher metabolism helped the nanobots build the crystalline structures inside the cells that made them crush proof. While the nanobots worked, my body twitched and heated in a way that reminded me of menopause, except every single inch of me grew warm, from the feet upwards.

When the heat rose up my neck, I realized with a touch of cold shock that the new implants must have already been installed, sometime while I slept. They wouldn't administer crush juice before replacing the implants. That would force them to go through the process all over again, so the nanobots could incorporate the new implants into their scaffold-

80

building.

I ate enormously and wished I could kiss the chef on the cheek in thanks for her talent. Before I could pull out my pad and check messages, sleepiness dropped over me.

"Damn it..." I breathed and staggered over to the bed. "I'm coming, I'm coming," I added, hauled myself onto the bed...and passed out.

Overall, the course of rejuvenation took thirty-nine standard days, which I only got to count up later, when it was all over. I was pronounced "done" and Dominica escorted me to the foyer of the clinic. As before, no one else appeared. The machinery moved smoothly around us, giving me the absolute privacy I had requested.

"You look wonderful," Dominica told me, before we stepped through the door into the public foyer beyond. "I hope you're pleased?"

I thought about the crush juice which was circling my system, and would for nearly two more years, until I excreted the last of the expired nanobots. After that, as reinforced cells were replaced with normal cells, I would start to "feel" high-gee conditions more and more, until forced to take another course. "I am very pleased," I assured her.

"You're sure you don't want to look in a mirror?" Dominica asked. This had bothered her immensely.

"I know what I look like at twenty-six," I assured her. "This is not my first time."

Dominica grinned, a very unprofessional expression full of mischief, that made her eyes light up. "You will look eventually," she assured me. "You can thank us, then." She opened the door. "Or recommend us to your friends, instead."

The soft-sell was the single marketing push the clinic had given me, in all the time I was there.

"I'll consider that," I assured her, and meant it.

I stepped out into the real world, feeling light, strong and much taller than I had before, which wasn't possible.

Juliyana was waiting. She smiled when she saw me...then her smile got wider. "Hot damn..." she breathed.

"Shut up."

"*Shit* hot damn," she said, circling me. "I feel like I should hit on you."

I rolled my eyes. "*Not* the most productive use of our time."

Juliyana came to a stop in front of me. She raised her brow. "Okay, next?"

My stomach rumbled. "Food," I declared. With a touch of regret I realized that whatever meal I ate next would not be close to the caliber of the meals I had been enjoying in the clinic. Although the clinic could afford to provide the best. By my count, I had eaten seven meals in thirty-nine days.

Juliyana nodded. "Stars, yes! What you want? My treat."

"A big steak," I said firmly. "Maybe even two."

8

JULIYANA HAD LEARNED HER WAY around the city while I was out for the count. She took me to a restaurant with a view of the starscape through steel glass windows, and honest-to-goodness tablecloths. I plucked at our tablecloth in disbelief.

"It's retro," Juliyana explained.

"It's antique, is more like it. I've only ever seen such things in pictures."

However, the food made up for any quirkiness in the decorations. So did the starscape beyond the window.

We both ate extremely well, to the point where I pushed back from the table and placed a hand on my belly. There was no soft paunch there, anymore, and a very full stomach lay just beneath the taut flesh.

We looked at each other and laughed.

Juliyana's smile faded. She generated a privacy bubble with her pad and leaned forward.

I refilled my glass of wine and leaned forward, too. With the privacy bubble in place we could shout at each other and no one would hear it, only people learn to read lips for this very reason. So we kept our heads close together and murmured.

"It has been an interesting few weeks," Juliyana began.

"You got the IDs?"

She nodded. "You're Maisie Carol. I'm Maariki Junia. They'll stand up to basic scans. It would have cost three times as much to have DNA records adjusted to match ID, so I didn't bother with that. It's not like we have to run on these forever."

"We can always figure something out later, if we need to. That will do for now." I could understand her concern about funds. Just a few days of travel as a civilian had reminded me how expensive it was.

"So what comes next?" Juliyana said. "Now you can use the freight lines, where do we go?"

"I was hoping you would have the answer to that from your research while I was gone."

She nodded. "I've spent a lot of time in records lately. The problem is, if Dad was not with the Imperial Rangers when he died, then he was clearly with the Imperial Shield. We can't just walk up to the Shield and demand answers."

"Our only line of inquiry now is Noam's CO at the time. Gabriel Dalton."

Juliyana winced.

"What is it?"

"Well, I did find out where he is. I mean, where he *isn't*. The man's a deserter, Danny."

"*Deserter?* Major Dalton?" I ran that through my mind, turning it over. "As much as I hate to admit it, the man did show some traits of a personality which could consider desertion a viable option," I admitted. "Did he duck out to avoid charges?" That seemed the most likely.

"I don't know. There's nothing in the records to say what happened. One day he was on the job. Next day he was gone. The last entry says he is wanted for desertion, after failing to report for duty three days in a row."

"Maybe we can track him down. I don't give a damn if he's wearing a uniform or not. I just want him to answer some questions. Where was he posted when he rabbited?"

"Annatarr," Juliyana replied.

"*Annatarr*?" I repeated, shocked all over again. The moon base on Annatarr had been *my* last posting. That was where I knew Dalton from. "Dalton was serving there forty years ago. Did he get a posting and come back?"

She shook her head. "That's where he was posted, forty years ago. That's when he bolted."

I drew a breath. "When? Exactly?"

Juliyana said, "A month after Noam died."

"A *month*..." I repeated. My heart thudded heavily. The pulse spike had nothing to do with an old woman blowing too much energy, anymore. "The timing is fucking suggestive."

"It's more than that," Juliyana replied. She tapped her pad. "He didn't just desert. He disappeared. Completely. I searched for traces of him—and I've grown good at it. He took a civilian shuttle from the moon across to the station. He bid for passage on a freighter heading for here, as it happens—New Phoenicia. He never got off the freighter. There's no wrist scan showing his ID. Nothing. For all I know, the freight crew shoved him out an airlock while they were in the hole. Which isn't possible."

Exposure to whatever existed inside the wormhole tended to destroy ships. At least, the scientists presumed that was what happened. Every year a few ships jumped into gates and failed to emerge at the other end. As loss of the ship and all passengers and crew was the cost of testing the theory, no one had tried.

This ship *had* emerged, but without a passenger.

"How many passengers got on, and got off?" I asked.

Juliyana grimaced. "Thirty, at each end."

"He changed IDs mid-flight," I breathed. That was the reason for Juliyana's grimace. Thirty passengers, thirty possibilities. She had spent her time tracing the movements of all thirty passengers, from that journey, through to today, trying to find the anomalies, the odd man out.

No wonder she needed steak.

"It's our only lead," I pointed out. "We have to chase down all the possibilities. Starting tomorrow, I'll help you." I yawned, suddenly. They had warned me I would spend a lot of time sleeping for a while. I was going through a type of reverse puberty.

Juliyana grinned. "Come on. I'll take you home."

"Home?" I asked, startled.

Home, it turned out, was a little house on a narrow street, with daylights and faux clouds overhead, currently blanked out so the real starscape could shine through the translucent areas of the dome. It was late.

Juliyana trudged up the rickety stairs and opened the door to one of the upper rooms. It was a bedroom, with a narrow bed and a dresser and not much else.

I put my sack on the dresser. "It looks perfect," I declared.

I slept like a teenager.

The next day we settled at the small table in the tiny kitchen with a pot of coffee between us. My screen emitter sat in the center of the table where we would collate our findings. Our pads and coffee mugs were in front of us.

Juliyana threw up a list of the thirty passengers of the *Yarrow's Pride* onto the emitted screen.

"Crew, too," I said. "Desertion is a capital crime." In fact, it was the *only* automatic capital crime. "He had nothing left to lose. Killing a crew member and taking his place would be nothing, after that."

Juliyana grimaced and put the crew list up, too. "Although you'd think the other crew members would have noticed the switch."

"Not if he did it at the very last minute. They might have found the body after they arrived at the station, but by then, the passengers would be gone. They wouldn't report it to the Rangers, either. They're freight grunts."

Freighter companies and spacers preferred to look after their own, even if murder was involved. They lived an exclusionary life.

"If he switched with the crew, then the passenger manifest would be short," she pointed out.

"Then we start with passengers, then check the crew. This thing has stayed buried for forty years. The trace won't be in any of the obvious places."

After three days of it, though, I began to wonder if the trace would be found at all. "Damn, Dalton really did just up and vanish, didn't he?" I breathed, scrubbing at my hair. I felt thick locks and waves. Wheat-colored wisps flicked in the corners of my vision, drawing my attention because they were not silver.

I stretched and felt the tightness of unused muscles.

"What are you doing right now?" I asked Juliyana as she frowned at her pad.

"Trying an idea." Her tone was remote. "Dalton couldn't have flipped IDs with another passenger, because thirty passengers arrived and thirty passengers left. Therefore, he picked up a completely new ID from somewhere. Right?"

"It's entirely possible he had the ID when he left, and only activated after he left the base," I pointed out. "That's how I'd do it. The moment the ship emerged from the gate and links were live."

She noted. "So my theory is that he anticipated that someone would try what we are doing—checking everyone. It makes sense that as soon as possible, he would dump the new ID and get a second one."

"New IDs that pass all the scans are not cheap. You found out for yourself."

She looked at me. "He was a Ranger, and he only had to acquire one ID. So maybe he bought a second one, the same as I did."

"Fair point." I got up from the chair, twitchy from lack of movement. "And you're testing that, how?"

She shrugged. "I'm looking up all thirty passengers' statuses for today, here and now. If he dumped the arriving ID, then it would make sense that there is no trace of it, forty years later. It would have stopped leaving traces, a day, a month, a week or more after he left the ship."

"It's a good test. Have you found anything?"

"I'm up to passenger number twelve. So far, they're all leading perfectly ordinary spacer lives. Three of them migrated to planetary status. Two are dead but led busy lives right up until they died."

"No sign that those busy lives were faked?"

"There are photos of the guests at their wakes. Full family trees of mourners."

"That seems somewhat elaborate for an ID he might've used for only a few days. Okay, then." I picked up my jacket from the back of the chair.

"Where are you going?"

I grimaced. "Just going for a walk."

"Right now?" Juliyana's voice was flat with disbelief.

"It's nearly midnight. I thought I'd look at the stars through the dome."

She just stared at me.

"Okay, I'm going for a drink." And I wasn't thinking of the little wine bar at the end of the street, either.

Juliyana's eyes narrowed. Then her expression cleared and she sat back. "There's a joint across the way from landing bay ten that is a likely place for spacers. It will still be open, too."

"That is the place I had in mind," I admitted. I did not finish my thought aloud. The little spacer–favored bar had a doxy den tacked to the rear, with a discrete sign at the back of the bar, between the whiskey bottles, displaying an up-to-date certification and warranty.

Juliyana lost interest. She turned back to her pad, and I went to get my...drink.

In the three days since I had left the therapy complex, I had slept very little, except for that first night, when I digested far too many grams of organically grown steak.

Since that night, we had been hunched over pads and staring at 3D data arrays turning over the table, while we tried to sort out exactly where Gabriel Dalton was hiding. Being able to go for hours without sleep was a function of the young. I was enjoying those benefits once more.

Once I had cooled off my gonads with some very sweaty fucking with a pleasant and well-endowed professional, I came back to the little house and dropped back into bed, now willing to pay my sleep debt.

I had forgotten about the dreams.

I think, in the farther recesses of my mind, I assumed they were a symptom of my advanced age. Andrain's geriatric research indicated that older people tended to linger inside their heads, revisiting old times and rejecting the far-too-modern times of their current days.

I figured that the dreams were my version of escaping a too-fast, too energetic reality.

This dream was different, right out of the gate. No beach. No anything, actually. The one thing that was the same was that no one was there.

In the empty box of nothingness, Noam stood with his shoulder to me, as usual.

"I wish you would fucking look at me, at least once," I said/thought.

Norm turned to me and raised a brow, the way I had seen him do a thousand of times before. "Will looking at you make you feel any better? Will you listen, then?"

It didn't bother me right then that he was talking to me. After all, it was a dream. Even though I didn't process that it was a dream right then. I have never had lucid dreams, and this certainly was not one of them.

"What am I supposed to be listening to?"

"Well, to me, at least. Spare some of your energy to consider a few things." He seemed amused.

It didn't occur to me that he was dead. Not in my dream. Yet there was a sense of wistfulness whispering through me as I stared at him. "Okay, shoot. What am I supposed to be listening to?"

"There is so much to tell you…"

"No shit," I said. "You left a fucking mess behind."

Clearly, this dream brain of mine had grasped that he was dead. Only the knowledge did not touch me.

Noam shifted his shoulder. An indifferent shrug. "Creativity is supposed to be messy."

"You were supposed to be a Ranger, following orders. What's messy about that?"

He swiveled, looking over his shoulder, as if someone was approaching. But there was nothing there. Nevertheless, he backed away from me. "Later," he said softly.

"Hey! You can't stay for five fucking minutes?"

I woke to the full glare from the daylights in the street outside blasting through my window, turning my narrow bed into a sweat box. I was gasping as I drew myself up against the headboard and clutched the damn sheet against my chest.

Noam had spoken to me! It was a coherent conversation. It even had some of the hallmarks of conversations we'd had in the past, where he irritated me and I sniped back. Our mother-son relationship had always run deep underground.

I shuddered. Only now that I was awake did I grasp the significance of the dream, the clarity with which I have been able to see him. Dreams weren't supposed to be like that. They were fragmentary, fleeting impressions. Sub-conscious detritus, as incomplete and stained as a midden. Only Noam had been as clear as any hologram.

I used the corner of the sheet to dry my face, then cast it to the floor, stalked into to the tiny bathroom and took a long shower.

By the time I emerged from the shower, I was starving hungry once more. It seemed like I was always hungry these days. I remembered the phenomenon from previous rejuvenations. I also knew that eventually, the hunger would slow down.

My newly revised metabolism could handle it, so I was not stinting myself. Not yet.

Even though it was still very early, and Juliyana was still deeply asleep, I stood at the basic printer, and had it produce a breakfast a king would not be embarrassed about. I pushed aside the pads and the screen emitter on the table and dug in.

I was only halfway through the meal, my stomach still rumbling, when I discovered I should have stayed in bed. My pad dinged for my attention. It was a real-live phone call.

From Farhan.

I hovered my hand over the pad for nearly twenty seconds before I connected. After all, he was family.

Farhan's brows shot up as the image assembled. "I honestly didn't think you would take the call."

"If you're going to spend money on an interstellar phone call, it seems only polite to answer it."

He was staring at me, taking in the details of my renewed appearance. I sat still, letting him look. After all, he had stared for years as my complexion faded.

"*This* is why you took the dividends?" he asked. "If I had known this was why you wanted the money, we could have come to an arrangement. You know the family has a scheme—"

"Which would tie me to the family barge for twenty-five years plus," I shot back. "I'm sorry, but right now I need to be able to move freely."

"I thought you had no interest in rejuvenating," Farhan said. He was still staring at me, his gaze moving over different points of my face.

"I don't suppose it will help if I tell you I will return the money later. Right now, though, I need to hang onto it. There something I must do."

"You mean, whatever you and Juliyana are up to."

"Yes."

"I was really hoping you would be reasonable about this." His voice was strained. "You know I have to drop the load on you for this. I'm accountable to directors and shareholders…"

I really hadn't been expecting anything else. "You aren't going to explain to me yet again about the family reputation and how I'm destroying it?"

"As you seem to have a complete lack of regard in that respect, I will not bother myself with a repetition," Farhan said. "Although I will state that I am disappointed, Danny. I thought I knew you well. Apparently, I don't."

He glanced at the corner of his screen. "Ten seconds left. I will save myself the energy and the money, as you have absconded with the family spare—"

The call cut off. An alert flashed to say the channel had been closed.

I pushed the pad away. By rights, I should have lost all my appetite and pushed the breakfast away, too. Instead, I pulled the plate back toward me and finished everything.

By the time Juliyana came downstairs, possibly woken by the smell of crisp bacon and maple syrup, all the plates were empty. The coffeepot was half-empty. She poured herself a mug from what remained and drank deeply.

She studied my face and the tools of our search pushed carelessly aside. "What's happened?"

"We'll have to move on, today."

She considered that, sipping coffee. "Okay, then."

I looked up at the ceiling. "Did you take a long lease on this place?"

"Day by day, payable once a week. I paid six days ago, so we can leave without alerting anyone. I'm guessing from your expression that it's time to use the new IDs."

"You pack." I stood. "For both of us. I'll head for the spacer bars and see what passage I can pick up for us."

"Where do you plan to head next?"

"Wherever the first reasonable offer is heading to."

Juliyana upended her mug, draining the coffee. She tossed the mug at the recycle maw and straightened.

I grabbed my jacket once more and headed out into the street. I walked swiftly through the still, quiet suburb to the main station concourse.

It was my intention to hit all the bars and restaurants, brothels and storefronts where spacers liked to hang out when they were on-station. The owners of these places earned the gratitude and loyalty of spacers, because they act-ed as clearinghouses for information which could not be included in any data network.

The freight of the Empire was left in the hands of civilian cargo lines. They were supposed to hold carry cargo, for their ships were fast and regularly subjected the crews to high-gee conditions. For that reason, spacers, like the Imperial military, were required to keep up their crush shots.

It wasn't long before enterprising ship captains realized they could sell empty space in their crew's cabins to any passengers who also happened to be up to date on their crush shots.

And thus was born an open, but still illegal, form of transport around the Empire. The Rangers turned a blind eye to the practice. Clearly, the demand was there, for anyone with crush status was usually in the freight game themselves, or they were military. There were times military personnel were happy to use the freight lines to transport unofficially, too.

Spacers in general had no patience for the ambling gait of the commercial crawlers, not after experiencing the freedom and speed of freight passage.

I certainly didn't.

Plus, the freighters headed to destinations which were banned to commercial passenger lines. That included military bases, Imperial facilities and xenophobic worlds who nevertheless needed external supplies because they were not self-sufficient.

It was the only efficient way to get around the galaxy, if you didn't own your own ship.

However, because freight travel was technically illegal, even though everyone did it, there were no official postings for berths. One had to know someone, who knew someone else, who was aware of a freighter with room and could hook you up with its captain in order to obtain passage.

Most of those conversations and hook ups took place in the bars and shops and cafés where I stopped by that morning. I spent a little money, left a larger tip and asked a few questions of whoever was behind the counter.

It isn't an instantaneous process. I would have to circle back to these joints to follow up on my original question. The first answer I usually received in response to the question of passage was accompanied by a blank look and an innocent expression, along with a declaration that they had no idea what I was talking about. Then I would thank them for their time and leave a large tip.

When I went back the second time, the innocent act would be dropped. If there was passage available, I would be introduced to a crewman, right there and then. Or I would be offered the chance to leave a message to be delivered to the ship, soonest.

There was always a danger that the berth they had available would be already sold by the time I caught up with someone from the ship. As travel by freighter was so common, though, if I missed the first opportunity, another would be along shortly. I just had to persist in asking.

I continued my rounds. I was braced for it to be a long morning, with my kidneys afloat with disgusting coffee and my stomach protesting over printed food passed off as freshly made. Except life suddenly got interesting, shortly after I had completed my first round of the most likely places to find passage.

I had rented a refresher to rid myself of some used coffee. Not for the first time, my reflection in the mirror startled me. It would take time to get used to looking at that young woman. She appeared to know nothing of the world.

I had never requested such a young cosmetic age before.

Youth was not an advantage in the military. It was better to look older and wiser, especially in the higher ranks.

It was while I was staring at the clean line of my jaw, with not a sag or sign of loose flesh anywhere, that I realized that no one had glanced at me with that startled second I had become accustomed to before the rejuvenation.

I was blending in, now. This deceptively young appearance would be useful.

I stepped out of the refresher. The door had nearly closed on me, locking me out unless I paid for another use, when I saw a tall man with useful shoulders and a military bearing, moving through the crowd on the concourse, his head turning as he searched every face.

Billy Kurzel, Agent At Large.

I eased back into the refresher and let the door shut, my heart thudding.

It could be purely coincidental that Billy was here on New Phoenicia. As one of the largest commercial hubs, it saw a lot of traffic, which would make it rich pickings for Billy and his ilk. He could be here merely to fill his quota of recruits.

Only, my gut said that wasn't the case.

Billy and the people he worked for were not going to give up on me without effort. They had already taken a swipe at me after I had told them no. That should have warned me they were determined.

Now I had a measure of exactly how dogged they were. They would follow me wherever I went, to continue their one -sided negotiations when they caught up with me.

 9

BILLY DID NOT KNOW ABOUT my rejuvenation. It was likely he would look right past me if he saw me, but I didn't want to take that chance.

I leaned against the shower stall and punched in a message to Juliyana.

Her acknowledgement came almost at once, which was a relief.

I renewed my rental on the refresher and waited inside until Juliyana tapped on the door. I stepped out.

Juliyana carried our two sacks, both of them bulging. I didn't remember mine being that loaded before.

She shrugged. "You said pack for both of us. So I used the space in your sack for some of my stuff. I've been here for weeks. I picked up some clothes."

I told her quickly about Billy.

"He doesn't know what you look like but he knows what I look like," Juliyana pointed out. "I hope he has reason to remember me," she added with a growl.

"All men are attached to their testicles. I guarantee he remembers you," I assured her. "I just didn't want you walking into him out there. We'll have to sneak off the station."

"Have you found passage yet?"

I thought of the barkeep with the barrel chest and a quiet manner. He hadn't bothered with the bullshit about not knowing what I was talking about. He had pocketed my tip. I had a feeling he was the most likely prospect to be able to connect me to a suitable freighter. "There is a bar, *The Oriental Monkey*, just up the concourse from here. Let's hit that one first."

"Yeah, I know that one," Juliyana said. "You said Billy was moving clockwise around the concourse?"

Like a great many very old stations, the core of New Phoenicia was a wheel which, once upon a time, had spun to impart gravity. That was before antigrav fields had come into common use.

Pseudo-gravity allowed entire cities to be built in space over their mother planets, for normal folk could live on the stations year-round without ill effect. Even freighters used pseudo-gravity, to avoid some of the nastier complications of long-term weightlessness and low gravity.

"Yes, he was moving clockwise," I told Juliyana.

She thought it through. "By now, he could have moved right around the ring. We may meet up with him as we head for the bar—assuming he's actually circling and not stopped somewhere."

"If he's stopped somewhere, it's not a problem for us. So let's assume he's circling. We'll go the long way around, which means we'd be following him, and won't come face to face with him." I picked up my sack. It should have been heavy, although the weight didn't bother me at all as I slung it over my shoulder.

"Around, then?"

"Around," I confirmed.

The mild-mannered barman did know someone who knew someone. When we walked into the bar, he jerked his chin at me, then jerked it at another patron.

The man in dirty overalls and spacer boots sat at a table by himself, watching the news headlines stream across the screen behind the bar. A half-eaten sandwich and a glass of something or other was in front of him.

I approached his table, while Juliyana hung back at the bar. "Can I get you another drink?" This close, I could see he was drawing close to his next rejuvenation. His whiskers were silvered and his jowls lose. His eyes were keen enough as they swept over me.

"You're not propositioning me, are you?" he asked, his voice gravelly.

I shook my head.

His gaze flickered toward the barman. As the bar was behind me, I could only presume the barman had silently indicated that I was safe to speak to.

The spacer relaxed and pushed the chair opposite him out with his boot. "Sure, I'll have another."

I waved to the barman, who was already pouring the drink out of a bottle with a label I didn't know. I sat down.

"You're looking for passage, then?"

"Depends on how soon you're leaving," I said.

His brow lifted. "Most people, it depends on where I'm going."

"As long as where you're going is away from here, I'm good with that."

He rubbed his chin, his whiskers rasping. "Is taking you aboard gonna be a problem for me?"

It was a fair question.

"Not if we leave here fast enough." I paused. "There's two of us."

His gaze shifted to Juliyana at the bar. "Your mother?"

"Granddaughter."

He snorted. "Serves me right." He considered me some more. "I can take two, if you don't mind sharing the room. The bunk'll take two."

"Not an issue. How soon are you leaving?"

"This is my last meal before dust-off." He nodded up at the barman, as the man put the spacer's glass of whatever in front of him. "And my last glass of Nightblack, too," he added. "We're a dry ship. I don't need the hassles, you understand?"

"Perfectly," I assured him. All Ranger vessels were completely dry, too.

"Military, right?"

"It shows?" I was surprised. This renewed body had the flexibility of youth, before parade stance had a chance to calcify the carriage.

"It's in the eyes," he told me. "Known my share of officers...yeah, thought so," he added, looking pleased with himself. He reached for his new drink. "Thirty standards from now. Bay thirty-four. I'll take your money when you and your granddaughter make it there."

I appreciated his honesty. Lots of spacers would have insisted upon taking my money now and not given a damn if we made it to the ship or not. Although, this close to dust off, the captain—and I was fairly certain he was the captain—has nothing to lose by waiting to see if we made it to the bay. His chances of finding another passenger to fill his empty cabin were extremely low given there were only thirty minutes left before their departure.

I nodded to him and got to my feet as he took a big slug of the glass of Nightblack. "Thirty minutes. We'll be there. Thank you." I paused. "Can I buy you another glass of Nightblack, to tide you over until you arrive at your destination?"

"Yeah, I could be talked into that." He hissed around the

bite of the liquor.

I moved over to the bar and paid for the man's drinks, with another tip for the barman. "Thanks for your help," I told him. I left the card he had slid back to me on the bar and put my finger on it. "There might be a man asking about two women looking for passage off-station."

The barman glanced at the card, then at me. For the first time I saw the mock innocence on his face. "Two women?" He shrugged.

I pushed the card back toward him. "Keep it. The change is yours."

He made the cards disappear as he finished pouring the captain's second drink.

Juliyana handed me my sack, I nodded at the barman, then at the captain, and we left.

"Bay thirty-four, about twenty-eight minutes from now," I told her as we merged into the clockwise moving stream.

"You figure Billy has the landing bays staked?"

"I would, if I were Billy." I looked around for navigation signs. A big station like Phoenicia had them everywhere. I spotted the readout and looked in the direction of the lower-digit bays. "It could take us all twenty-eight minutes just to get to the bay," I said. "It's at the far end of the city."

The remote location made sense. The big commercial lines paid over the odds for central bays. The military got preferential placement, too. Freighters and their ugly cargoes were placed out of the gaze of passengers and residents. The freight bays were a good two kilometers away.

Juliyana rounded on me, her expression concerned. "Billy doesn't have to stake out all the bays. He just has to stake out the shuttle that will get us there."

"He doesn't know we will use freighters," I pointed out. "He still thinks I'm an old woman, forced to use the commercial crawlers."

"That depends. His information was good enough to find you the moment you turned down rejuvenation. His sources are probably just as good on this station. I bet he works here a lot, rounding up his recruits."

I pulled up a schematic of the city on my pad, irritated. I should have anticipated this myself. It had been too long. I was out of practice. I studied the map, locating the clump of landing bays we needed to reach and the layout of the Mag-line which would get us there.

I looked up at Juliyana. "Are you feeling energetic?"

"What does that mean?"

I held the pad out to her and traced the route with my fingernail. "This will get us there."

"It's not a shuttle line, it's just streets and avenues." She tilted her head. "Avoid the shuttle..."

I nodded. "Walk, jog, run, walk. Less walking than running."

Juliyana shortened the straps on her sack and shrugged it into a more comfortable position. "Time is ticking."

We ran.

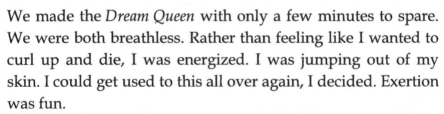

We made the *Dream Queen* with only a few minutes to spare. We were both breathless. Rather than feeling like I wanted to curl up and die, I was energized. I was jumping out of my skin. I could get used to this all over again, I decided. Exertion was fun.

The captain, whose name was Newman, we discovered, was not waiting for us on the loading ramp. His 2IC was a spare, withered woman with a deep voice and no sense of humor, called, hilariously, Joy.

I was very grateful she was expecting us. She was the type of second who followed procedure, no matter what, to make up for Newman's casual style of captaincy. If Newman had failed to advise her we were expected, she would have turned us away.

She waved her pad over each of our wrists, and I held my breath. Now we would learn if the new IDs we had paid for were worth the money Juliyana had spent on them.

Joy turned the pad to check the readout. "Right, Maisie and Maariki. Your crush status checks out. Up the ramp, to the back of the bay. Turn left into the main gallery. Find someone there. They'll point you to your cabin." She smiled, a mirthless expression. "Welcome aboard."

We were directed to the cabin by distracted crewmembers, who were hurrying along the gallery, intent on their responsibilities. The working freight ships had minimal crews, sometimes slicing the personnel down and redistributing responsibilities so each crew member was doing the work of two or three others. During a long haul, that was not onerous. During departure and arrival, and especially while hooked up at the station, where they offloaded and uploaded new cargoes, the crew barely slept.

It was no wonder Captain Newman had sought alone-time in the bar with a glass of his favorite tipple, just before take-off. It was possibly the only rest he'd had since arriving at New Phoenicia.

The ship was clearly preparing to leave. The reaction engines rumbled, making the whole ship gently vibrate.

The cabin we were directed to was as cramped as promised. The bunk doubled as a gravitation shell for two, even though for the standard acceleration of the freight ship, we wouldn't need it. It was there in case extremely high gee maneuvers were required. There were few times when such a need arose. Crush juice let spacers withstand a lot. I could re-member only a few occasions from my time on military carri-ers when we had been ordered to our shells. Usually, sharp acceleration and deceleration only occurred if the ship was trying to evade something. In the military, that was usually another ship, or another ship's weapons.

A freighter might have to dodge unexpected and extremely large objects, like asteroids which were not mapped, or even other ships who were out of their shipping lanes.

While we were still making our way to the cabin, the ship moved away from the station and kicked into gear. I drew in a breath, as inertia tried to press the front of my rib cage in to meet my spine. It was an illusion, of course, although it had been a long time since I had experienced high gee. I paused, breathing steadily.

Juliyana lifted her brow at me. "Okay?"

I nodded. I was still breathing. The nano bots were doing their job.

We continued walking, both automatically falling into the wading stride one used when under high acceleration. Cap-tain Newman was not hanging around. As we stepped into the cabin, I felt the tiny lurch which ships gave when they moved through an array gate and into a wormhole.

I threw my sack on the floor beside the bed. I didn't expect to have to touch either of them before the flight ended. Only then did it occur to me to check our destination.

Juliyana was ahead of me. She stood at the concierge panel, making herself familiar with the ship's directory and services.

"Where are we heading?" I asked.

She tapped a few more times, then said, "Devonire."

"Never heard of it. That might be a good thing."

Juliyana tapped a few more time. "Devonire III. Single de-parture point station, over a single city, servicing a continent of farmers. No other major exports besides produce."

It would make sense that a freighter would be heading for such an outpost. A single note economy would rely upon imports of everything else.

I resisted the temptation to pull up my pad and consult the archives on the size and capacity of the space station. Now we were in the hole, I couldn't access the usual networks.

The ship's concierge held permanent archive in its memory, which allowed the crew to access information they needed while in the hole. Each time the ship emerged from a gate, the gate would pass on the most recent communications squirt, which would include archival information which was automatically fed to the concierge.

"How big is the station?" I asked Juliyana. "Did the ship update data before it left? What other ships are due at the station when we get there?"

Juliyana made a small sound which might have been smothered irritation. "They have a whole three landing bays," she said, her tone admiring.

"Don't be like that," I chided her. "I realize it's not New Phoenicia…"

"The *Dream Queen* is the only ship due to arrive this week."

"Good. We'll have the run of the station to ourselves. When I get a chance, I'll find out from Newman where they're going next. We need to start looking for a freighter that's heading in the direction we want."

"And what direction is that? The last known destination of Gabriel Dalton was New Phoenicia, and we just left there." Her jaw sagged a little as a new thought occurred to her. "You're not thinking we should try to reach Annatarr, are you? Not after Farhan has promised to rain mayhem down upon us."

"Annatarr is a military base," I pointed out. "There are no

law-enforcement battalions there."

"And you expect the Rangers to pay any attention to that division? They never have in the past. I'm combat and I've arrested my fair share of petty criminals, too."

I seethed for a moment. It was fucking inconvenient to have been pushed away from New Phoenicia. It didn't help that our research had been interrupted, either. "Perhaps Devonire has a hilton we can rent. We can hunker down and nail the records. Find that trace. Then we'll know where we're going."

In the back of my mind I was thinking that Devonire was a remote and out-of-the-way place. Who in their right mind would think of looking for us there? We were traveling on the new IDs, which no one knew was us. As difficult as it was to find a trace of Gabriel Dalton running under a false ID, that same degree of difficulty would also hamper anyone looking for us.

"I suspect we may have just bought ourselves time to properly figure this out," I told Juliyana.

"Yeah, you said Zillah's World would be nice and quiet, too," Juliyana said, her tone dry. "I'm going to find food. I got up way too early this morning and I've been moving since. I need breakfast."

I felt the need to apologize and squashed it.

Things were moving, as Juliyana had said on Zillah's World. Life got interesting when that happened.

As I had eaten breakfast already, I stood in the middle of the cabin and considered if I should try to catch up on my sleep after all. Juliyana hadn't said how long the schlep through the hole would be. Devonire was a near-neighbor in astronomical terms so it was likely the trip would take double -digit hours.

Only, I didn't feel the need for sleep. I was wired, zapping with energy. Glowing with it.

Noam stepped into my lateral view, moved a few more steps and turned to face me. "Hi again. Thought she'd never leave. We have a few moments, now."

I didn't feel any concern about him standing in front of me like that. Instead, the sensation swept down upon me that something was behind me...coming closer. Something was about to happen.

My heart zoomed up into the run-for-your-life level. Adrenaline painted a coppery taste in my mouth.

The sensation of doom washed over me, making every hair on my flesh try to stand up in a prickly parade. Coldness touched me.

"Noam..." I wasn't sure if I spoke aloud or not. "Why are you here?"

"I've been here all along," he told me. "I've been trying a long time to speak to you. There's a lot to say, and I don't know how long I've got until—" He jerked his head toward the door of the cabin. "Shit..." he breathed.

And disappeared.

Juliyana thrust open the door. "They've invited us to dinner, Danny—" she begun.

I heard her, but was incapable of replying. I sagged, and just barely got my hands out to stop from falling on my face.

I was sweating, my heart threatening to explode out of my chest. "Noam..." I croaked.

Juliyana gripped my arms and hauled me to my feet, then shuffled me over to the bed and dropped me on the end of it. She crouched to look me in the face.

"Noam, what?"

"He was just here," I squeezed out of my uncooperative throat. "Talking to me."

10

JULIYANA DIDN'T BELIEVE ME, OF course. Even I had trouble believing it, and he had been right there in front of me.

I'd been an old woman so recently, I think the effect still lingered in her mind. Juliyana fussed. She dialed up the medical AI on the concierge panel and connected it to her pad and ran diagnostics, even though I told her more than once I was fine, nothing wrong.

Which was a small lie. I felt very tired, when only moments ago, I had been pulsing with energy.

The AI directed Juliyana through a series of scans and probes. Just like a real doctor, it said nothing until it'd had a chance to consider everything properly. Unlike real doctors, though, it could collate and analyze the mountains of data points it had collected and consider them in gestalt, plus consult every medical resource available to it in the hole...all in a few seconds.

It cleared its "throat" and said in a pleasant tenor; "It appears you have suffered a petit mal seizure—what laymen call a waking seizure."

Juliyana put her hands on her hips, looking less than happy.

It matched how I felt. "These are not the old implants," I pointed out. "They were causing the seizures, before."

"Perhaps not." The AI spoke with a pedantic tone which matched every doctor I've ever met. "It is possible the epilepsy is independent of the implants. As you no longer have the old implants for me to examine, I can only make assumptions based on the data I have to hand. It is also possible the implants were merely enhancing the seizures. You said they were classic incidences?"

That is what Andrain had called them. "Yes. Grand mal."

"Modern implants have a neutral impact on brain polarity and energy. It is possible your new implants are ameliorating the seizures, so they are reduced to petit mal, instead. I can prescribe an anti-seizure inoculation which will hold you over until you have emerged into regular space and can consult a specialist."

"No," I said quickly.

Juliyana raised her brow. "You said these things were killing you," she pointed out.

"That was before," I said. Even to me, my tone sounded testy. "Noam was right *there*," I added.

Juliyana rolled her eyes. "Hallucination. You were having a seizure."

"It isn't typical to hallucinate while seizing," the AI interjected, its tone studied.

"The anti-seizure inoculation," I said, staring at Juliyana while I addressed the AI. "What are the side effects?"

"Many and varied, including increased seizures," the AI said, happy to be able to answer a question properly at last. "Brain fog is typical. Headaches, slowness of thoughts. Impact on cognition has been recorded throughout medical history. No medication has ever provided relief and *not* made the patient feel groggy. Also, increased appetite and over the long term, slowed metabolism, both of which contribute to significant weight increase—"

"Stop. Thank you," I said, looking at Juliyana.

"Shit..." she breathed.

"Exactly."

"Are the petit mal seizures life-threatening if left unmedicated?" Juliyana asked the AI.

"Not generally," was the reply. "Although they are usually considered to be pre-cursors to a full seizure, which in Danny's case, may be fatal, according to her previous physician. Without a full medical history to hand, I cannot be more specific."

Juliyana stirred. "Thank you. Dismissed."

The concierge panel lights blinked out to the single glowing green point to indicate it was listening.

Juliyana crossed her arms. "Then there's nothing that can be done. You can't medicate, and you can't predict when you'll have the next one."

"That's the way I heard it, too," I agreed. I got up. Everything felt normal, once more, yet I was still baked. "How about we get that dinner you were yammering about, when you came in?" Food would help.

We emerged from the gate thirteen hours later. In that time, I ate, slept a solid eight hours, and ate again.

I was back to feeling twitchy with good health and an overload of energy. One of the side benefits of rejuvenation is that in the second and subsequent go-rounds, you don't for a second fail to appreciate youth while you have it. I found myself smiling a lot. I got permission to use the ship's gymnasium and worked myself up into a glowing sweat, stressing my well-developed muscles.

I could deadlift a ridiculous amount, more than I ever had. The off-duty crewmembers watched me from the corner of their eye, just as interested in the weight I was moving around. I didn't laugh out loud at the male crewmen who reached for the upper end of the weight stacks and turned red in the face proving they could sling more weight than me. They didn't know they were responding to cues which came out of antiquity, that humanity had never got rid of and wouldn't while reproduction remained a sexual process.

The rejuvenation therapy had been worth the outrageous price. Right now I was fully inclined to recommend the clinic to anyone who asked. I was unused to luxury level therapy. Ranger-provided rejuvenations were standardized — there were very few options one got to pick. The Imperial Rangers wanted their soldiers to be fit, strong and healthy, and that was it. Senior officers had a few more options, including cosmetic age, but less than the average grunt thought we got.

We were less than an hour from emerging out of the hole when I ended the session — not because I was drained, but because I thought it prudent to shower and change before we disembarked from the ship. Every time we had stepped onto a station lately, it had proved eventful, with no time to linger for basics like showering and eating.

This time, though, events came to our attention *before* we reached the station. The first I knew of it was when I was re-packing my overloaded sack. The concierge gave a little cough and said; "Captain's compliments. Will you step along to the flight deck, as soon as you can."

Passengers were rarely invited onto the flight deck. They got underfoot and distracted crew with inane questions if they did.

"Problem with the IDs?" Juliyana suggested, looking up from her pad.

"Newman wouldn't give a damn about that." I sealed my boots and got to my feet. "Only way to find out is go see him as directed." I didn't for a moment consider the request optional. If I didn't respond, a crewmember—possibly more than one—would come to find me and make sure I presented myself.

I checked the layout of the ship on the screen the concierge thoughtfully displayed. The flight deck was at the end of the main gallery, as I had expected it to be. Even though a flight control deck could be placed anywhere on the ship these days, most ships followed the ages old practice of placing the deck at the top or at the front of the ship. "Front" was often subjective—and could only be figured out by finding the outlets of the reaction engines and tracing a line forward along the ship from them. The *Dream Queen*, though, was elongated, and had a pair of stubby articulated guns facing forward, making the leading edge of the craft very clear.

The deck was cramped. The five deck crew manning the controls all rested casually against newish-looking shells which they didn't need. The modern shells were smaller, yet there still wasn't a lot of room on the deck.

This deck was a donut model, all control dashboards facing the center, where the screens could display any view needed, plus schematics, and clear headshot views of the other members of the deck, if needed.

Newman beckoned with his fingers, as I paused at the entrance to the deck.

I made my way around the back of the shells. No one bothered to glance at me. They were busy, now we'd emerged from the hole. There was plenty to do between now and docking.

Newman pointed at a screen. "You said leaving New Phoenicia would be the end of your woes."

I looked. The screen showed a long view of the Devonire station. It was as small as I had guessed from Juliyana's quick research. The three landing bays were ranged on this side of the station, facing the gates where all the traffic came from.

An old-fashioned cable setup hung from the bottom of the station, trailing down to the planet's surface. "Haven't seen one of those in years," I murmured, watching the glasseen pod rise up into the underside of the station.

"Check the bays," Newman said. "We've been cleared for the portside."

The portside bay was empty. The station was one of the old kind, where a ship had to nudge up against an outside port and couple with it. I hoped they didn't use molecule tunnels to hook up with the ships. I didn't like walking along a ramp which had nothing between me and fatal vacuum except for a thin membrane of invisible, coherent molecules acting as a shield. They said the molecule barriers simply couldn't fail because of the nature of the interaction between molecules and vacuum. If that was the case, then why didn't more people use them? They're cheap enough.

I'm guessing too many people felt the way I did, including those who made decisions about a station design.

The surprising aspect of the station was that both other landing bays were in use. "The *Queen* is supposed to be the only ship arriving for a week," I said.

Newman pulled at the softer skin below his chin. "Recognize either ship?" He tapped the keyboard. The view pulled in tighter upon the two ships snuggled up to the station.

Glasseen connector tunnels. Thank the stars.

I focused upon the ship at the starboard landing bay. It was a thick, blunt design, solid all the way through, with no projections or spindly extensions which could be snapped off or sheered away. There were regular shapes all over the hull, and all of them would have a purpose, too. The ship had that sort of spare, elegant design about it. Nothing for show or

113

decoration. Just utilitarian efficiency. Despite the blocky shape and sparseness, there was an elegance to the dimensions.

"Can you focus on the starboard side?" I asked Newman.

He tapped. The lens shifted and the view expanded.

Now I could see details. Big reaction engine cones—*very* big in proportion to the size of the ship. That sucker would *move* under that sort of impetus.

The hull itself was strangely colored. The standard subdued glow of gray carbon steel showed here and there. Carbon steel was the material most external hulls were made of these days. Everywhere else, the hull was a matte ochre red. I frowned, peering at the mottled color, wondering what *that* was about. Then it clicked.

"Rust," I breathed. "How the fuck does a ship get rusty in space?"

"Good question," Newman said. "You don't know the ship, then?"

I took in the four rail guns mounted top and bottom of the ship and shook my head. "Independent party, I guess. I don't know them, sorry."

He nodded. "It's the other one I wanted to ask you about." He nudged the lens. The screen dissolved into a mash of pixels, then resolved once the lens stopped moving. The lens focused on the big ship which took up the center bay. The center bay was the big one. The ship had got this bay because it wouldn't have fit either of the other two.

I traced the lines of the ship. The entire ship was matte black, a non-reflecting material which in space would make the ship virtually invisible, except for the negative space it would make from blocking the stars behind it.

Two long, independent arms ran forward from the body of the ship, both of them three times longer and nearly half

114

the width of the body. They were independent troop drop ships, which would detach from the main ship to get infantry to the surface...or mechs, or armed crawlers, or whatever was required down there. While attached to the ship, their front end cannons could be aimed and fired by the main flight deck weapons officers.

I swallowed. "An Imperial Ranger armed carrier."

Newman was watching my face. "Friends of yours?"

He was being ironic, yet for all I knew, I did have friends on the ship. Only, the way Newman meant it was also true. I pushed my hand through my hair. "That's a combat vessel. The combat battalions have no interest in me." Which was true as far as I knew.

"Meaning the police battalions do?" Newman rasped, looking unhappy.

"They're not here for me," I assured him. "It's a coincidence. No one knew we would be on this ship and..." I plunged on, "...and *no one* knows what names we're using."

Newman considered this, his old eyes narrowed.

"Fifty minutes out, boss," one of the crew said softly.

"I wouldn't bank on no one knowing you're here," Newman said. He pointed at a tiny woman frowning at her screens. "LeOnde says the ship's security feeds were raided before we made it into the hole."

LeOnde nodded and looked up. "It wasn't subtle. They accessed the footage showing the cargo ramp, in the last three hours before we left."

I stared at her unhappily. "The footage shows our faces as we came on board," I guessed. Even though we were traveling under false IDs, a smart AI could still go through visuals and match faces to ours on file.

LeOnde gave me a taut smile and went back to her dashboard.

Newman was back to tugging the flesh beneath his chin. "The heavy hand meant they didn't care if we knew. It usually means some sort of official agent, with the authority to raid private feeds. And lo, the Rangers are here." He waved his hand at the screen.

I carefully said nothing. No point in committing myself. I already knew where Newman was taking this. I would be thinking the exact same thing, in his shoes. I was a passenger who would draw too much official attention upon his ship. Nothing he was doing was illegal, that I knew about, except for carrying passengers, which every freighter did as a matter of course. He was like most honest civilians, though— nervous in the face of authority.

"I can't take you on from here," Newman said. "We part ways at Devonire."

I nodded at the expected announcement and turned to look at the screen again. The lens was adjusting as the *Queen* drew closer to the station, shifting focus. The black ship looked lethal...and it *was* lethal. Everyone thought of the dreadnoughts and the super-maneuverable frigates as the powerhouses of the Imperial fleet. Carriers, though, were designed to protect ground troops and were damned good at it. Yet they could also use that firepower against enemy ships with an effectiveness as devastating as any dreadnought's.

The shitty bonus for me right now was that most of the time, carriers had at least three or four cadres of infantry aboard.

My lucky fucking day.

According to Newman, this wasn't the coincidence it looked like. I wanted to point out to him that I'd faced two major coincidences lately. This would be number three...if it was chance at all.

"You'd better go sort out your exit," Newman said.

That was going to be tricky. If it had been an internal landing bay like those at New Phoenicia, I could have used an external hatch to climb out, move carefully around the ship and use one of the admin doors to the bay to ease out, all without raising the attention of any official parties monitoring the ship.

Only, we would be connected by a tunnel to the station itself. Any external hatch was just that, an exit to pure vacuum.

We *had* to use the cargo door. It was the only one which would be connected to the station.

"Thanks, Captain," I murmured. No point getting pissed at him. None of this was his fault, and he had been as fair-handed as he could be. "I'll settle with your purser and square things away."

"That'd be Joy," he called after me. "You'll find her in the mess."

I found my way to the mess. Joy *was* there, and frowning over three pads, all battered and scratched, and muttering to herself.

The thrill of administration. I shuddered, and pulled her attention away from cooking the books, to dicker over the price of our passage. I used one of the un-anchored cards to pay what I thought was an exorbitant rate, but was probably about average, then hurried back to the cabin.

"We're about to dock and the Rangers are already waiting for us," I told Juliyana.

"Fucking Farhan," she muttered. "He really did drop the boom on us."

"Looks like. Although there's no point getting pissed at him. He's watching out for the family in general, which is exactly what he's supposed to do." I picked up my sack. "Devonire is a standard first stage vertical sub-station design."

Juliyana got to her feet. "First stage modules have external docking. We have to exit exactly where they're going to expect us to appear. They'll be waiting for us."

"If they're here for us at all, and that's not a given," I told her.

"Why else would they be here?"

"It's a combat vessel. A carrier. That's overkill for what they think is a family thief." I frowned. "All the station's support services and maintenance will be in the bottom tiers."

"Run like hell and get lost down there?" Juliyana hazarded.

"There's also a cable down to the surface..." Although the cable car itself would rise up through the station to the higher levels, where it would dock with the internal quay to offload passengers. "What I'd give for a suit right now..." Without enviro-suits, we were limited in what we could do.

"Suits would just slow us down," Juliyana pointed out.

True.

We moved back along the main gallery to the armored door of the cargo hold. Joy stood there with the dour man who had supervised the closing of the cargo bay when we had left New Phoenicia. His name was Harry, as far as I had been able to pick up from the dinner we had taken with the crew just after take off. Both Harry and Joy were waiting with patient expressions. The cargo bay door was tightly closed, with red lights showing all over the armored exterior. It was locked and sealed to contain atmosphere.

It was standard procedure when connecting to an external docking bay. The connection of the tunnel was an inexact affair, because the docking collar had been designed to dock with the broadest number of ship models as possible. It would clank and hiss and attach and detach a number of times while it found the best purchase against the ship's hull. Then the tunnel was filled with atmosphere, and the doors at either end could be safely opened.

Yet accidents could happen. The collar might not fit exactly and the opening of either door could create a gust which knocked the collar loose, exposing the airlock on the station and the cargo bay to explosive depressurization.

So everyone stood on the other side of the bulkhead doors until the tunnel was properly opened, tested and announced safe.

"You're eager to leave, then?" Harry asked us. He didn't sound at all interested in the answer. He was being polite to two passengers whom he was never going to see again.

"Yep," I said.

Joy considered us with her downturned expression. I wondered if it was just the natural set of her mouth. Some people had downward curving mouths, and when they relaxed, they instead looked unhappy. "You know there's Rangers out there, right?"

How much had everyone guessed about us? Or were all civilians, not just spacers, reticent about dealing with authority?

"I am aware," I admitted unhappily.

Juliyana exchanged a glance with me.

Harry took in our expressions and scratched under his ear. "Ya know, there's a pair of miniature cargo drums sitting right beside the left-hand side of the bay doors. The blue ones, right?"

I nodded. I knew what he was talking about. They were pale blue vertical, rectangular sealed crates, the cheapest type of freight, used by families and individuals for heavy stuff which couldn't go via the bulk parcel services.

"Carry one of them," Harry said. "Up against your chest.

No one would see your face unless they wanted to."

"I'm not that strong," I pointed out. The drums had to weigh more than me and Juliyana put together, when they were loaded.

"They're empty dead-head, this trip," Harry said.

Thank you, I mentally breathed. "Where do you want them parked, beyond the lock?"

"Anywhere you put 'em down will be fine. We can find them again, and it's not like there's anything in them we have to deliver." He shrugged.

The cargo bay door gave a little beep.

"Pumping," Joy warned.

The tunnel was attached and atmosphere being pumped in.

My gut tightened.

"Best come over this side," Harry said. "Soon as the door opens wide enough, you can go."

We moved over to his side. The cargo bay door's readouts were flashing notifications and warnings about insufficient pressure beyond the door—not that we could open it, now, anyway. Nothing would unlock the door, short of a nuclear blast, until the air equalized on the other side.

Then all the beeps and alerts and flashing lights turned off. Silence.

Juliyana pulled in an unsteady breath, her gaze fixed on the door. Her feet were spread in a ready stance.

A heavy thud of titanium bolts opening sounded inside the door. Then the hiss and breaking of the seal around the door as it shifted. A pause to let the air into the interior of the seal, to break the vacuum which held it locked.

Then the door rumbled to one side.

As soon as the door was wide enough to get through, Juliyana slipped through it and was gone. I followed her.

Juliyana had sensibly moved around the edge of the cargo bay, where a corridor of space was kept free, instead of down the center lane which was also kept open. The cavernous room had cargo carriers stacked up nearly to the ceiling.

I jogged after Juliyana. No need to move at top speed yet—I had glimpsed the outer door of the station at the other end of the tunnel—it still wasn't open yet.

I found Juliyana at the edge of the cargo bay doors, which were fully retracted. She hoisted one of the two crates up into her arms, as if she had expected it to be heavy. It *looked* heavy, because the shell was reinforced with thick ribs. Yet Juliyana nearly threw the crate over her shoulder.

Forewarned, I picked up the other crate. It was as light as a feather. We stood by the doors, watching the outer station airlock door, waiting for it to crack open.

With a hiss and a sigh of old pneumatics and pumps, the door cranked open. I could hear the wheels grinding, somewhere inside, and gears moving on metal tracks with a heavy ratcheting sound.

There were people on the other side of the door, becoming steadily more visible the wider the door opened. I scanned them. Dirty overalls, basic blues, browns, greens. None of the charcoal black uniforms I was braced for.

"Ready?" I breathed.

"Fuck no," Juliyana breathed back. "Only way is forward, though."

True.

"Don't run until we have to," I warned her as the door came to a shuddering halt. I stepped out onto the interleaved metal plates of the tunnel. The sheath around the tunnel was opaque, so I could see basic shapes, but no details. I walked along the tunnel, my boots making the plates shudder and yaw. I wondered what the really heavy cargo containers did to the tunnel when they were lorried over to the station.

I hitched the barrel up into a more comfortable position and kept walking. A woman with ruddy cheeks and a put-upon air stood at the wide door, a pad in hand. The chief stevedore.

I wasn't concerned about her stopping us for formalities, for all of those would have been sorted out while the *Queen* moved from the gates to the station.

"In a hurry, then?" she asked, her voice gruff.

"Hot date tonight," I murmured as I stepped up onto the station floor and felt solidness beneath my feet.

The other workers who had been milling about the door were drifting away. Their job of coupling the ship had been done.

The air lock was the same size as the external door. Another door exactly the same dimensions was on the other side of the ten-meter wide airlock. It was closed. Instead, a man-sized door to the left, in the side wall, was propped open. It had similar warnings and locking mechanisms to the main cargo door. The workers were leaving through it.

I turned toward the door.

"Welcome to Devonire," the stevedore told me. She made it sound like a curse.

I grunted, a wordless acknowledgement.

"Thanks," Juliyana said, her voice strained.

I stepped through the door and only then realized that the crate wasn't just obscuring my face, it was also blocking my view. There was a whisper of sound and the sensation of a very large space around me. The ceiling was up high. The main level of the station would be as open as possible, with a central core where the cable car passed through.

To my flank, on either side, I saw bright lights and white walls — standard neutral station décor. Observation windows

122

to my right, which was the direction of the other two ships' landing bays. Four combat Rangers in their dark uniforms stood at the windows, peering at the newly arrived ship.

My heart seized. My breath, too.

I turned in the opposite direction, which put my back to them, and started walking swiftly along the curved wall. If I kept following it, I would move out of their sight. Then I could put the crate down and go looking for a way down to the lower levels—or up to the cable car pier. *Something...* although my options were severely limited right now.

"We look stupid carrying these," Juliyana muttered.

I agreed.

"Hey! There she is! Andela! Juliyana Andela! Halt!"

"Fuck, they don't even realize it's me," I bitched.

"They're going to know in a second," Juliyana said.

We kept walking.

"Andela! I said *halt!*" one of the Rangers bellowed. Around us, the few people lingering on this level of the station were whispering, wondering what was happening.

"There's only four of them," Juliyana said.

A shriver bolt singed the floor between us and my heart gave another dance of fright and concern. They had opened fire among civilians pretty damn quick. They weren't even sure it was us, damn it!

"Four of them, two of us. Through them, then?" I said.

"That's what I'm thinking."

Going through them would ensure they didn't get up again for a while. That would give us time.

"On my count," I said. "One, two...*three.*"

I put the crate down thankfully, spun, and sprinted back toward the four Rangers, who were also breaking into a run after us.

I saw their eyes open as they realized we were bringing

the fight to them. I didn't fool myself, though. These were combat-trained cadre. We had to surprise them if we were going to put them down. "Temporary stopper only!" I yelled at Juliyana and leapt at the first of them as he came within reaching distance.

It was a short fight, and brutal. It had to be. Killing them outright would have been easier and quicker, but I wanted them still breathing when we were done. That required sleeper holds and numbing strikes…and moving fast to maintain our surprise factor, which didn't give us much of a margin, but it would have to do.

My first dropped to the ground with a sigh. The second was reaching for me, which made it easier. I slid under his arm, came up behind him and rammed my pointed knuckle into the nerve junction under his ear.

His arm dropped, numb.

Another strike to the side of his knee and his leg bent, unable to hold him up. He staggered, tried to thrust out the leg that wasn't working and fell over.

Juliyana stood breathing hard over her two, who were moaning and rolling on the ground. Then she looked over my shoulder and *her* eyes widened.

I spun around.

There was an open area by the wall which hid the cable car shaft, filled with tables and chairs. Bar on one side. Café on the other .

Nearly every chair was filled with Rangers, who were now leaping to their feet and reaching for their shrivers.

"Fuck," I breathed.

A whistle sounded, so piercing it made me wince. I spared a glance to the right.

A man stood farther down the concourse, waving toward me. Civilian clothing. Long utility coat. A mass of unruly brown hair and piercing blue eyes. Square chin.

"Move it!" I yelled at Juliyana and sprinted in his direction. He waved us on, his arm movements picking up speed.

We sprinted, ducking between and around civilians, who were doing their best to get out of the way and not moving nearly fast enough. Their sluggishness preserved our asses. The Rangers wouldn't shoot at us if there was a chance they could hit civilians.

The man stood where I judged the starboard landing bay doors were—the landing bay with the rusted-up hulk with the clean lines and rail guns.

He moved toward the doors and we drew closer. I don't think I had got around to taking a breath since I had broken into a sprint. There wasn't time.

He pulled open the man-sized door and held it open as we got there. I skidded on the floor—moving too fast—then pushed off with my hand and dived through the door, my heart screaming.

As I dived, a shriver bolt tore through the air over my head and sizzled against the interior of the air lock.

The man bolted the door and pressed his hand against it. "That won't hold them long," he said. "Move it."

"Who the fuck are you?" Juliyana demanded.

"Later," I told her. "Quickly. Onto the ship."

We followed him over to the other side of the airlock and onto the flimsy tunnel leading into the guts of the rustbucket.

Thudding on the outer lock door. Yelling, barely heard.

I didn't fool myself. They were Rangers. One of them even now would be screaming at the station's traffic controller, demanding they open the bay door remotely.

We thudded across the tunnel and into the dark interior of the ship. As soon as we all hit solid flooring, he yelled, "Shut the doors! Get us out of here! Maximum speed!"

"Aye, captain," came a disembodied voice—a man's tenor, with a snap in it that said he was hurrying.

The door of the ship slammed closed behind us and the seals hissed.

"I'll have to break the connection to the station," the pilot added.

"Do it," he told her. "Do whatever it takes. Just get us to the gate and into a hole, before they get that carrier of theirs unhooked and coming after us."

"I can outfly that carrier," the pilot said, sounding amused.

"I believe him," the man added. "He's cocky, but he knows his stuff."

Even as he spoke, the rumble of engines shivered the floor beneath our feet.

There was the softest of jolts as the ship moved.

I was impressed. From cold to moving in…what? Ten seconds? That was impressive. Maybe the pilot, whoever he was, had kept the engines in trickle-over state, ready to go, just in case.

Our savior leaned against the wall with one hand and let out a deep breath. He raised a brow at me. "Hello, Danny."

"Hello, Gabriel," I replied.

"Gabriel *Dalton*?" Juliyana said, her hand flashing to her bare hip. "You've got to be fucking kidding me."

11

"LATER," DALTON TOLD JULIYANA GRUFFLY. He turned and ran along the corridor we were in—a long, loping stride which swallowed ground quickly. "We still have to beat that carrier to the gates," he yelled over his shoulder.

"*Dalton*, Danny?" Juliyana said, turning to me, her hand gripping her hip.

"You heard him. Later," I told her. "Let's get out of here, first." I took off after Dalton.

The ship was bigger than I had first thought it to be. It took a few minutes to make our way to the bridge. I guess any ship, when parked beside an Imperial carrier, tended to look teeny in comparison.

The corridors were refreshingly wide, lined with lockers and utility cupboards, and other services panels—blank walls weren't left blank for long on a ship. Sooner or later something was bolted to them, or hung on them, or cut into them. Space was always tight.

The corridors we ran through were empty. Was everyone on the bridge? The corridor echoed as we followed Dalton. It didn't curve, but it did jig to the left then back to the right, following the spine of the ship. It meant the bridge was to-ward the front and centered.

Then up a ramp, and the bridge opened up before us.

There was no one there. Not a single fucking soul. "What the hell?" I breathed, looking around the area.

Dalton strode forward, toward the triple screens at the front of the deck, as if the empty deck was not a surprise to him. The screens were set to show the forward view, which at this point displayed Devonire station sliding to our starboard as the ship turned, preparing to blast toward the gate. The gate was in sight already—a giant, bio-mechanical ring hanging in space, looking quite small from here.

It had taken Newman's ship over an hour to cover the distance between the gate and the station. It was a lot of time for the carrier to catch up with us—or just shoot us out of the sky at their leisure. Their mauler cannon bolts could travel faster than they could, a fact I had relied upon in the past when I had been standing beside the captain's shell, directing his efforts.

"Lyth," Dalton said as he reached the control panel in front of the wide three-part screen. "Is the carrier away yet?" He leaned on the panel and looked into the screen and down to the right.

With a jolt, I realized they weren't screens at all.

"They're *windows!*" Juliyana breathed, beside me, sounding as winded as me. "Actual fucking windows..." She looked up and around the empty deck. There were stations for more crew than Dalton—at least one was navigation, for it had the flat tabletop where the 3D stellar maps could display. The other posts could be a variety of things—I'd figure that out later. There were too many mysteries here to unravel, and higher priorities to deal with first.

The engines kicked up a gear, becoming a steady, low rumble we could hear now, not just feel through our boots. The ship leapt forward. The view on the screen showed the gate steadily growing larger. Gee force pressed against me, making me shove a foot backward in response.

We were going to make the gate a shit-ton faster than

Newman had managed with his trusty freighter.

What *was* this ship? I studied the details, trying to figure out what model it was. I had never seen a deck like this, before. There was no name plate for the ship rivetted to a bulkhead, which was usual. I hadn't recognized the long lines of the ship when I had studied it in Newman's viewscreen on approach to the station, either.

The railguns top and bottom and on both sides, said this was not exactly a civilian ship. Freighters and private craft *did* carry arms and weapons—it was only sensible—but they didn't advertise them the way this ship did.

I had never seen another ship quite like this one before.

"The carrier is just pulling away from the station," the disembodied voice informed Dalton. Only, Dalton wasn't standing straight. He bowed, still gripping the control panel, this time for support, not leverage. He moaned.

I waded forward, for the ship was accelerating hard, putting all of us under immense pressure. "You're flying without crush juice!" I yelled at Dalton. "How fucking stupid can you *be*?" I moved right up to his side.

He shook his head, a fractional movement. Pain etched on his face. "No, no—I'm juiced. It's just…" He grimaced and closed his eyes.

"Old?" I guessed.

Dalton didn't answer.

"Computer, slow your rate of acceleration right now!" I yelled.

"No, I'm fine," Dalton said quickly. He straightened up slowly, with great effort. I wasn't fooled. He was still feeling the force in every cell.

I wasn't his keeper. I didn't try arguing again. He could crush himself to death if he wanted to—later. For right now I needed him whole.

"I said, computer, slow the fuck down or you'll kill one of your passengers," I shouted.

The ship slowed and the pressure instantly eased. I took a deep breath, enjoying it. "Thank you," I told the thing. *Lyth*, Dalton had called it. "Ships' AI," I said to Juliyana. "Automated everything, run by the computer core."

"Risky," she breathed.

I had to agree with her. Managing a ship this size and complexity with only the help of a single AI was a sure way to end up floating dead and cold in deep space somewhere, because you only had two hands. Automation didn't and couldn't deal with everything adaptable humans could, with their opposable thumbs.

I looked though the view windows, still marveling that they were actual windows. This close, I could see the forward ends of the ship protruding from either side of the bridge position, thrusting forward like the twin troop craft attached to the front of the carrier we were leaving farther behind with each passing second. These were elongated diamond-shaped protrusions, bristling with antennas and dishes and other probes on their noses.

Dalton saw the direction of my gaze. "Drop ships," he said. His voice was hoarse and he pressed the heel of his hand against his chest, massaging it. "At least, that's what Lyth tells me. Also, when they're cradled by the ship, as they are now, they can act as backup bridges, if something should happen to this one."

"A nice redundancy," I murmured. "Status on the carrier?" I added, lifting my voice a little to address the AI.

"Lyth, you can speak with Danny," Dalton added.

"It won't catch us," Lyth replied, sounding amused.

"Its mauler cannon might," I pointed out.

"Not in five seconds, it won't." This time the amusement

was more than apparent in its voice.

The gate filled the entire view from top to bottom. Soon, it would be larger than the windows. We would have to lean forward to see all of it.

Juliyana came up to my side. "This is *too* easy," she murmured.

I had to agree with her. "Later," I murmured back. "Once we're in the hole, you can hold him down and I'll dig out answers, 'kay?"

"Deal," she breathed.

Dalton tried to look amused. The pain lines around his mouth ruined the effect. He shoved his hands into the pockets of his coat and said, "Capacitor ready, Lyth?"

"Of course," Lyth replied. "Transitioning into a wormhole is a bit difficult without one."

Juliyana laughed and smothered it. "I like its attitude."

"Relax, people," Lyth added. "I got this."

For a ship at maximum speed, the vibrations coming through the deck and the low rumble of the reaction engines was mild, yet the gate loomed large. Now I could see the complex details around the thick circle of bio-mechanical technology. It glinted dark blue and black, silver and gray in the light from Devonire, as all gates did.

As we watched, the space inside the gate turned aqua blue and opaque. The wormhole had been formed. At the same time, the capacitor whined, building up for the high-energy jump through the gate.

AIs always coordinated the jumps through gates. It required precise timing. The completed formation of the wormhole and the full charge of the capacitor needed to occur to the same moment, with only a split second leeway in either direction.

The aqua surface shimmered.

I saw the probes and the fine noses of the drop ships push through the surface and disappear a fractional beat of time before the blue washed over us and the ship shivered, as all ships did.

We were in the hole.

All of us took a deep breath and let it out. Even the AI gusted out a noisy exhalation.

I turned to Dalton. "What the fuck are you *doing* way out here, Dalton? And where the hell did you get this ship?"

He snorted and turned away from the windows. They were showing nothing now. The view would be blank until we emerged from the hole once more. Looking at the nothingness of a hole for too long was unnerving, and some people actually got nauseous if they stared at it for too long. Most ships turned their big screens to other views once they've made the jump. These were *window* screens, though.

"You might want to install blinds or something over those windows," I told Dalton. "Save us from getting dizzy."

"Oh, yeah," he said absently. "Lyth, could you take care of that?"

"Absolutely," Lyth said, his tone accommodating.

The windows turned opaque.

"Nanobots in the Glasseen," Lyth announced, sounding proud of himself.

I would have to deal with the AI-with-an-attitude problem later. I stared at Dalton. "Why were you on Devonire?" I demanded. A question at a time, if necessary, to get it out of him. It was deeply disturbing to me that he just happened to show up where we did. Did he know we had been looking for him?

Juliyana did not seem to be in a hurry to tell him that, either. She moved over to the navigator's table and parked one hip on it. It was her right knee hanging over the end of the table, which put her hand within inches of the blade she had in her boot.

Dalton moved over to the shell facing the window. A pilot's chair, if ever human, manual helm control was needed. He leaned his shoulder against it, crossing his arms. He made it look casual, although I wondered how much propping up he needed. Gee force pressure could have lingering affects.

"I found the ship," Dalton told us.

"*Found* it?' Juliyana repeated.

"He stole it," I interpreted.

Dalton shook his head. "No. I really didn't. It invited me aboard."

"Invited…" I rolled my eyes. "What, it sang out to you as you happened to be passing, and you thought, why shouldn't I step on board a strange ship? It surely can't belong to anyone else. Ships float abandoned all over the empire, after all."

"That's pretty much what did happen," Dalton replied, his jaw flexing. The blue eyes seemed to grow a bit harder and brighter. He was irritated.

Well, that made two of us.

I glanced at Juliyana and her folded arms and steady stare. Make that three of us.

Dalton said, "First, it wasn't floating anywhere. It was parked in a junk park in the bowels of Badelt City. Second, I was led down there by…shit…" He stood up. "You'll believe this as much as you'll believe I had no idea you were arriving on Devonire just now, but…" He paused, measuring me. "I was moving fast," he began.

"Running away," Juliyana amended.

"There was a sudden flux of Rangers onto the station. Combat battalions—I know too many of them, so I...*moved*," he told her, his irritation growing enough to show in his voice. "I turned randomly, trying to get lost. The city is a maze, anyway. As I ran, doors started opening, and lights would flash to get my attention. The first time I dived through a door that opened, it shut right behind me. I figured if whatever the fuck was going on was going to be that help-ful, I'd go wherever it wanted me to go."

"Which was down to the junk park?" I guessed.

"That's where I ended up," Dalton replied. "Then the ship waved at me—"

Juliyana gave a hard laugh of disbelief.

Dalton's jaw tightened. His eyes narrowed. Then his lifted his gaze up a little. "Lyth, it's time to do that thing you do."

"Sure, Gabriel," Lyth replied.

Nothing happened. I raised my brow at Dalton.

"Hi, Danny Andela," Lyth said—from *behind* me.

I whirled.

Juliyana bolted off the table, her hand flashing to her hip, her eyes wide.

A stranger stood there. He was two meters tall, with black hair which needed trimming, a lean physique and a know-it-all grin, which grew broader as I studied him. "Boo!" he add-ed.

Juliyana sucked in a little squeaky breath.

"Hologram," I murmured. It was a damn good one. I couldn't see any shimmering edges, or transparent sections. Lyth looked as solid as me.

Lyth shook his head. "Wrong. Sorry." He leaned toward me, picked up my wrist and gripped my hand and shook it.

I tore my hand out of his grip and backed up.

"He's harmless," Dalton said. "So far," he added, with a

134

judicious tone.

"Android?" Juliyana breathed, moving closer to the thing, gazing intently. "Only, how did you get around the Laxman Syndrome?" She circled the thing, which turned to follow her arc, a smile on its face.

"I don't know," Dalton said, his tone sharp. "I know nothing about this ship. Lyth—this one you're looking at—was standing on the boarding ramp of the ship, waving to me as I moved through the junk park. I could have had a battalion of rangers on my ass, so when he invited me onto the ship, I took the opportunity."

"You're *all* wrong," Lyth said happily. "Not android, therefore no need to get around anything tricky."

"You stepped onto a strange, junked and abandoned ship and managed to pilot it to Devonire?" I asked. Although, the junk status explained the rust on the exterior of the ship. Junk parks were damp, unventilated places. Even carbon steel eventually succumbed to the moisture.

"I didn't do a damn thing to pilot it except ask for permission to dock when we got here," Dalton said. "The ship flew itself."

"That's impossible," I shot back, still watching Lyth as it spun to follow Juliyana's circle around it.

"Stay still, damn it," Juliyana muttered.

Lyth grew still but twisted its chin to watch her circle... and kept twisting. I gasped as its head swiveled right around on its neck, with no apparent damage.

Dalton sucked in a startled breath, too. "Damn..." he breathed.

Lyth looked even more amused. I would have said it was enjoying our discomfort—no, it was enjoying showing off, only ship AIs didn't have emotions.

Juliyana halted her circling. It wasn't giving her any more

answers than we had so far. "Okay," she told the thing. "Explain your nature so we can understand."

"It would be easier to demonstrate," Lyth said, his smile growing warmer.

"Demonstrate, then," Juliyana told it.

Lyth melted into a puddle on the floor, with flowing traces of colors which had made up his appearance swirling like paint in water.

We all stepped out of the way.

The puddle didn't spread the way normal liquid did. It remained exactly where it was...then it shrunk. The colors disappeared before the puddle itself did, turning it to a black, non-reflective mass that...evaporated.

I stepped closer to the place where the puddle had been. We all did.

Dalton prodded at the space on the treaded floor with the toe of his boot. "He did that last time," he said.

"If you'll step back a moment," Lyth said, from the overhead speakers.

We all stepped back.

Lyth grew in front of us once more. I watched it build from a small spill of the complete black, developing size, then details and finally colors...and Lyth stood there once more. He spread his hands, as if to say "see?"

"So yeah, he waved at me," Dalton said. "And said I should come aboard, that he could get me off the station without alerting the Rangers."

"What *are* you?" I demanded.

Lyth put his hands together in a surprisingly elegant movement. "I am an outward extrusion of the ship. I *am* the ship. You stand aboard the *Supreme Lythion*. I am my hands, my heart, my tools, for..." He shrugged his shoulders and fell apart.

136

It was like watching a child's container of marbles all poured out upon the floor, to bounce and roll and find room for themselves, jostling and knocking together.

Only these marbles were all five-centimeter high versions of the full sized Lyth.

"This is how I can fly myself," Lyth said, from overhead. "If levers must be pulled or buttons depressed, I can do that..."

The thousands of tiny Lyth figures moved over to the navigation table and ran up the leg to the surface. A bunch of them moved over to the control panel and formed into a disembodied finger, which carefully pressed the power grid.

The navigation table came to glowing life, showing the planetary bodies of an unnamed system, circling a blue-white sun.

The finger turned it off again, then flowed back to the rest of the little figures, which flowed down the leg of the table and back to the space where Lyth had been standing, before.

They came together and rose up into Lyth's shape once more. "Of course, most of the functions in this ship don't require a human hand to manipulate them. The ship was designed so I could manage them all. For those few functions which require touch, I can still take care of them."

"Why?" I demanded sharply. A ship that could fly itself and control its own internal functions was far too powerful, in my estimation. I felt deeply uneasy just standing on the deck of the thing.

"Why, to serve you," Lyth replied, his smile fading. "That is my purpose."

"What if your purpose was corrupted, and you decided taking a knife to my throat would serve others?" Dalton asked, his voice raspy. I recognized he felt the same concern I did.

Lyth swayed toward him, raised his fist and punched his jaw...only the fist didn't make contact. It splintered apart and flakes dropped to the ground, to float over to Lyth's boots and be reabsorbed.

His hand reassembled. "Impact against any solid-state mass, beyond a certain velocity, destroys this structure's cohesion."

"Velocity..." Dalton murmured, his fingers up against his untouched jaw. He rubbed it and dropped his hand.

"Yes, but you could kill us all because you control the ship," Juliyana replied. "You could expose the interior to vacuum. We'd be dead in three minutes. That doesn't require velocity."

"Why *would* I do that?" Lyth asked, his tone reasonable. "You are my guests." His brow furrowed. "Besides...it would be, well, *wrong*."

"An AI with ethical subroutines," I breathed. "Amazing."

"And hands, too," Dalton added.

"You should think of this body as merely a tool," Lyth said. "I can reassemble myself into any object—probe, hammer, sensor—"

"You can form intelligent circuits?" I said sharply.

"*I* am the intelligence," Lyth said, its voice coming from the overhead speakers.

"This form has sensors in every nanoparticle, which combined together provide feedback which I can process," the Lyth in front of us added.

"Nanobots," I breathed, as the essential nature of the thing became clear to me. "Acting in concert."

"I can reach into the smallest spaces in the ship," Lyth added. "In this form, I can move around the spaces designed for humans."

"Have you been Turing-tested?" Juliyana asked, looking at

the ceiling where the speakers emitted.

"I have no consciousness," Lyth said. "The self-awareness you profess to as humans escapes my understanding. I have been taught human mannerisms and learned how to interact with humans in ways which reassure them and allow me to serve them to the fullest capacity."

"You *like* interacting with us," Dalton added.

Lyth sobered. The warmth in its eyes faded. "It has been a very long time since I had company," he confessed. "I regret the absence."

"Damn, I think it was lonely," Juliyana breathed.

"Is that why you offered to get me off the city, Lyth?" Dalton said. "You wanted company?"

Lyth frowned. "I was told to bring you to Devonire."

"*Who* told you?" we all said together. Juliyana and Dalton sounded as alarmed as I felt.

"I don't know," Lyth said.

"You followed the order, anyway."

"I always obey human requests, unless they put my existence in jeopardy. If a human is in danger, even my existence can be disregarded."

"Orders of priority," Juliyana murmured. "Standard AI ethical foundation."

"How did your orders arrive?" Dalton asked Lyth.

Lyth frowned. "Voice communication."

"Authenticated?"

"Yes. It was a human speaking to me. Their responses measured beyond Turing standard." Lyth smiled. "You must understand, I am particularly sensitive about *who* I take my orders from. I check carefully when I am first confronted with what appears to be a human, to ensure I am not being deceived."

"You tested us?" Juliyana asked.

"There is no need to test any of you," Lyth said airily. "Dalton felt pain under high acceleration and Danny's metabolism has slowed in the last few minutes, indicating she is both hungry and tired. While you, Juliyana, are simply a delight to behold." Its smile was warm as it considered her.

Juliyana's lips parted. It wasn't often I saw her left with nothing to say.

Then my stomach rumbled loudly, and all three of them turned to look at me.

"Damn, he was right," Juliyana said.

"Tell me you have a galley on this thing," Dalton added.

"Follow me," Lyth said, and strode across the bridge deck toward the exit ramp.

I followed everyone else with a touch of reluctance. I *was* starving, only there were still a few million or so questions which needed urgent answers, before I could relax enough to eat.

Yet the ship with the answers was walking away from me. I had no choice but to follow.

12

LYTH PLACED A STEAMING PLATE of curry in front of me, diverting me with the aroma of spices.

My stomach rumbled again. I detached the fork from the rim of the bowl and ate quickly.

Gabriel sat at the big table, his head resting against the tall back cushions of the bench we were both sitting on.

Juliyana sat on the other side of the table, on a matching bench, with a lower back, so those of us on this side could see beyond the bench and across the rest of the galley.

Lyth orchestrated the printer, producing meals for Juliyana and Gabriel. "There are no fresh food supplies," it explained. "Although I can store fresh food over the long term, and even longer if the preservation options are activated. The capacity of the storage is a function of—"

"Yes, yes," I said, cutting it off. I pointed my fork at Dalton. "How long since your last crush shot, Dalton?"

"Two years ago," he replied, his voice tired.

Juliyana lowered her spoonful of stew. "What sort of shit did you buy?" she demanded. "Two years isn't nearly long enough for the nanobots to even begin to expire, even in the cheapest juice out there."

He cracked one eye open to look at her. "You sound just like your mother."

"Danny is my grandmother," she replied tartly and returned to eating.

Dalton fully opened the eye. "You're Noam's daughter?"

Juliyana lowered the spoon once more. "Why do you think we were looking for you?"

I winced. That was a card I had wanted to hold for now.

Dalton sat up. "You were looking for me?"

"That's for later," I replied. "First, I have a few questions of my own."

Dalton held up his hand, looking at Juliyana. "You were looking for me? Why were you on Devonire, if you were looking for me? No one knew I was there—even I didn't know where I was until Devonire traffic control reached out, when the *Lythion* emerged from the gate."

"We had to leave New Phoenicia in a hurry," Juliyana said. "We took the first passage to anywhere else."

"An anywhere which just happened to be where I was..." Dalton muttered.

I was looking at Lyth. Dalton was, too.

Juliyana put her spoon down and stared at the thing, too. "There's been way, *way* too many handy coincidences, lately," she said softly.

Lyth had taken the last seat at the table. Now he looked offended. "I am a shipmind," he said. "I just follow orders."

"From this mysterious human you can't name," Dalton said. "What if this human reaches out again and tells you we're a threat to your existence?"

"Can't happen in the hole," Juliyana pointed out.

Lyth turned to her. "It couldn't happen beyond the array, either." His tone sounded as though he was anxious for her to believe him. "Not anymore."

"Why not anymore?" I asked.

"Because you are here," Lyth said simply.

"What, we outrank any other humans because we're sitting in you?" Dalton asked.

"You outrank any other human orders, because that was what I was ordered to do," Lyth said. "I was to imprint your voices and follow your instructions."

"*All* of us?" Juliyana said. "How did this person even know where we would be? *We* didn't know."

"We knew for the eighteen hours we were in the hole," I said. "None of this makes sense and right now I'm too hungry to care. So I repeat my original question, Dalton. Why is your crush status so weak?"

Dalton sat back against the high bench once more. "What do you care?" He closed his eyes.

"I care, because you're on this ship and I have no idea where we're heading—"

"Greater New Hamburg," Lyth slid in.

"—or what will face us when we emerge from the gate," I finished, with a hand palm up to Lyth, silently telling him to stow his comments. "If we have to dodge another carrier or, stars save us, a dreadnought, then you're going to feel it."

"Hell, Danny, I didn't know you cared," Dalton drawled.

"I care that you won't be a bit of use to me in that situation, and that you'll die before I have my answers."

"Is there a medical AI on the ship, Lyth?" Juliyana asked him. She was phrasing her questions as if the Lyth appendage was not the ship itself. Hell, we were all referring to it as "him".

"An up to date one," I amended.

"The AI has been updated in the last fifteen seconds, since you made your first enquiry," Lyth told Juliyana. "It has the sum total of human biology and medical knowledge at its disposal and is waiting to assess Gabriel, as soon as he is ready."

Dalton opened his eyes. "I am not sick. I have no intention of being prodded."

"There's *something* wrong with you," I said. "I want the active status of everyone on this ship before we emerge from the gates. I already know Juliyana's."

Dalton didn't move. "You left the Rangers forty years ago, but you're still giving orders."

"Then consider it a request with imperatives attached," I told him.

"This is *my* ship," Dalton began, sitting up once more.

"I think Lyth would disagree with you." Juliyana's tone was serene. Her hand was beneath the table, out of sight.

"Actually," Lyth said, his tone conciliatory, "Colonel Andela outranks you, Major Dalton."

"And Lyth *did* call you a passenger," I pointed out sweetly.

"He called *all* of us guests," Dalton shot back, his long finger stabbing the tabletop, next to his untouched sandwich.

"He is taking my orders, and I outrank you," I replied.

"He's taking my orders, too," Dalton growled. He looked at Lyth. "Right? The mystery man told you to follow our orders."

Lyth nodded. "Only, someone must command the crew of the ship, and—"

"Now we're *crew*?" Juliyana said, dismay on her face.

Lyth looked surprised, then upset. "Are you *not* crew? Will you...leave me?"

"Oh for crying out loud," I breathed. "A heartbroken ship is the last thing we need. Lyth, snap out of it. Juliyana isn't going anywhere for a while. Dalton, if you're not going to eat that sandwich, push it here. Then shove your male ego out the airlock and go with Lyth. Submit to whatever diagnostics the medical AI deems necessary so you don't keel over next time the ship yaws."

He didn't move.

"I mean it, Major. Move your ass," I added, keeping my face immobile and giving away none of the tension in my gut.

Juliyana was vibrating with the same wariness. Gabriel Dalton had been a brilliant soldier on the field of battle — smart and relentless. He would persist against overwhelming odds, never giving up. It was a quality which couldn't be trained into soldiers and I had learned to spot it in soldiers under my command and foster their natural skills with enhanced training.

So Dalton was physically dangerous. I needed to clip his maverick streak right now. He'd spent forty years living outside a chain of command and had to get used to it once more.

Dalton opened his mouth to say something. By the tightness of his jaw and the heat in his eyes, he wasn't about to salute me and obey.

"Don't be a fool," I raged at him. "If you haven't figured it out already, this ship is something we've never seen before. It's advanced well beyond anything even the Rangers have got. The medical AI has to be of the same caliber. Why *wouldn't* you want to take advantage of the resource?"

Dalton closed his mouth. His eyes still glinted with anger.

"I judge you've spent forty years running under assumed IDs, scrounging for a living," I said. "You've learned to grasp opportunities as they swing by, or you would never have walked onto the *Lythion*. Don't turn this chance away because you don't like who is telling you to take it."

I kept my gaze steady, drilling into his.

Dalton broke first. His gaze shifted from mine. "Makes sense," he said gruffly. He shoved the plate of sandwich at me and got to his feet. "Come on, bot-boy. Show me where to go."

Lyth glanced at Juliyana, clearly torn about leaving her company.

I rolled my eyes.

Then Lyth split himself in two and formed two three-

145

quarter scale versions of himself. One stayed beside Juliyana. The other stepped in front of Dalton. "This way," it told him and headed for the exit of the galley.

When the door shut, I dropped my fork and gave a great gusty sigh.

Juliyana considered me. "Guess you're the captain then, Captain." She put her knife on the table and turned her attention back to her meal.

"Danny will do," I replied, as evenly as I could. I sighed. "And now my curry is cold."

Lyth printed a fresh half portion of curry for me and recycled the rest. While he was waiting for the printer to produce the meal, Lyth abruptly sprouted to full height. He glanced at me. "I left Dalton with the doctor and I'm listening in recording mode in case the doctor needs me for anything."

He brought the bowl over and put it in front of me. "Enjoy." He sat once more.

I detached the fork from the rim and ate. These were not Cygnus print files at all. I'd never tasted this before.

In between forkfuls, I questioned Lyth. "Tell me about this human who told you to come to Devonire and take Dalton with you."

"I've told you what I know," Lyth said. His tone said he was being frank. "The communication was direct, live and the message bullet reinforced. I could not break the encryption."

"You tried, then?" Juliyana asked.

Lyth grimaced. "I did. I felt no more comfortable than you did about accepting an order from someone I didn't know, although the order was simple enough. I was to attract Dalton's attention when he came close enough to the ship, urge him to come aboard, then take him to Devonire."

Lyth had become agitated when we suggested we would be leaving the ship and not returning. I coupled it to this revelation. "You were pleased to have the company," I surmised.

"Yes!" Lyth said. "And the orders wouldn't bring harm to him. When I saw Dalton was actually trying to escape Rangers, it meant taking him away would actually serve him, so I was pleased to oblige. I squeezed out of that mausoleum and dived into the gates as quickly as I could..." Lyth paused and looked uncomfortable.

"What else?" I coaxed.

"Dalton passed out," Lyth admitted. "I didn't have the capacity to do more than negotiate with the gate and jump, so I did not scan him then. Afterwards, he refused to let me or the doctor examine him." His gaze met mine.

It was remarkable how a pair of black eyes made from nanobots could appear so lifelike.

"I am impressed you made him do it," Lyth added.

"Dalton was a Ranger," I said. "He follows orders if they make sense. I just had to make them make sense."

"Wait," Juliyana said, pushing her empty plate away and wiping her mouth. "You said *you* negotiated with the gate? You paid the fees and taxes, too?"

"I didn't have to." Lyth frowned. "I wasn't asked. I did not notice the omission at the time. I did not have to negotiate or pay fees when I took the three of you back through the Devonire gate, either. It was simply never raised. I knocked and asked the gate to form the wormhole and it did." He looked from Juliyana to me. "That is very strange, isn't it?"

"Look who's talking." I tapped the table, thinking. "You also said the medical AI—the doctor—was updated straight after Juliyana suggested Dalton use it. We're in a hole and communications squirts can't reach us here. So how did you update anything?"

Lyth frowned again. "I don't know. It was automatic to reach for updates, and they were available, so I handed them on to the doctor." He shrugged, a human gesture.

"That's *impossible*," Juliyana breathed.

"Manifestly not," I said. "The AI *was* updated."

"Unless Lyth got mixed up. Maybe he updated the AI just before we jumped."

Lyth gave her a gentle smile. "I assure you, I was far too busy to update anything right then. My subroutines were at full capacity computing the jump. I only updated when you spoke of the medical AI. I do not need to convince you, though, for you will check the logs yourself."

Juliyana smiled reluctantly. "I will," she admitted. "No offense, but if you're malfunctioning, you would not be aware of it."

"Yes, do run an independent diagnostic, Juliyana," I said. "I want an operational status on *everyone*." I looked Lyth in the eye.

He pressed his hand to his chest. "I'm part of the everyone," he breathed, looking rapturous.

I rolled my eyes. "What can you tell me about yourself, Lyth? Where did you come from? How old are you? How long were you in the junk park?"

Lyth blinked. "I have downloaded all the boring statistics to your implant, Colonel. The same information is available via the concierge AI, which you can access via any of the staterooms. So I will give you the thumbnail version now. I was designed by Girish Wedekind, eighty-three years—"

"I know that name," I interrupted.

"Wedekind was stark raving mad," Juliyana said. She had her hand to her temple, so I knew she was accessing the files Lyth had downloaded. Of course he would have given her a copy, too. "He designed the dreadnoughts the Rangers are still using today—an earlier version, although the model has never fundamentally changed. Wedekind turned into a recluse after that. The fame and the claims for his designs sent him over—at least, that's what everyone thinks. No one heard about him for decades, then he suddenly showed up, announcing he had made a special ship."

"I was the sum of all his passion and creativity," Lyth said softly. "He poured everything he had into my design." His small, warm smile faded. "Then he revealed me to all of humanity…"

"And they laughed," Juliyana added softly.

"They said I was ugly," Lyth said. "They never got to properly understand about the *inside* of me. They looked only upon my appearance."

"No offense, Lyth, but from the outside, you do look… well, blocky," I told him.

Lyth nodded. "A symmetrical block. A dimensionally appealing one. They did not understand the elegance in the spare details, in the negative spaces. They misunderstood."

"Quite likely, they did," I told him. "I'm guessing you were displayed to the Emperor, the Shield and the Rangers, yes?"

Lyth nodded.

"Soldiers only understand function, not form," I told him. "If you didn't melt a frigate into vapor, they wouldn't have been impressed."

"I wasn't given the chance," Lyth said.

"Does that mean you *can*?" Juliyana asked, sounding interested.

"I wouldn't know," Lyth replied, his tone bland. "I've never tried."

I thought of the railguns on the exterior. Given the true size of this ship, now it was away from a carrier and not diminished in comparison, I judged the guns were heavier than I had first measured them to be. "If any ship was capable of destroying a frigate in one shot, it might well be you, Lyth, although that is not an experiment you should run. The Emperor gets pissed when people break his toys."

Lyth nodded. "I will wait until you tell me I can try to melt a frigate."

"What happened to you after the Emperor sent Girish Wedekind away?" Juliyana asked curiously.

I wanted to warn her not to anthropomorphize Lyth too much. It was just a smart AI, designed to ape human emotions. As it was advice I should follow myself, I said nothing.

"Girish ordered me to park myself at Badelt City," Lyth said. "So I did, even though I was sad he was leaving. He never did come back."

"You've been in that junk park for eighty-three years?" I asked.

"Eighty-two years, six months, two weeks and two days," Lyth said. "Terran Standard, that is."

No wonder the empathetic thing pined for company and was running about making sure we were happy, to ensure we wouldn't want to leave.

Lyth sat up. "Major Dalton is finished and is asking to speak to you," he told me.

"He can't come here?"

"He is receiving treatment," Lyth replied.

"You'd better show me the way to the infirmary," I told him. "And don't do that splitting thing, huh? It makes me feel like I've had one too many cocktails."

Lyth pouted, but obeyed.

13

DALTON SAT IN A COMFORTABLE chair in a large room with subdued color on the wall. The color extended to cupboard fronts, drawers and counters. The light was low. Dalton even had his feet up on a hassock. His long coat laid over the back of the chair and his sleeve was rolled up. His arm was extended, with a cuff around the thickest part of his forearm.

Lyth moved a matching armchair over in front of Dalton and patted the back of it, indicating I should sit.

The cushions were *very* soft.

Then I tried to get up again. "The chair wasn't here just now, when I came in." Even the fastest printer known couldn't print and grow a chair in seconds.

Dalton smiled grimly. "It gets even weirder," he assured me. "The walls move."

"Major Dalton is mildly claustrophobic," Lyth said. "I made adjustments."

"Lyth is the most advanced ship Girish Wedekind ever designed," I told Dalton. "You're really claustrophobic? How'd you get in the Rangers?" Rangers had to squeeze into pods, crawl through tunnels, and breath each others' body odor for days at a time while on missions—claustrophobia should have bounced him right out the recruiting center door.

"I wasn't, then," Dalton said. "There was a thing a few years ago…" He scowled. "Doesn't matter," he growled.

I looked at the cuff on his arm. "What's that?"

"I don't know," Dalton said, in the same tone. "Every time I try to say no to something, the AI parrots at me about how advanced it is, and how the treatment it can provide me is the very best available outside the most exclusive clinics anywhere in the empire." His scowl deepened. "You primed the damn thing."

"Lyth did, I suspect," I replied. "I've never spoken to the AI. So, what is the problem then? Can it fix your crush status?"

"Not here," Dalton said.

I looked at Lyth. "The AI can't administer crush juice, even in an emergency?"

Most shipboard medical AIs could supervise crush shots—it was a basic function, as everyone on a ship needed high level crush status at all times.

"I *have* crush juice in my system, still," Dalton said. "The problem is…" He trailed off, looking disgusted.

Lyth tilted his head, as if he was listening to something I couldn't hear. "Ah!" he said. "Major Dalton underwent rejuvenation eleven years ago. The therapy did not properly extend his telomeres."

I looked at Dalton, surprised.

He shrugged. "What can I say? Bootleg rejuvenation is expensive. I got what I paid for."

I felt a touch of…something. I squashed it. "Your cells are too old for the crush juice to work, and you can't have another shot because the nanobots in that shot will fight with the ones you already have."

"Yeah, that's about what the doc said," Dalton drawled.

How fucking ironic.

"You don't have to look like that," Dalton growled.

"You've been on the run for forty years, Gabriel," I told him. "You've defied the odds. No one runs that long. Everyone gets caught eventually."

"In case it isn't obvious, I'm not exactly thriving." He lifted his arm with the hard cuff around it. "In fact, I was pretty close to rock bottom when Lyth found me." He looked away from me.

Lyth had the sense to keep his mouth shut.

"When we hit station side, we'll do something about the rejuvenation," I told Dalton.

He looked at me once more. "No. No favors."

"I need you fully functional."

"I'm not your junior officer anymore."

"You were never a *junior* officer," I assured him.

"Why exactly were you dodging the Rangers, anyway?"

I sat back, startled. It wasn't the change of subject it appeared to be, but it *was* an unexpected direction. I had forgotten how Dalton's mind sometimes tore off on strange tangents, seeing oblique connections and bizarre associations.

"I've been thinking about it," Dalton said. "We know why I want to avoid Rangers—"

"I know the external reason, but I need to know the motive behind it," I replied.

"You, first," Dalton said, then shut up. His eyes narrowed as he studied me, seeing if I would meet him halfway.

He was right. He was no longer a Ranger officer reporting to me.

And I was no longer the Colonel he had reported to. I had to shift to match the changed circumstances. "I diverted my family corporation's annual dividends payment and bought a rejuvenation and crush juice with some of it," I told him. "The family CEO informed the police battalions, who are now looking for me."

Dalton's eyes grew very wide. "*You* stole money?" He started to smile. "Damn, you actually *have* changed, haven't you?"

"I haven't changed. But I *am* adapting to the circumstances," I replied as calmly as I could, even though my pulse had jumped. I didn't like being called a thief, even though that was exactly what I was—at least for now. I pushed the concern aside. "Why did you desert your post, Dalton?"

"Why did you steal the money and rejuvenate?" he shot back. "Rumor said you were sitting on your stellar barge, waiting for the end."

"I was," I replied as calmly as I could. We could go around and around all day, trading I-dare-you's. I cut through it, instead. "Juliyana found orders transferring Noam to the Imperial Shield, a year before he died. They carried my chop."

Dalton grew still. "*Your* chop…"

"I found the real orders, the ones with your signature."

He sat back. "*That's* why you were looking for me. You're looking into Noam's death."

"There's something odd about it," I told him. "At least, Juliyana thinks so, and she has a lot of documents that suggest it."

"Suggest it, or you just *want* them to suggest it?" Dalton asked. His voice held none of the usual harsh notes.

"So why did you bolt, Dalton?"

His expression closed over. "I got a message that said it would be a smart move to fade over the horizon. It was a source I trusted…so I faded."

And he had been fading ever since.

"Just like that?" I asked. "No questions?"

"Just like that." He gazed back at me, unwavering.

I recognized that I would not get anything more out of him right now. "Lyth, how long are we in the hole, for?"

"There are another eighteen hours, thirty-three minutes and forty-seven seconds remaining before we emerge," Lyth

154

said smoothly, his tone polite and impartial.

I nodded and got to my feet. "Finish your treatment. We can talk later," I told Dalton. He needed time to unclench. "Lyth, you mentioned staterooms. Show me one of them."

"Good luck with that," Dalton said, as I left.

I found out what he meant very quickly, for Lyth walked me along the corridor we had followed when we first arrived. It ran down the flank of the ship and only jigged to the center to lead directly to the bridge deck.

"You may choose any door," Lyth told me.

I peered at the half dozen security doors along the corridor and frowned. "I don't remember seeing all these doors before." I had never fully lost the habit of mentally mapping doors and routes and exits through strange environments. I would have remembered these.

"They were not here the last time you traversed the corridor," Lyth told me.

I glared at him.

"They're just doors," Lyth added, his voice soft. "Here." He moved over to the nearest one and waved his hand over the keyplate, as if he had biometrics it could scan. The door opened. Only in the back of my mind did I process that he had just opened the door for his own avatar.

I stepped up to the open doorway, curious.

The room beyond was blank, featureless, and *huge*. "Who uses this place? The fucking Emperor?"

"Too large?" Lyth said.

The walls moved and shifted.

I staggered back a step or two. "What the..." I moved back to the doorway and would have propped myself up against the frame, except I suddenly remembered that the door had-n't been here a while ago, either. I made myself stand there, my arms crossed, watching the walls...*flow*.

It was the same type of movement Lyth had used when he turned into a finger and pressed the navigation table power-on button.

"You mean, this entire ship is made of nanobots?" I breathed, awe stealing all the strength from my voice.

"The exterior walls are hardened carbide metal, to with-stand the rigors of space."

"And they're rusty," I added, my tone dry.

"Not for much longer," Lyth replied serenely. "I'm restor-ing the outer epidermis as we speak."

He meant it literally. "Right *now*?" I asked. "Out *there*?"

"How do you scratch an itch?" he asked me, his tone curi-ous.

"I just scratch. I don't think about it." I nodded. "Okay, got it. The epidermis is just you. But these inner walls...even the corridor wall, they're made up of your nanobots?"

"No. My nanobots are smarter and have inbuilt sensory and communications functions. The bots that the walls and everything in the living section of the ship is made of are pure construction bots. They move, grip and hold still when they're told to."

"By you."

"Yes." Lyth smiled. "So...is the room of sufficient dimen-sions to suit you?"

I looked again. The walls, still blank and featureless, were considerably closer together, yet the space was still larger than my apartment on the *Judeste*. "I could learn to live with it," I said cautiously. "You created an armchair..." I added. A thought struck me. "Was the galley even there before we got there?"

"It was there before you got there," Lyth replied. "For a few minutes, at least."

I had an even more horrible thought. "Was my curry made of nanobots, then?"

"The printer is a perfectly normal printer," Lyth replied. "The bots just move it with them, as required."

"The *energy* needed for something like this..." I murmured.

"Every time the nanobots move, they create kinetic energy, which is drained from them to avoid damaging them, and stored for future use. I never run out of internal energy." He was very proud of that. "So...what furniture would you like in your room?"

"A bed, for now," I told him. I was just about to add that I needed pillows and sheets and a thick eiderdown over the top to snuggle beneath, when a bed rose up from the floor, looking unformed and lumpy. The surfaces smoothed out, developed details, grew flat and colored themselves in, until finally, a bed stood there. It was large enough for at least two people, with lots of pillows *and* a thick comforter.

"I could get to enjoy this," I said. "Once you've made something like the bed, can you change it?"

"It is easier to scrap it, disperse the nanobots, and start again," Lyth admitted. "But changes are certainly possible whenever you want them. Do you want me to change anything now?" The comforter on the bed shifted through patterns and rainbow colors.

"As long as it is warm and soft, I'm fine," I said quickly. "I had a sack with me on the deck..."

"Fetching it," Lyth replied, his tone remote. "It'll be here in a moment. I've added a concierge printer, there." He nodded. One of the walls now featured the dark face of a concierge and the maw of a printer beneath. "The concierge is *not* me, so you may deal with it with complete privacy."

"I appreciate that," I said honestly.

"If you require any changes, the concierge can arrange them. Ask for whatever you need."

A semicircular hole a meter high appeared at the bottom of one of the walls, next to the bed. A platform on wheels rolled out of the hole. My sack was on top of it.

I pushed my surprise aside. Why *wouldn't* the ship just push aside nanobots and take the quickest route to where it needed to go?

"I'm never going to sleep, wondering if a wall is suddenly going to shift or open up and let something through." I glared at Lyth. "Humans like stability," I added.

Lyth pressed a finger to his temple, as if he was thinking hard. "I have settled the matter with the concierge," he told me. "If you tell the concierge to lock your room settings, no one else may change them — not even me. Then you will be assured that nothing will move unless you wish it to."

"That works for now," I said, although I was going to have to contemplate how one related to a space that could change to anything in an instant.

But right now, the bed beckoned.

"Juliyana is asking for you," Lyth said.

"Tell her to get some sleep," I replied, moving toward the bed. "I'll talk to her in eight hours." I frowned. "What is the ship time, right now?"

"Whatever you want it to be," Lyth replied.

Of course.

"Then in nine hours, it will be six in the morning. Tell the others, please."

"Goodnight, Colonel."

"Danny," I growled. "I haven't been Colonel Andela for a long time."

"Good night, then, Captain Danny," Lyth said.

I gave up.

Lyth went away, the door closed behind him with a soft hiss, then gave a tiny chirp to indicate it was locked.

The bed was perfectly soft and snuggle-inducing. I was woken by the light in the room shifting toward dawn, until the sun rose, blazing, up one wall and roused me to full wakefulness.

Yeah, I could get *very* used to this.

14

THE GALLEY WASN'T WHERE I left it.

I was positive the door had moved a few meters up the passage from where it had been. But the door looked the same and when I approached it, it opened as it had before.

I stopped on the sill for a moment, to absorb the differences. Last night, the galley had been adequately functional, with the table and two benches, the printer maw and some recessed cupboards and drawers on one wall.

I wasn't sure where the printer was anymore, but for a moment, that wasn't my concern.

I stood in an antique edifice I could vaguely remember having seen before, but only in images. Where I stood was approximately in the middle of it. To either side was a row of tables with padded benches on either side of them, with a clear space running down the middle. On the other side of the corridor was a high counter with round stools in front of it, screwed to the floor at regular intervals. The counter was clear in places, but there were islands of things—in my surprise, I didn't absorb the details, only that there were glass domes and cylinders displaying what was inside.

From somewhere in the room, music was playing very quietly. A muted voice sang too softly for me to hear the lyrics. I was positive I'd never heard the song before, yet it seemed familiar, anyway.

The wall that the corridor behind me had in common with

this place was dazzlingly bright. I took another step forward to inspect the wall.

It *looked* like a glass window, running the length of the long room, with metal supports spaced across it. On the pane immediately next to the door, words had been painted in a rainbow arc, but they were in reverse, a display for whoever might read them on the other side. My brain said there was no "other side" to the illusion, but damn it, there were people out there in the sunshine, walking by. And there were ground vehicles that looked nothing like anything I had ever seen before. The only reason I knew they were ground vehicles was because a woman in very odd clothes settled behind the controls of one of them, started it, and steered it away from where it had been parked. The vehicle would be forced to follow the paved road because it had inflated wheels.

The sound of people walking by, the vehicles, and even further away, birds and high childish voices calling to each came through the "window".

Overriding all that, though, was the smell of brewed coffee…and hot food. I thought I could detect the scent of maple syrup.

"Danny," Juliyana called.

I had been aware of her and Dalton sitting to the left, when I stepped in. I pulled myself away from the fascinating view through the window and walked along the corridor to where they were sitting and settled on the bench beside Juliyana.

Dalton held out a thick piece of card toward me, with text and decorations on it.

"An analogue menu," I murmured.

"Not exactly," Dalton said. "If you double tap what you want, that orders it."

"I told it what I wanted and it wrote it there for me to tap and confirm," Juliyana said. "Now we're just waiting for it to arrive."

I tapped on the eggs. Then I added waffles because the smell of warm syrup was making my mouth water. And coffee, because that smell was divine, too. The menu wrote a big green check mark next to each item I tapped.

I handed the menu back to Dalton. "Is this place your idea?"

"I asked the concierge if it had seen images of old Terran diners," he said. "Apparently, it has."

Juliyana smothered her laugh.

I just stared at Dalton.

He gave a defensive shrug. "I like history, okay?"

"*Military* history, sure," I said, for I remembered his interest from the days when I had known him on Annatarr.

"History, period," Dalton said. "I've branched out. Time can stretch when you're hiding from everyone."

A young brunette woman in a pink dress, overlaid with a white apron, came up to the table carrying a heavy tray. "Morning, ladies and gents. Let's see here. There's coffee, coffee and…mm, coffee." She put thick mugs of coffee in front of each of us. "The rest will be right along, 'kay?" She winked at Dalton and headed back behind the counter and into what looked like a rear room—a kitchen as antique as this place, I supposed, but it wouldn't really be there.

Dalton got a silly grin on his face as he watched the waitress move away.

"You realize you're ogling Lyth, right?" Juliyana told him.

Dalton's smile faded. "I'm enjoying the ambience, alright?"

Juliyana laughed.

"Actually, I'm right here," Lyth said. The façade he had been using last night moved up to the end of our table. "May

I join you?"

"Coffee, honey?" the waitress called from behind the counter.

"Yes, please," Lyth told her and sat on the end of the bench as Dalton straightened up and shuffled closer to the window and its distracting view. He put his hands on the table and looked at me. "I presumed you would wish to discuss our immediate future."

The waitress put an identical cup of coffee in front of Lyth.

We all held our breath, watching as he picked up the mug and appeared to sip it.

And the level of coffee in the mug was lower, when he put the mug back.

I stuck my finger in the dark liquid, felt the sting of hot coffee. I moved to put the finger in my mouth and suck off the coffee, watching Lyth all the time, waiting for him to protest that I should not. He just stared steadily back.

"Danny, no," Juliyana said quickly as I closed my lips around the damp finger, proving she'd had the same thought I had, that the coffee and the mug was just more of Lyth — nanobots split off and made to look like the coffee we were drinking and the cups holding that coffee.

"Tastes exactly like real coffee," I said, as Dalton and Juliyana watched intently.

"That's because it *is* real coffee," Lyth assured us. "But we're getting distracted," he pointed out.

I blinked, and tried to push away the question blazing in my mind, namely, where the hell he put the coffee he was "drinking"? "Yes," I said, regrouping. "Juliyana and I have spent a lot of money and a lot of time trying to find you, Dalton. You arriving at Devonire is a coincidence I'm still not happy about, but that's immaterial for right now. The larger question is where do we go now? I've had some thoughts about that—"

"Back up a few steps, Danny," Dalton said. "You need to fill me in on this whole Noam thing."

"No, we don't," Juliyana said, her tone flat.

"The fuck you don't," Dalton shot back. "This is *my* ship—"

"Danny outranks you," Juliyana interrupted.

We were back to that. I slapped the table to get their attention. "Just shut up for a moment, will you?"

"No," Dalton told me. "I was here first. It was an abandoned ship. It's mine by salvage rights."

"You can't even steer the thing," Juliyana shot back, looking amused. "I'd say you belong to the *Lythion*, not the other way around."

"*Shut up*! Both of you!" I cried.

They shut up. Dalton glared at me.

Lyth raised his hand. "I may be able to offer some clarity on this issue."

"Go," I told him.

"My orders were to collect *all* of you. I just happened to scoop up Dalton first—no offence," he added, glancing at Dalton.

Dalton pushed back into the corner of the seat, angled so he could glare at all of us. "None taken."

"I was also instructed to obey all of you," Lyth added. "That would imply that if any of you own the ship at all, you all have equal rights. And as the more experienced officer, Danny should lead." He paused. "A democratic leader," he added. "One that we all agree to follow."

"Democracy doesn't work," Dalton growled.

"Representative democracy does not," Lyth returned. "Perfect and pure democracy *does* work, but it rarely exists. Right here, it does."

I hid my smile as I watched Dalton squirm. Lyth was doing all the work for me. "Are you voting me in as captain, Lyth?" I already knew he had. He had called me Captain Danny last night.

"I believe that was the general thrust of what I was saying," Lyth replied.

"I vote for Danny, too," Juliyana said swiftly.

Dalton's face tinged red and he drew a breath to protest… but the waitress chose that moment to come up to the table with another tray heavy with steaming plates giving off delicious scents.

Dalton had been neatly distracted. We all were. We all ate—even Lyth did, and I *really* wanted to know what he would do with the food and liquid he was taking in.

I was nearly through my breakfast, which was delicious. It shouldn't be, for the food was printed and printed food never tasted quite the same as freshly prepared organics, but it *did* taste marvelous. Maybe it was the false sunshine and the airy notes of music drifting in the background, or the distant sound of a bustling ancient city…who knows? I just know it was one of the best meals I've ever had…and I had eaten chef-prepared operatic-quality meals at the clinic on New Phoenicia.

Dalton pushed his plate aside before I was finished and gripped his coffee mug in both hands. "You're captain for now," he told me. "I've been outvoted. Fine. No problems. You can be captain as long as you're on the ship. But when we get out of this hole, we're diving straight back into another one. I'm taking you back to your barge, lady, and dumping you on it." He glanced at Juliyana. "Both of you."

Juliyana put her chin on her fist. "Why did you run away from the Rangers, Dalton?'

"None of your fucking business," he shot back.

"He was warned to take a dive, so he did," I said.

Dalton crossed his arms. "Can we get more coffee?" he bitched, looking for the waitress.

Juliyana didn't move. She kept her gaze on Dalton. "Answer me this, Dalton. You've been running forty years plus. Did you never stop to ask yourself *why* you're running?"

"I'm running because I'm wanted for desertion," he growled. His glance flickered toward me.

"I'm not the still-active Ranger here," I pointed out.

Juliyana smiled. "I'm off-duty and on hiatus," she replied. "So let's be frank. The desertion is just the symptom. The reason you ran is the crux. It fits a pattern."

"You think you know why I ran, huh?"

"I don't believe even you do," Juliyana replied. "You just *think* you do. I don't care why you think you ran, though. The interesting thing is that just over a month after Danny resigned, you had a sudden need to disappear and never be found again. Have you considered, Dalton, that either throwing you into a brig for whatever you think you're running from, or, as actually happened, having you run and stay wanted and off the grid, was exactly what someone wanted?"

Dalton put his coffee mug down. Slowly. He only just found the table with the bottom of it, because he was staring at Juliyana. "You're saying Danny was forced to resign?"

He was *not* stupid. I gave him that.

"Danny thinks she resigned of her own free will, but what if everything was set up to push her into a place where she thought resigning was the only viable option? What if you were pushed into a place where you thought running was your only option?"

Dalton leaned forward. He was hooked. "*Why?*" he demanded, his voice showing a hint of strain.

"It got both you and Danny off the board," Juliyana replied. "You were Noam's CO. Danny was throwing her weight around, trying to exonerate Noam, to find out what really happened, because she doesn't believe he went mad, either."

"And what about you?" Dalton said.

"I was already off the board. I was stripped of all rank. I've been stuck in maintenance on shit assignments in every small corner of the Empire ever since."

Dalton winced. "Damn..." he breathed.

"Anyone who had a reason to want to learn the truth was dealt with," Juliyana finished. "Even Darcy, Noam's partner, has been neutralized."

"Only, I wasn't digging into what happened to Noam," Dalton pointed out.

"You *did* know he had been reassigned to the Imperial Shield," I said. "You're the only person in the Rangers who knew. So they caused you to run, and changed the orders so it looked like I issued them."

"Why you?" Dalton said. "Why not just destroy the transfer orders?"

"It would discredit me, if I ever tried to claim again that Noam was not the cause of the Drakas disaster." I grimaced. "The orders would make it look like I was crazed with guilt for shoving him into an assignment that drove him mad." I shrugged.

Lyth said softly, "No, the orders were changed so that Juliyana would come to find you."

We all stared at him.

"You *know* that?" Juliyana said.

"I cannot demonstrate that it is true, but it is the simplest explanation. Danny had already been judged as a mother crazed with grief and forced to resign. There was no need for additional measures. The real orders were too easy to find. All they needed the false orders to do was prompt you into acting."

"You know something about this, Lyth?" I asked warily.

Lyth shook his head. "I've been stuck in a junk park for nearly a century, cut off from *everything*. This is the first I've heard of Noam Andela's actions at Drakas—although I am now up to date with the public records...such as they are."

He had been quietly processing all the public data while we had been convincing Dalton he hadn't run of his own free will at all.

Dalton scrubbed his face with both palms. "This doesn't make any sense," he said. His voice was hoarse. He didn't like the idea that he had been manipulated any more than we did. "So I knew he'd been transferred to the Imperial Shield. So what? How is that a threat? I signed transfer orders every fucking week."

"Do you know who he was reporting to in the Shield?" I asked. "The orders didn't say."

"Transfers to the Shield *don't* specify CO or unit," Dalton said. "You know that as well as I do."

"But you *do* know who he was assigned to," I replied. I was absolutely certain of it, because Dalton was the type of officer who not only asked questions he shouldn't, he made sure he had sources who could give him the answers. He had never been a soldier who could blindly obey. He questioned everything. It was the reason he had still been a Major despite a thirty-year career in the Rangers. He knew how to work within the system...to a point.

Juliyana leaned forward eagerly. "*That's* why you were made to run," she added. "You knew too much."

Dalton swallowed. "You'd better tell me everything." This

time, it wasn't a demand. It was a plea.

I left the three of them in the diner, with Juliyana holding their rapt attention while she went through all the evidence and suggestive documents she had on file. Although, the only ironclad proof of any wrongdoing was the transfer orders with my chop on them, alongside the real orders.

We needed proof, something that would stand up under the blaze of public scrutiny and not look like the pair of us—or Dalton, for that matter—were delusional from our long-term denial of Noam's fate.

I was starting to have some ideas about that. The *Supreme Lythion* dropping into our laps as it had would open up our options in ways I was only just starting to encompass.

My room was as I had left it…only the bed was made. Oh well, I could live with that much intrusion. I went over to my travel sack, which was still sitting upon the wheeled platform on which it had arrived last night. My pad had more data I could add to the discussion back in the diner.

"Danny," Noam said urgently, behind me.

I whirled, my heart shooting straight up into the infarction range. "Noam…"

He moved toward me, looking as real as the bed he was skirting. He held up his hands. "Now you're here, we really need to talk."

"You're not here," I told him. "You're just my mind blowing a gasket." I felt sticky and prickling and panicked. But I clung to what I knew—what I *thought*—was happening, for it helped me anchor myself.

"You're right. I'm not exactly here," he said. "But this is the only way for now I can reach you. You have to listen to me, Danny. They're coming for you."

More doom and gloom. More scary forecasts. I shook my head. "No. No more. I'm tired of this." I made myself straighten despite my blood pressure making me hunch in and clutch at my chest. "I want you to leave, Noam."

"No, you don't. Not really." His tone was wise and gentle.

"What more do you want?" I cried. "I'm doing everything I can to figure out what happened to you. I've...fuck, I've rejuvenated, stolen money to do it, and now the family want my neck. The Rangers are after me, and not just for the money, anymore. I'm tired of being smacked around by this, Noam. Every move I make, someone tries to swipe at me. I just wanted to die in peace, and now I have another ninety years of the empire dumping bullshit on me..."

Noam just looked at me, the corner of his mouth lifted. My heart ached. I'd seen that amused, tolerant expression so many times before!

"*Did* you go mad?" I whispered, my eyes prickling.

"Did you *really* give up?" he asked.

Truth time. I'd been here before, lately. "No," I whispered and felt the veracity of it in my gut. "No, not really."

Noam nodded. "That's what I thought. Ask Dalton about Michael Powell Moroder."

What the fuck...! I stared at him, my thoughts racing with more than the sensation of doom that always accompanied his arrival.

Noam glanced over his shoulder. "Michael Powell Moroder," he repeated, then walked away.

Through the wall.

I sank onto the bed, my pulse sounding like canon fire in my head and my whole body shaking with the adrenaline overload.

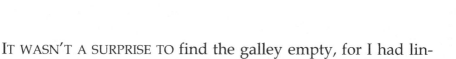 15

IT WASN'T A SURPRISE TO find the galley empty, for I had lingered in my room, recovering, for longer than I had originally intended to be there.

The galley looked the same as when I had left it, which was surprisingly reassuring. I still wasn't sure I liked the idea of a living space that changed outfits more often than me.

I looked for a concierge panel, or even the printer, which was usually next to one. I couldn't spot either, so I raised my voice and tried anyway. "Lyth, where is Dalton?"

He said from behind me, "He's in his room. I'll show you the way."

I turned and followed him back down the corridor to one of the other doors that had appeared on the inside wall of the corridor. I glanced at the lockers and drawers in the corridor itself. "Are they decorative?" I asked Lyth.

"The outer hull wall is as solid as any non-gaseous or non-liquid form," he replied. "But they *are* all empty," he added. He stopped at a door three down from mine and gestured to it.

I glanced at the doors in between. "Juliyana has one...who has the other?"

"Perhaps I do," Lyth looked mischievous.

I rolled my eyes and raised my knuckles to the door, then shifted my hand to the keyplate and pressed it. "Dalton, it's Danny. We need to talk." I looked at Lyth. "*If* he lets me in to talk, I need you to leave us alone for a bit."

"Concierge only," Lyth promised. He turned and walked away.

I put my fingers against the keyplate once more. "Dalton. Gabriel. It's important."

After a moment, the door slid open.

I did a doubletake on this threshold, too. The room was not a room at all. It was a dock on a still lake, with mist-shrouded and tree-carpeted mountains on the other side. A cool breeze drifted off the water. Lapping sounds came from beneath the planks of the dock and I could *smell* lake water, faint but distinct. To one side was a rickety table and a single round-back chair, beside a battered and scratched printer maw enclosed inside an object I had only seen in history videos—a refrigerator, I think they called them.

On the other end of the dock was a comfortable easy chair, facing the water and the cloud-wreathed mountains. Behind the chair was a hammock, hanging from posts on either side of the dock.

Dalton sat on the edge of the hammock, perfectly balanced. He'd had practice in sleeping in one, clearly. "I came here to think," he complained.

"Think? Or brood?"

He scowled. "*Think*," he said firmly. "And if I wanted to, why shouldn't I brood? If you and Juliyana are right about Noam, then I've lost forty years plus, fucked up my health, risked dying most days of the week, and it was for *nothing*. I was in the wrong place at the wrong time and signed the wrong set of orders." His tone was deeply bitter.

"Not for nothing," I said firmly. "If you were just the average officer, you'd still be signing papers somewhere, safe because you don't ask questions when told to jump." I paused. "You did *something* that goosed them, Dalton."

172

He breathed heavily. A gusty sigh.

I changed subjects—just for a moment. I looked at the reflection of the crags on the surface of the lake, admiring it. "Damn, you're really running with the full options, aren't you?" I studied the snow-covered peaks behind the front ones. "Is this from Terra?"

"Shostavich," he said. "My home world."

"You're ball-born...I didn't know that."

"There's a lot you don't know about me." He glared at me, waiting.

I leapt. "Michael Powell Moroder." I watched his face carefully.

Dalton's jaw sagged. He caught it up. *"Where did you get that name?"* he demanded, striding toward me.

"Then you *do* know it."

"Where did you hear it?" Dalton repeated. His hands flexed as he stood before me and I had the distinct sensation he wanted to shake me to pop the answer out. "No one had that name, not in connection with this."

"Who is he?" My own heart was thudding once more.

Dalton's jaw worked. He swore softly. "Noam's reporting officer in the Shield." He turned away and stalked over to the railing at the edge of the dock and leaned on it. The dock actually creaked under his feet, as if it really was a genuine plank structure resting on a lakebed. "You shouldn't have that name. There's no way you could. I've never told *anyone*." He was speaking to the water.

"You were keeping it," I said. "The ace up your sleeve."

Dalton turned and rested his butt on the railing and crossed his arms. "Where did you get the name?" he demanded. "The man who gave it to me is dead."

I built up an instant lie, about contacts inside the Shield. Only it wouldn't hold. Dalton was a master of networking and favors, and *he* likely didn't have a contact inside the Shield. No one did. They're a shield for a reason. They're impervious to the entire empire.

Dalton waited me out.

I shrugged. "Noam told me."

His eyes narrowed. "If you knew all along, then why chase after me at all? Why not go straight for Moroder?"

"I found out, just now."

Dalton's arms loosened. Then he said carefully, "Noam told you...just now?"

I realized I had crossed my own arms. I deliberately lowered them. "I know how it sounds. But is that any weirder than this?" I lifted my hand up toward the mountains. "Is it any stranger than a ship plucking you out of the depths of a stellar city and spiriting you to a remote station where I just happen to show up?"

Dalton rubbed the back of his neck. "Okay, point made. So...Noam just...what? Sent you a message?"

"I don't know how it works," I admitted. "I have..." Damn it, I couldn't hold back now. "I have waking seizures and when I do, I see and hear Noam. I thought it was my brain getting scrambled by the seizure, showing me what I wanted to see."

Dalton tilted his head. "I can understand that." His tone was calmer.

"Only, just now, Noam gave me a name I've never heard in my life. You just confirmed it is a *real* name, and someone connected to the Shield."

Dalton grew very still. "You're *sure* you've never heard the name?"

"Never. Not with the three names in there, like that. Maybe there are dozens of Michael Moroders running around the Empire and I just happened to dredge up the name of one of

174

them from seeing it on a roster or who knows anywhere? But *this* Moroder? Out of all of them?"

"Yeah, it's a stretch," Dalton admitted. "So, if you didn't come up with the name yourself, who gave it to you?"

"At the moment, all I know is that Noam did. As it's a legitimate lead, we have to follow it, Dalton. We have to find where Moroder is now and go talk to him. Face-to-face, no data across the array for the Empire to pick up. Anyone mixed up in this will have been tagged by the Empire. They'll be alerted if anyone reaches out to them."

Dalton shook his head. "We should be reaching out to Cygnus Intergenera."

"*Cygnus?*" I let out the shocked breath I'd sucked in. "Why the fuck would we talk to them? If we can even find anyone to talk to in the first place? We'd get the corporate runaround. Appointments, meetings, lackies—they'll never say no, but they'll tie us up in red tape for years and never give us what we want."

"Only if you try to use the official channels," Dalton said dismissively. "The war Noam was in, the battle he blasted out of existence, was the Empire against Cygnus. You and I and Juliyana—even Lyth—are being nudged into digging through what happened, and if we survive long enough to go public with what we find, Cygnus stands to gain the most out of that."

I considered it. "You think the Emperor is behind this, too."

"I think someone really high up in the Shield is behind it," Dalton replied. "The Emperor doesn't control their every movement. Although legally, the Shield and the Emperor are the same thing. If we prove the Shield were involved in a massive coverup for whatever reason, Cygnus will then sue the Emperor's ass and get back control of the array, then happily return to squeezing the Empire with trade tariffs and gate fees."

"It's an interesting theory," I admitted. "Aren't you at all interested in *what* they're covering up?"

"No," Dalton said flatly. "I couldn't give a flying fuck. This isn't my passion project, Danny. I just want my life back. Demonstrating to anyone who cares to listen that the Imperial Shield deceived the entire galaxy is enough to do that."

"What they're hiding is the reason you lost your life in the first place."

"I still don't care. I stopped caring a long time ago."

I let him keep the lie intact, and shifted ground. "Moroder is an easier lead to follow."

"You think?" His tone was withering. "He's *Imperial Shield*. We're better off heading directly for Rozsa Chang."

"The CEO of Cygnus?" I shook my head. "I admire the scale of your thinking, Dalton, but we would never get near her. She's as armor-plated as the Emperor."

"You think she wouldn't take a call from Danny Andela if we could put your name in front of her? You think she would refuse a call from anyone called Andela?" He paused. "We're heading for Sh'Klea Sine. That just happens to be where the Cygnus board meets."

I considered the logistics, juggling factors. "That's the problem with you, Dalton," I said, letting my irritation show. "You grasp at lateral issues and pull everything off course. You always have."

"We'll be *right there*." His voice was low. Intense.

"You take short-cuts. I doubt the regulation has been written that you haven't tried to break in one way or another. You get perverse delight out of it."

"You made your disapproval of me well known on Annatarr," Dalton shot back. "And that's irrelevant —"

176

"It proves my point. Running full tilt at Cygnus is the wrong move."

"Why?" he demanded. "You can't force me to follow your orders now, *Colonel*. Explain yourself. If you can get beyond 'because I say so', I'll be the most shocked man on the fucking ship."

"I *am* the captain!" I shot back.

"And you just proved my point." He shook his head.

I drew in a ragged breath. Damn it, he was getting to me. "We can't afford to steer by committee," I said, trying to keep my voice calm and reasonable.

"And I can't afford to follow you without question. It's *my life*, Danny. Don't you get that?"

That was the old Gabriel showing. I recalled in a flash an occasion when he had questioned my orders, justifying it with the one reason I had a hard time arguing against. "It's *my men*, Colonel," he'd ground out.

Dalton's men had always been stupidly loyal to him—well beyond the regard other Rangers had for their CO. The way Dalton challenged everything was part of the reason why. "The source who tipped you off, who told you to run and keep running…they were under your command, once, weren't they?"

Dalton's cheeks hollowed out. His jaw flexed.

I nodded. "You guarded their backs. Now they have yours. Still."

"Not now," he murmured. "Not anymore."

"Because they think you deserted," I breathed, as the pattern shifted and dropped into place. "We can do both at once," I told him. "Chang *and* Moroder. We have to figure out where the hell they are after forty years and how to reach them. Lyth should be able to help with that. Whoever's location we find first, that's who we tackle first."

Dalton looked surprised. Then he grinned. "You realize that Chang's schedule is public property? Lyth will find her in seconds. Hell, he's probably listening and has already pulled up this month's public agenda."

"He promised he wouldn't listen."

"You believed him?"

"I believe he is terrified we won't like him and decide to leave."

Dalton's eyes narrowed. "Yeah, I know something about that feeling," he said softly.

I floundered for a response, startled by the confession.

Then Dalton got to his feet. "Thirty seconds talking to you cures me right away," he added. "Maybe you should have a heart to heart with Lyth. Fix him right up."

I outlined the task for Lyth and asked him to find a way to reach out to both people—Chang and Moroder—then report back.

Then I went to find Juliyana, who wasn't in her room. I got lost in the back end of the ship, which was a labyrinth of utility rooms and corridors, and two other sub-levels that I didn't go near. Finally, I said impatiently to the air over my head, "Lyth, where the fuck is Juliyana?"

Lyth did not assemble himself behind me, as he had before. Instead, the ship spoke in his voice. "Follow the mouse. It'll take you to her."

A fist-sized lump grew on the floor two meters ahead of me, then turned into the universe's most indestructible rodent and scurried ahead, tail up. I followed it back through the maze, recognizing points I'd already passed, then into a new section. I put my hand against the wall on my left. Cold.

The walls in my room were not hot to touch, but they weren't cold, or even cool. "This is the exterior portside hull, isn't it?"

"It is," Lyth admitted.

The mouse ran over to a door in the interior wall and melted back into the floor and disappeared. The door opened… onto the void of space and a star field.

"Come in, Danny," Lyth called, from inside the void.

I saw his silhouette…and Juliyana's. They stood on an observation deck, staring up at the starfield. That was why he had not personally escorted me to this place. He didn't want to leave her side.

I tabled that discussion for another time and went over to them. "What are you doing?"

"Mapping out scenarios," Juliyana murmured. "We're jumping randomly around the empire and have been for weeks. I thought it might be prudent to take a breath and actually plan where we go next."

"That's what I've been doing," I said. "What's that blinking star?"

"Sh'Klea Sine, our destination," Lyth said.

I frowned. "The scale is too small. Can we scale up and get an overview?"

The stars receded, as if they had been sucked down a tunnel, to be replaced with even more stars.

"It doesn't help," Juliyana said, her tone apologetic. "The starfield is fractal. You can drill down and still be overwhelmed."

"Then kill the starfield and create a representation. Lyth, clear the view, and show only the Sine system, and Sh'Klea itself."

The stars disappeared. A green and blue world appeared. Over it, considerably scaled in size, hung a geo-stationary, sprawling city of domes and towers winking in an out-of-view sun. Also not visible was the gate, where we would emerge in less than three hours.

"Is this from your archives?" I asked Lyth curiously, for the detail was amazing.

"It is as the city appears right now," Lyth said.

"You mean, this is the view from the gate?"

"Correct."

"How do you do that, Lyth?" Juliyana asked him. "I've never known a ship that could do that before. Your data is always updating, too."

"I don't know how," Lyth said reluctantly, as if the confession pained him. "I just can."

"More of Wedekind's brilliance, perhaps," I said. I turned back to examine Sh'Klea Sine. "The docks are internal. We can't see who is there."

The view was overlaid by a bulleted list that scrolled slowly. "The current list of registrations of ships berthed at Sh'Klea Sine," Lyth said.

"You *are* still working on finding Chang and Moroder, aren't you?" I asked him.

"Absolutely," he assured me. Then he added, "You've noticed the Imperial registrations in the list, yes?"

I turned back to the list of ship names hanging in the air in front of us, over the twinkling city. "None of them are familiar to me, but it's been a while. Pick them out for me and tell me their classifications."

Four names were highlighted. "They're all falcon class," Lyth said.

"Dreadnoughts," Juliyana concluded, with a heavy sigh. "Waiting for us?"

"Sh'Klea Sine is the financial and banking capital of the empire. It's unlikely four dreadnoughts would pull up beside it for shore leave, not all at once," I said. "They don't know we can see ahead to our exit," I added.

"They're waiting for us," Juliyana said.

"Lyth," I said. "What regiment do the dreadnoughts belong to?"

"The seventh."

Law enforcement. "It's a good bet they're there for us," I said. "Only how they know we're coming…" That was another impossible problem for another time. "We can't linger when we arrive," I added. "No matter how much Dalton wants us to. We're going to have to turn on a molecule and dive right back into another hole."

"Dalton can't handle that sort of flying," Lyth said. "Not yet."

"Then we pack him in a shell until we're back in the hole."

"He won't like that," Juliyana said.

"He won't like *not* being in a shell more," I replied. "I'll break it to him," I added.

16

WE WERE BOTH RIGHT. DALTON complained and bellyached even when he was in the shell Lyth had prepared for him on the bridge. It wasn't the captain's shell in front of the windows, but one just off to the side. Combat shells let the soldier remain upright and on their feet until gravity itself pushed them into the shell and cushioned the force. Most of the time, I had forgotten that the cushioned wall at my back was actually an inertia shell, ready to take over and shield me when needed. In all my years of active ship duties, I had never once had to use the shell. The crush juice had been up to the task.

"Sixty seconds," *Lythion* warned from overhead as Lyth set the controls on the shell.

"At the most, you'll feel ten percent above one gee," Lyth told Dalton. "The shell won't automatically render you unconscious."

"Thank the fuck for that," Dalton said heavily and relaxed into the shell.

I thought I understood his frustration. He'd been relying on his own resources for a long time. Now he had to let go and let us get him out of trouble.

"Don't fuss, Dalton," I told him, keeping my voice airy and unconcerned. "This is a basic maneuver. We'll be back in the hole so fast, you won't have time to take a breath."

"Actually, it will take forty-seven seconds to—"

"Not now."

"Yes, Captain."

Dalton scowled even harder.

"Emerging," Lyth warned.

I rested my shoulders against the cushion behind me, bracing myself. From the corner of my eye, I could see Juliyana settling against the shell by the console I had designated as the weapons console.

The blank nothingness of the hole was replaced by a starfield and a blinding white sun, before the screen polarized and the sun become an orange disk. Dazzled, I blinked my eyes. "Around and back in, Lyth. As tight as you can."

The reaction engines made the ship vibrate under my feet. With the full navigation grid online, the ship was shivering with eagerness to move. The sun slid to our left, moving out of sight, as the ship turned in a tight arc.

I could feel my body trying to move to the left, too. I braced my feet and ignored it.

Sine III came into view, a bright jewel of a planet with a deadly atmosphere. Sh'Klea Sine hung above it.

"Any movement from the landing bays?" I called.

"All four bay doors are on alert," Lyth said. He stood next to Dalton's shell, his gaze ahead. Then he snapped upright.

"Incoming traffic!" Lythion said, his tone urgent.

"Hold on!" Lyth added.

Incoming meant a ship was emerging from the gate behind us. Normally it wouldn't be an issue. Normal ships emerged, then raced at best speed toward the city. We had looped around, though, and were very nearly facing back the way we'd come. In a few seconds, we would see the gate we had just emerged from...which put us directly in the path of the ship which had just emerged.

"Swing under it!" I shouted. "Then up into the gate behind it! Move it!"

The twin noses of the ship dipped—I saw brighter stars rise above them. The *Lythion* maintained the hard circle, even as it dipped.

Three seconds later, the ship we were dodging came into view, the massive gate behind it. Matte black, sleek and deadly.

"It's a carrier!" Dalton shouted.

"Their cannon is adjusting," Juliyana added, her tone calm. She slid her fingers over the console, preparing.

"Do not fire," I said urgently. "Do *not* provoke them." We could still slide under them. We were so close we had the element of surprise on our side. The carrier would think we were attacking, right until we ducked under them. It was too large to turn as fast and tight as we were. We'd be back in the hole before they figured out what we were doing.

"Ten seconds until we pass under them," Lyth warned.

The cannon was pointing directly at us now, a black, deadly snout. Nothing showed in the black throat, yet.

Even to me, it seemed as though we would ram the carrier. My breath caught and held. I griped the edge of my shell, wondering if Lyth had miscalculated. At the very last second, we grazed under the carrier. If we had been in atmosphere, the wake of our passage would have rocked the bigger ship and tossed around everyone inside it.

The gate loomed and appeared to be leaning away from us because of the angle of our approach.

"Capacitor ready," Lyth said softly.

The gate glowed, the center aqua blue and peaceful, beckoning us.

"Entering," Lyth added, as we drove through the pond and into the blankness of the wormhole behind it.

I blew out my breath and relaxed.

Juliyana met my gaze. "The carrier. Was it following us?"

"Through null-space? I would have said that was impossible, two days ago." I grimaced. "One more thing we have to figure out," I added.

I went over to Dalton's shell. It was completely closed. "Lyth, open it, please. Wake him gently."

"Inertia was too high, at the end, there," Lyth began as he started the wake cycle on the side of the shell.

"You did fine, Lyth," I told him.

The shell gave a soft popping sound then retracted on either side. The protective gel which had covered Dalton completely pulled aside with it. Dalton looked like he was asleep. The shell stole one's consciousness, which I think Dalton would be relieved about, as he was already mildly claustrophobic. He wouldn't have liked the sensation of being smothered which a fully closed shell imparted.

He drew in a deep breath and opened his eyes.

I gave him my warmest and most reassuring smile. "We're safely in the hole." I held out my hand. "Come on, I'll buy you a drink."

He took my hand and stepped out of the shell and shuddered. "Make that two."

We all headed for the diner. There was no discussion. We just gravitated there like electrons.

We slid into the same booth we had used that morning.

The waitress came over with her tray and placed heavy-bottomed glasses in front of us. Each had five centimeters of liquid in it. "I figured you could use a belt," she told us and winked and went away.

Dalton was the first to knock back his shot. He hissed and

placed the glass very carefully back on the table.

We followed suit. Even Lyth made a show of gulping his whisky, drawing the air over his tongue like a true aficionado of grain alcohols did.

Juliyana held her empty glass up to the waitress, tapped it, and held up four fingers. Then she turned back to us. "They're tracking us. Somehow."

"Not possible," Lyth said.

"A lot of impossible things have happened lately," I said. "Best not make that argument unless you can back it up."

"I can back it up," Lyth said. "It is impossible for anyone to track us inside a wormhole, because we're not in proper space. I could prove that with mathematics, but I doubt you'd understand it."

Dalton snorted and patted Lyth on the shoulder. "Way to make us all feel inadequate."

Lyth looked alarmed. "But you really wouldn't understand…" he said quickly.

"I'm sure we wouldn't. Relax, Lyth. We'll take it as a base fact for now that we can't be tracked inside the array. So how *did* they know we were coming?"

Juliyana pressed her fingers to her temples. "The data…" she said.

We all looked at her and waited.

Juliyana sat up again. "Look, we've been making queries for hours and hours, all of it sensitive data, right? We didn't stop to question how the *Lythion* could suck up live data like we were in ordinary space. We just used it because it was very, very convenient. So all these delicate questions were put out there into the data stream."

Dalton wiped his finger around the bottom of his glass, picking up the last of the excellent whisky. "And we've already agreed that anyone involved in the Drakas disaster

186

asking about anyone else involved in it would ring alarms across the empire." He looked up. "We must have rung every alarm out there."

"Yes, but that doesn't explain how they knew where we would emerge," Juliyana said, in a tone that said she was working it out, arranging pieces.

"It's a *wormhole*," I said. "Lyth doesn't know how he gets the data, but we're in a hole with two ends—the data must come through one of them."

"The arrival gate," Lyth said. "The hole collapses behind us."

I stared at him.

"That's something I could have lived without knowing," Dalton growled.

Juliyana pointed at Lyth. "*That's* how they figured out where we were going to emerge—or maybe they figured we were already in normal space, because they don't know we can get data in the hole. They tracked the origin of the query and it led them to the gate at Sh'Klea Sine. So they raced there. Any ships on the other side of the galaxy would have got there before us, ready to greet us."

I turned to Lyth. "You have to stop pulling in live data," I told him. "Right now."

"It could already be too late," Juliyana pointed out.

"Right *now*, Lyth," I insisted.

He nodded. "Done." Then his brow smoothed out. "By the way, there is something else you should know." His tone was grave.

* * *

Lyth took us to the room/space where he and Juliyana had been peering up at the starfield, which showed an interesting tendency toward conservation of energy. He could have simply shifted the diner around to show us his findings. Or perhaps he was sensitive enough to understand that my preference for my room to remain frozen extended to other spaces, too.

The representation of Sh'Klea Sine was gone. In its place was another station — one of the vertical ones with a fat belly and hundreds of levels — a bit like the *Umb Judeste*. An ochre rock of a planet hung above it, with the light from a red sun bathing both.

"Wow…" Dalton breathed, clutching his whisky glass to his chest, his chin up.

"That's our destination?" Juliyana asked. "I don't recognize it."

"I said to stop pulling data, Lyth," I snapped. "What part of that did you not understand?"

"I'm not pulling data," Lyth replied. "This is an archival file of Polyxene. You'll notice it isn't moving? We also won't have updates on who is there to greet us, either."

Was that a touch of grumpiness in his tone?

"Small joint," Dalton said, with the air of recall. "But they still have seven bars on the main concourse."

"Also, you should know that when we arrive, we can't swing around and dive back through the gate," Lyth said. "We *must* dock. The fuel cells will be close to depletion by the time we arrive."

I absorbed that and nodded, telling myself it was just another mission parameter. "So, what did you want to show us?"

A dozen documents and images laid themselves out over the top of the display of Polyxene, their corners covering others, layer after layer.

"You might want to slow down a bit, Lyth," Juliyana said

with a diplomatic tone. "We don't read that fast."

"There is no need to read any of them," Lyth said. "I have already done so and have collated the data."

Dalton pointed. "That's Rozsa Chang's public itinerary," he said, as the blizzard of documents ceased.

"This month's, yes," Lyth said. "That was my starting point."

"You found where she will be," I said.

"That will be impossible, captain, as the public documents are fabrications."

We all looked at him.

"You mean, all the little Cygnets drooling to glimpse the president check these documents, hurry to where she's going to be...and she doesn't turn up?" Dalton's tone was incredulous. "And *no one* bitches about that?"

Lyth shook his head. "The closer to the actual date, the more accurate the documents are — that's quite normal, really. Humans are woeful at predicting what they will be doing and more inaccurate the farther ahead in time they are predicting. But in this case, I believe the inaccuracy is deliberate misdirection."

"Why do you think that?" I demanded.

"Because for any one day of President Chang's *real* agenda, only one or two events actually happen. Often, they are public events where Dalton's Cygnets can see her — and those events are scheduled at the very last minute, sometimes with only hours of warning."

"Security," Juliyana murmured.

"Security...and something else," Lyth said.

The documents hanging in the air in front of us moved around, showing pages with tables. They flipped in a mesmerizing cascade. "I could only draw that conclusion by comparing where President Chang had *actually* been against her public agenda."

"You tracked her real movements?" I asked.

"I didn't track her movements, but the traces those movements left behind. She uses three different identities to move around anonymously. The correlation with her known movements gave me the names, and I tracked them back."

More documents popped up. Landing bay fees. Gate fees. Bioscans. A dozen different stations, stellar cities and commercial hubs. The last document showed Sh'Klea Sine, which lay directly behind us. "Passenger Sprita Niessner passed through bio scanning every second month. Those dates coincide with the Cygnus board meetings, but Niessner is not a board member." A list of board members overlaid the bio scan list.

"Lemme guess," Dalton said. "Chang has never been documented arriving at Sh'Klea Sine, but the board meeting minutes says she was there."

"Correct," Lyth said.

I looked at Dalton. "You were saying it would be easy to find out where she'll be, I recall?"

He scowled. "You're telling us all this to explain why you can't figure it out, Lyth?"

"Oh, I can predict where she will be with a degree of accuracy, and the closer in time that location is to us, the more confident I can be about the prediction. Which means you may have to sit and wait for her to come to a location near you. But that isn't why I wanted you to see this."

The documents shifted again.

"I was curious," Lyth said. "So I went back forty years and put together Chang's real movements, as best as the documentation allows. I draw your attention to these dates and locations."

This time, dozens of documents arrayed themselves so

they were readable, with highlighted lines of dates and locations, and durations of stay.

"This is Chang?" I asked, for the name was not hers.

"This is an identity she was using in that decade," Lyth said. "I verified it the same way I verified the Neissner ID. Then I cross checked all other people of interest surrounding Noam Andela's death and established that some of them also regularly used false IDs."

"Shit, and we spent *days* trying to find just Dalton," Juliyana murmured.

The original dozen documents ranged across the air shifted, so that similar documents were paired with each one, also with highlights.

We examined them for a moment. "The dates, times and locations match," I concluded.

"Who is Addilyn Blanchard, Lyth?" I demanded, for that was the name of the ID that matched Chang's movements.

Lyth's gaze was steady. "Ramaker III, First of the Tanique Dynasty."

Dalton and Juliyana stared at Lyth, their jaws slack.

I felt the same freezing shock, but it was a superficial layer floating over a sense of inevitability. "The Emperor was meeting with her. Almost weekly."

Juliyana bent and put her hands on her knees. "The stars in their firmament... Everything I dug up *said* there was a connection, but I kept dismissing it. I didn't think...I thought it was impossible, that I was being paranoid." She gave a strained laugh and pressed her hand to her mouth.

Dalton drained his whisky, set the glass on the floor and turned to study the documents once more. "Lyth, focus on that one." He pointed.

The document zoomed larger. Lyth helpfully pulled the corresponding document's highlighted line over to this one and floated it just beneath the first.

"Thanks, but it's the letterhead that interests me," Dalton told him. "Napoli Incorporated." He turned to face us. "It's not widely known, but the information is out there. Lyth can confirm. Napoli is the parent corporation that owns and controls Fantasy Inc."

Lyth intoned, "Fantasy Inc. Pleasure Resort is controlled by a consortium of business interests. Napoli Incorporated holds a majority share and has administered the resort for the last one hundred and three years."

I felt my mouth turning down. My gut was joining it. "Chang and the Emperor were having an affair..."

Juliyana kept breathing deeply, still bent over. Her breath grew shorter.

Dalton looked around. "Lyth, I need a drink. *Now.*"

The walls of the room were disguised by the optical display, but a spotlight picked out a section of one wall, which was blank. As we watched, the surface of the wall shifted, and a printer outlet appeared, as if it was rising up to the surface of a pool. Which, in a way, it was. The construction nanobots had flowed across the printer's façade, making way for it.

Dalton tossed his glass into the recycle maw and picked up the fresh drink that formed on the print tray. He took a big mouthful and swallowed hard and turned to face us. "The fucking Emperor and Chang *arranged* the whole Drakas thing..." His voice was hoarse.

"We don't know that for sure," I pointed out. "Lyth, how long do these two identities parallel each other?"

"For three years after Drakas," Lyth replied. "There are no other identities that I can conclude belong to either President Chang or the Emperor that follow the same pattern."

"They used each other up, then parted," Juliyana said.

She drew upright with a heavy inhalation. "They both got what they wanted." Her tone was bitter.

"Got *what* though?" I asked. "Cygnus lost face, lost lives, lost most of their military, and control of the array into the bargain...Chang wouldn't have arranged that loss."

"Wait," Dalton said. "Wait just a moment. Aren't we falling into confirmation bias here? We wanted to find something, and Lyth found it, because he was looking for it."

"I didn't tell Lyth to go back into the past," I said. "I only asked him to find Chang *now*. Confirmation bias helped Lyth find it, that's all. We were looking for it and no one else is—they don't even suspect this connection exists."

"So they were fucking. So what?" Dalton said, his tone angry. "It doesn't mean what you think."

"No?" My tone came out cooler than I had intended. "The most powerful man in the empire and the most powerful businesswoman in bed together...you really think they restricted themselves to conversations about sweet nothings?"

"Why are you pissed about it, Dalton?" Juliyana said, her tone curious.

His answer was to drain the glass. He tossed it at the recycle maw, a powerful overarm throw. The glass tinkled, then was evaporated out of existence.

"I think we're all reacting to the indigestible fact," I said. "The Emperor and Chang were not the enemies we thought they were. Not then, and probably not now, either, despite lawsuits, wars and constant outbreaks of hostilities. That puts everything about Noam's death and the Drakas thing into a different category."

"No, it doesn't," Juliyana said firmly. "It merely confirms what we suspected and didn't want to believe—that people were working against our interests and those of the public and covering them up. We just can't cope with the fact that it was the Emperor himself doing the deed."

"Shit, I said almost the same thing to Danny, a few hours ago," Dalton said, crossing his arms. "Imperial Shield, maybe. The Emperor, no way." His shook his head.

"It might be the same game, but the stakes have changed," I said. "They're bigger now."

"They were always this big," Lyth said. "Now, though, you are aware of their magnitude. That is a good thing. It is information you can work with."

I drew in a breath. "How long until we reach Polyxene?"

Lyth grimaced. "Twenty-seven hours. I picked the closest location, so our time in the hole was longest."

"It will serve," I decided. "It will give us time to sort out our next step."

"You can't seriously be thinking about tackling the Emperor himself?" Dalton said, his voice strained.

"Directly? No." I kept my gaze on his face. Dalton was the doubter, the questioner, and I needed him working with me, now. "We thought we were chasing two different things, Dalton. Chang and Moroder. Now they're indirectly connected. Chang is a dead end. We could put lasers under her fingernails and she wouldn't hand over her connection with Ramaker. It would destroy her career and any life she values. She's too hard a nut to crack. So we go after Moroder and we see where it takes us."

"Then you *are* going after the Emperor...indirectly," Juliyana said.

I could feel some of the energy and tingling restlessness returning to me, now I'd got over the shock of it. "Lyth just pointed out that nothing has changed, except now we know the scale of what we're dealing with. My reasons haven't changed...have yours?"

Juliyana considered. "I think knowing this has just set

them in reinforced plasteel."

I looked at Dalton. He nodded. "You know why I'm in this. It hasn't changed.

"Good," I said. "Because yes, I am going after the fucking Emperor."

"Which he literally is," Dalton added.

Of the four of us, it was Lyth who laughed the loudest.

17

ONE CAN ONLY WORK SO long before mental fatigue sets in. I lasted thirteen hours more before I found myself dithering over which screen I should look at next and finding it an impossible decision.

I dismissed all the screens I had arrayed and rubbed my scalp, feeling the exhaustion register. My face bones ached. But I was too wired to sleep, yet, even though the bed was right behind me. I could fall backwards where I stood and I was sure the bed would move to catch me. But I also knew my own body. I needed downtime, first.

I moved around to the portside of the ship and the room where the stars had been arrayed. "*Lythion,*" I said, as I walked. "During the next set of daylight hours, have this stellar room moved closer to the front of the ship, please."

"Noted, Captain," *Lythion* murmured back from the overhead speakers.

I was adjusting with disgusting speed to the luxurious possibilities of moving rooms and walls and furniture.

"Oh, and arrange the starfield in the room for me, will you? Any starfield."

"The room is already in use, Captain."

The door opened and I could see a heavy starfield beckoning. Reluctantly, I went in.

Juliyana was the occupant. She had made some adjustments. The plain floor/observation deck had become a mountainside lookout. Deciduous trees I could not name ranged on either side, whispering in an unfelt late evening breeze.

A fire crackled in a stone circle, and Juliyana rested in a fold-up camping lounger, wrapped in a plaid rug, a mug in her hand that steamed gently.

I hesitated.

"It's fine. Come in, Danny," she said.

To her left, an identical chair rose up from the earth and formed properly. A folded plaid blanket laid on the seat.

One of the wheeled platforms bumped over the flattened grass and weeds, up to the chair. It held another steaming mug.

"Coffee at this time of night?"

"It's hot chocolate."

I settled on the chair and put the blanket over my knees. It wasn't cold, but the blanket just felt right. The chair was at the right angle to lean back and study the stars.

"The hot chocolate is the perfect touch." I picked up my mug. The wagon melted into the ground. "I thought Lyth might be here, too."

Juliyana grimaced. "I wanted to be alone."

"I can go," I offered.

"I don't mind you. You're…" She frowned. "I want to say you're peaceful to be around, only things happen around you all the time. I guess…you know how to stay silent, when you need to."

I stayed silent and sipped, gazing up at the stars. There was no moon to steal their light and no nearby city to throw up a masking glow. It was a pitch black night sky. Stars reeled in their circuits. Nebula glowed pink and purple and red.

I didn't recognize any of the constellations, but the thick

white mass of stars banding across the sky I did know. "The galactic hub," I murmured.

"It's beautiful, isn't it?" Juliyana replied just as softly. "This place is perfect. Seeing this—it's just what I needed right now." She hesitated, then added, "I love the stars. Space. I love being out there." She glanced at me self-consciously.

"You don't need to apologize. Star-faring is in our blood, you and I. I didn't join the Rangers to be a soldier, or even for the free rejuvenations. I joined because it would get me into space, out there." I nodded at the stars.

Juliyana gripped her mug in both hands and stared at the contents. "I've been on permanent below-surface duty since Noam died."

"That's pretty standard for grunts," I said as gently as I could.

"The bowels of ships, the basements of buildings, the deepest interiors of stations." She said it in a monotone, looking up at the stars. "They won't put me back in the combat cadres. They won't leave me in a unit long enough to make friends or even prove myself. I get moved around, every few weeks or months, with my record just ahead of me, priming COs to distrust me right off the bat."

"But you've out-lasted them, so far."

She nodded and lifted her chin to indicate the stars. "Because of them. Because I want to be out among them once more." She looked at me. "So fuck 'em. Fuck everyone. I won't cave because they're prejudiced assholes. I will see this thing through and I *will* get out there once more." She drained her cup with a convulsive jerk of her wrist.

When she thought I wasn't looking, she turned her chin and discretely wiped the tear tracks on her cheeks.

I let her have her privacy, while I picked out the nearest

stars, trying to see if I could discern globular bodies with my newly restored vision.

"Whatever it takes, huh, Danny?" Juliyana said. Her voice was normal.

I kept my gaze on the stars. "All my money. The backpay, danger benefits, health…all of it."

"All the money which is gone now?"

"Yeah. I used it for bribes." I glanced at her to catch her reaction, then away, my heart thudding harder that it needed to. "Bribes, travel, 'investments'. None of it worked. I couldn't even get his remains back, let alone a millimeter of truth." I kept my chin up as if I was studying the heavens but closed my eyes. I don't think I've ever felt quite so foolish and exposed.

After a moment, Juliyana said, "You *did* try, then!"

The genuine pleasure in her voice made me look at her, startled.

She was smiling. "You let me think you didn't give a damn."

"I didn't. Not after all this time. Although I'm here — *still* here, despite what we know, now, so I guess I really did mind, after all."

A soft coughing sound came from overhead. *Lythion* spoke, his tone apologetic. "I thought you should know. I've found Moroder."

"Acean isn't a station at all," Lyth explained, as we stood around the navigation table on the bridge. "It's Alkalost's moon — an airless, point one gee orbiting rock."

A crescent edge of a green world turned beneath a moon radiating sunlight. Then the view shifted to focus upon the moon and the sunlight faded as the moon revolved to reveal the nightside. The view focused in, while I hoped Lyth was still using archives for this. I would have asked, only I had jumped on him once before, and if he was more stupid than the average AI, and *was* using live feeds, then it was too late to do anything about it. I concentrated on the display, instead.

Low, half-buried buildings were revealed, most of them bunker types — windowless, armored against weapons and radiation, and impenetrable. The buildings were connected by a star of enclosed catwalks. I've seen dozens of barracks that look exactly the same, but they were in atmospheres, or under domes. This place looked bleaker than hell.

"It is an Imperial Shield research and manufacturing post," Lyth continued. "They use pseudo gravity in the living areas and research labs, but the manufacturing plant takes advantage of the near-absence of gravity. It makes it possible for a single grunt to move heavy objects around."

"What do they manufacture?" Dalton asked, as he studied the moon and rubbed his stubble-covered chin. His hair was ruffled. I suspected Lyth had pulled him from deep sleep. As I could no longer reem him out for slovenliness, I ignored his appearance.

"I couldn't absolutely confirm what they build there," Lyth said. "The data is obscure and conflicting. The research center projects are easier to find, and quite unremarkable, which makes it likely that the research function of the base is a blind."

"A fake front over a pile of misdirection?" I asked.

"Yes, which leads me to the inescapable conclusion that this is one of the locations where the Shield puts together array gates."

"The actual gates themselves?" Juliyana said, her interest

deepening. She frowned at the rotating moon. "You mean, we've uncovered the location?"

I could understand her incredulity. Where and how the Shield put together the jump gates was a closely and ruthlessly guarded secret. The myths about the manufacturing process had driven gossip for as long as the empire had existed.

When I was a child, we had scared each other into shivers by describing how the gates were made of spare parts of humans who had died, melted onto metal...and sometimes not so dead humans were used, and their screams were how ship AIs found the gates.

The gates *were* biomechanical—the Imperial Family had never denied that. How the biomass integrated with the mechanics was where the secret lay. Also *why* biomass was needed at all...

One could take advanced education degrees studying the jump gates and the array, yet only the most gifted academics were ever invited to undertake such study. The degrees were administered by the Imperial Shield, of course. Public handbooks outlining the degrees showed a range of subjects surrounding the array and the gates, but nothing about the function of the gates themselves. It was likely another deliberate omission, because even course subject titles and descriptions might hint at processes they didn't want to share.

"This *might* be a construction location," Lyth told Juliyana. "It would not be the only one, if it is. But it could also be a way-station that only constructs a component of a gate."

"That, I can confirm," I said. "I've seen the family records when the Carranoak barge found McCreary Landing. Imperial Shield ships came through the barge gate and put together the gate for McCreary Landing right there in space. And there were fourteen ships—each with a separate part. The gates are only put together into a functioning whole in their final position."

Juliyana looked disappointed. "I wanted to see how big they really were."

"Two kilometers across," Lyth said. "Except the barge-towed gates, which are much smaller."

Juliyana rolled her eyes at him.

Dalton made an impatient sound and pointed at the revolving moon hanging over the navigation table. "So, Moroder is on this station...somewhere. It looks small standing over it like this, but there are a lot of places in those buildings where he might be. We can't land next to the front gate, lean out and beckon him over. And we can't sneak in there and hunt for him. They're going to notice the *Lythion* floating overhead, and that's presuming we can make it past all the security layers guarding this place."

"You can't get in there," I said. "It's Imperial Shield and a gate facility. We won't get near it in this ship, even if Lyth knows how to fake Imperial ship IDs—"

"Not yet, but I'm working on it," Lyth said.

"—and you can't get in there by devious methods," I finished. "We can't coax Moroder to come to us, either, because the Shield will saturate any travel he takes off the moon with tethers and tracking and security screens that will probe down to the DNA level anyone who comes near him. *Any-thing* that entices him off-planet will make them suspicious."

Dalton scowled. Juliyana chewed the inside corner of her mouth, looking unhappy.

"You can't get in," Lyth said, "but Sagai Skylark can."

"Who the fuck is that?" I demanded.

Dalton laughed. And kept laughing. He swung away from the table, holding his sides, his shoulders shaking.

Juliyana frowned, watching Dalton. Then she looked at

Lyth, her expression demanding an answer.

Dalton swung back. "Oh, let me," he said, sounding breathless, smiling hugely. His gaze met mine. "Sagai Skylark is an exotic dancer. And she *does* resemble you." His smile radiated even harder. "Especially with the right makeup and jewelry and...clothes." His gaze shifted down and back up to my face.

My cheeks burned, which irritated the shit out of me. I glared at Lyth. "I can't pretend to be her and just turn up. It will raise their suspicions, too."

"Sagai Skylark has consented to putting on a performance at the base," Lyth said. "The contract was signed over a year ago — she is so in demand that her calendar is filled far ahead."

"Please say this is the only way," Dalton begged Lyth.

"I believe it might be," Lyth replied.

Dalton gave a happy sigh.

Which did nothing to allay my irritation. "One," I said heavily, "they will scope her DNA when she arrives, to make sure she's who she says she is."

"I can get around that," Lyth said. "A simple switch of records — purely temporary."

I wanted to growl. "Two," I added, "there is a real Sagai whatever out there. What do we do with her? We can't have her turn up on the base, too."

"I can take —" Dalton began quickly.

"No, Juliyana can do it," I interjected. Then I grimaced, for I had committed myself. "I don't want you anywhere near the woman," I told Dalton.

"Besides, Major Dalton should be there to question Moroder," Lyth said.

"I'm supposed to put him in my pocket?" I asked and wondered if Sagai's clothes even had pockets. I suspected not.

"There are two side airlocks where personnel can enter the base, but they can only be opened from the inside," Lyth said. "I can overcome the locking mechanism so that security is not alerted to the opening, but it is a pre-Accord lock. It requires a human hand to actually open the doors."

"Me," I concluded. Before the Ordi Accord, which had been signed five years before I resigned, all airlocks anywhere required manual manipulation for safety reasons. A human had to open the door because computers could be overcome. In a little war between the Ritomari and the Ordi, the Ritomari military forces had extorted the Ordi to open the airlocks by holding shrivers to the heads of their children. The Ordi overrode the computers and exposed themselves and the military base to explosive decompression. The entire Ordi force had died in three horrible minutes.

The Ritomari regimental commander who had devised the strategy was tried by the Imperial high court and executed, which didn't comfort the Ordi greatly. The Accord was reached and signed by every state in the Empire inside a year, agreeing that the human factor must not be mandatory in the control of airlocks.

Apparently, the Imperial Shield considered itself above such laws. Or they just hadn't got around to upgrading.

Either way, it made them vulnerable.

"So, Dalton comes with me as a stagehand or something," I begun.

"Manager, would be better," Lyth said.

Dalton grinned.

"But he stays on the ship, while I go into the base, which means security will be watching the ship."

"Watching you, more like," Dalton said, his voice dreamy.

"Security will passively watch the ship," Lyth said. "When

the nightline reaches the base, Dalton can slip out of the ship and walk around to the airlock, where you can let him in."

Dalton's smile evaporated. "Wait…it's airless out there!"

Lyth nodded. "You will be wearing an environment suit — non-reflecting of both heat and infrared, so you won't show on scans."

"I don't *have* a suit," Dalton shot back, his face turning red.

"You will have in about three hours. It's nearly done," Lyth replied.

Dalton's jaw worked. "I *hate* suits!"

It was my turn to smile.

"Okay, then," I said.

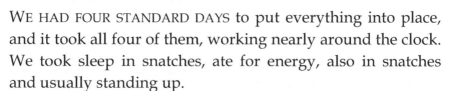

18

WE HAD FOUR STANDARD DAYS to put everything into place, and it took all four of them, working nearly around the clock. We took sleep in snatches, ate for energy, also in snatches and usually standing up.

I learned a lot about Lyth's capabilities in those four days.

First, we docked at Polyxene. Juliyana was the only one to step off the ship and that was to fake a signature on the invoice for solid state mass for the reaction engines and the secondary service engines that ran everything else on the ship that wasn't part of the free-flowing living section...although Lyth's construction nanobots diverted excess energy to help with the draw, too.

The entire time we paused at Polyxene, Lyth remained on the bridge, a still figure remotely monitoring the landing bay doors, the security feeds and watching for any alerts telling us we'd been coupled to the ship that had blasted its way back into the gates at Sh'Klea Sine.

"We need to develop unofficial fuel sources," Dalton observed, watching Lyth's unmoving shape.

"Later," I said, in agreement. "Right now, we have other priorities."

"They won't matter a damn if pulling up at a station for fuel lands us in an Imperial net."

"Then *you* find that source for us," I said, irritated.

"I will!" he shot back and stalked off the bridge.

I felt a teeny bit sorry for him. He was suffering proactive claustrophobia, anticipating what, for him, would be the horror of being enclosed in an airtight suit. We had all carefully avoided telling him the suit was made of Lyth's construction nanobots, pre-programmed to hold their shape even away from the reach of the ship. He'd find that even more terrifying.

After Polyxene, we took a three-phase jump to Keeler IV, which was Sagai's homebase. The jump-jump-jump shaved fourteen hours off the direct jump, for we crisscrossed the empire in giant strides. Most ships went direct and put up with the time in the hole because they had to pay gate taxes, landing fees and more, all of which piled up when you crisscrossed. As the *Lythion* seemed to be able to circumvent the gates' demands for compensation, the only factor we needed to take into consideration was the duration of the jump. That made the back-and-forth viable and this insane scheme doable.

Juliyana slid through the Keeler landing bay doors into the station proper, a small pack over her shoulder, while we waited...and finished preparations.

Two hours later, she jogged back onto the *Lythion*, and reported in somewhat breathlessly to me. She wore the simple uniform of a deliveryman, and the shirt was ripped at the sleeve. I didn't ask for explanations.

"Done," Juliyana told me. "Secure. Let's get the fuck out of here."

Somewhere in the depths of the station, Juliyana had stashed the real Sagai Skylark with food and water, and a pad that would self-actuate in two days and let her send out a cry for help.

Lyth didn't wait for my command. He connected with traffic control, got permission to leave, opened the external door, and lifted off.

Dalton held out a heavy duffel bag to me. "It's time," he said gruffly. He had a bigger bag over one shoulder.

I nodded and took the bag.

Lyth parked himself over Acean, carefully positioning himself so that whoever tried to take a look at the ship would be dazzled by the red sun directly behind him. "You'll be out of range if you don't leave in three minutes," he warned us via the dropship's interface. "Good luck," he added.

I let Dalton take the controls. It would give him something to do and take his mind off the next few hours.

He piloted with more skill than I presumed he had, even though the ghost AI resident in the drop ship did most of the work. "You've been hanging out on freighters," I said.

"Worked on more than one," he said, still gruff. "It's the only way to stay hidden, long term. Now shut up, I have to make nice with Acean security. And you have to get ready."

Dalton spoke to Acean control without engaging imaging. He was polite, even charming, as they traded IDs for the drop ship and the station. I moved to the back of the ship and changed into the flamboyant daywear that Sagai Skylark was known for. Lyth had provided clothes, a full profile, and personal details—enough for me to get by for a few hours.

The performance was scheduled for eight hours from now. The nightline was due six hours from now. I had no intention of giving a real performance. I am as graceful as a block of ice. It was going to be close, though...

Dalton put the dropship down right on top of the marker and shut it down.

An articulated arm of metal rings extended out toward the

airlock on the closest side of the ship. We watched it unfold and lengthen. There was nothing between the rings.

"Perfect," I breathed. "A molecular barrier."

Dalton grinned. "Better you than me." He raised a brow. "You look fantastic, by the way. Red suits you."

I glared at him.

"You should pout your lips when you do that," he added. "Then you'll have Sagai down perfectly." He reached and prodded the control panel. "Door's open, Colonel. Enjoy."

I consoled myself with the fact that *I* didn't have to go out in a suit made of nanobots. I climbed down the steps into the fragile atmosphere inside the molecular barrier, to await the welcoming committee—a bunch of uniformed men doing their best not to drool.

I took a very deep breath, plastered a smile on my highly rouged lips and waved enthusiastically, while letting my hips cock coyly.

It was a very long six hours.

I'm sure there were women on the station, but I never saw one. Even the lesbians stayed away because Sagai's core fans were heterosexual men with impossible fantasies. I did my best to tease them while avoiding the wandering hands and colliding bodies, and constantly checked the time.

A festive barracks dinner was provided, with me at the head of the table next to the station commander, Asucar, who was due for rejuvenation.

A great fuss was made of making sure I was introduced with suitable hand holding and cheek kissing to every senior officer on the base of the appropriate gender. One of them was Moroder, who seemed just as taken by Sagai as everyone else. He was a thin man with a proportionally thin moustache and mousy hair swept back from a high forehead. His eyes were as sharp as his nose.

I made sure to rub up against him with no more or less fervor than I had the other officers.

I've never been as eager to escape a regimental dinner as I was to plead for time to prepare and get out of *that* room. I was escorted by Moroder himself to a little room with a counter and a hastily erected mirror. "The common room is just on the other side of the corridor," Moroder explained to me. "We will be running your retrospective to...what do you say? Warm up the audience? We have put the lights as you requested, and the first row of benches is twenty-five meters from the back of the room. It isn't much of a stage, I'm afraid."

"All the world is a stage," I said blithely. "I am a professional, Lyle. I can adapt." I fluttered my overly long lashes at him.

He nodded. "I will leave you to prepare." He pointed to my duffel bag in the corner, which contained more makeup, teeny costumes I had no intention of donning and items which would have been mistaken as stage props by whoever searched through the bag while I was eating. The stage props had raised my brows and made me even more thankful I didn't have to actually perform for the hyenas out there. I could hear the buzz building in the common room from here, and there was still ninety minutes before the performance was due to start.

"Thank you!" I called after Moroder. "Oh, where can I find you, if I need something?"

Moroder pointed down the corridor outside the door. "My office is along there. My name is on it."

"You won't be in the auditorium?" I pouted.

"I will be there for your performance," he assured me and left, closing the door behind him.

I gave him time to walk away. While I was waiting, I

moved over to the duffel bag and pulled out an elongated prop, grimacing at the size and shape. I found the reset button on the base, pushed my thumbnail against it and shoved.

The prop melted. I nearly dropped it, got both hands underneath it and watched the nanobots turn into a perfect facsimile of a Ranger's standard issue combat knife. More of Lyth's creative programming.

I pushed the knife into the built-in sheath on my hip. The feathers hid the hilt. I eased open the door and looked up and down the corridor. This would be the hardest part. I had to move around the station without drawing men like a magnet. The feathers and ruffles and transparent fabric were not even close to discreet.

The air lock was in the opposite direction to Moroder's office. I went in that direction…and didn't meet a soul.

Then it hit me. Everyone was in the auditorium, waiting for Sagai to appear.

Five minutes later, I was inside the utility room with the airlock. The airlock itself was tiny—barely enough for one man to cycle through at a time. That was a good thing in this case. It would be quicker to fill with air once Dalton stepped into the chamber.

I waited, my heart running hard, all my senses straining to hear anyone approach. I remember time stretching out like this on other missions and battles—particularly on the run-up to the start.

The lock clicked and hissed as the atmosphere vented. I held still, waiting to see if any alarms sounded, or people came running to investigate.

Nothing.

I moved over to the wheel and waited for the green light, then cranked the wheel. It was heavy. No accidental spin would open that door. It took deliberate effort.

The outer door jutted a few centimeters, then a black glove slid over the edge of it and hauled it open enough to let Dalton's black-suited figure through. He turned and shut the door, hauling on the interior wheel, then cranked it closed until the lock dropped and showed red once more. Air pumped back into the space.

I was already at the outer door. As soon as it cycled and lit green, I turned it open.

Dalton stepped in and I shut it behind him. He pulled off the helmet, looking very unhappy.

"You made it," I assured him. "You don't have to go back that way," I added. "I know where Moroder is, too—a bonus."

"Only I can't clump about the station in this," Dalton pointed out. "Lyth missed something in this grand plan of his—I thought of it, halfway around the base."

"No, he didn't miss it," I told him. "Turn around, let me get at your air pack."

"Why?" But he turned anyway.

I found the control panel Lyth had demonstrated to me and punched in the code.

Dalton sucked in a shocked breath as the suit moved around him. It flowed and shifted, until it resembled one of the midnight blue Imperial Shield officers' uniforms.

Sweat dotted his temples. "I walked around out there wearing *nanobots*?" he breathed.

"We figured you'd rather not know until later."

He swallowed and nodded.

"Sweep your hair back, make it look like you *tried* to comb it," I added and took him back through the station. As we approached the room I should have been in, I pointed to the door into the common room, where even more noise was coming. Dalton nodded.

There were men lingering in the corridor now. They were, I presumed, trying to find a pretext to see Sagai. When they saw her walking toward them, they all straightened and puffed out, while trying to make it look like they hadn't seen me at all.

Dalton moved up and held out his elbow and I slid my hand under his arm and smiled up at him, to the acute disappointment of every man we passed. They were so pissed about it, they didn't register Dalton at all, except as bigger, broader-shouldered competition.

I stopped at the door with Moroder's nameplate and Dalton silently moved to one side. I knocked and pushed into Moroder's office in a flurry of feathers and panic. "Lyle! Hells bells, Lyle, the mirror just fell off the wall! There's glass *everywhere!*" I flapped my hands at him, as Moroder rose to his feet, confusion playing on his face.

"Oh, you have to *help me*, Lyle," I said breathlessly, moving closer.

He figured it out, but not soon enough. I pushed the injector against the side of his neck just as he realized my hands were moving *around* him instead of over him and tried to jerk out of the way.

He stiffened and grew still, breathing hard.

"You won't be able to move until that wears off," I told him. "Also, you can't speak just yet." I pushed the used injector into the same pocket the knife sat in. "It'll just hurt if you try, so don't bother."

His throat worked, proving he was an idiot. His face creased in pain, as he said with uncooperative lips, "*hooo?*"

I went over to the door and opened it. Dalton slipped inside, moved straight over to Moroder, scooped him up over his shoulders and moved out again. I turned the old mechanical lock on the inside of the door and shut the door again.

CAMERON COOPER

We moved farther along the corridor, away from the dressing room and Moroder's office. This was the front administration section of the base, but everyone was off duty for the day and most of them were in the common room already. The place was deserted.

"Morale's low," Dalton observed. "No one working overtime."

I moved over to the door where I had entered earlier and put my hand on the grab bar and waited.

When Lyth remotely pushed the bar down, as a signal, I shoved the door open and moved out into the molecular tunnel. Right then, I didn't give a damn about the nothingness on the other side of the metal rings. I was braced for someone to shout at us — which couldn't happen in zero atmosphere — or for shriver bolts to sizzle by us. Nothing happened, though. Lyth had short-circuited their security feeds and if anyone *was* watching the feeds instead of the frank retrospective on Sagai Skylark that was by now running in the common room, then they would see nothing.

We hauled Moroder up into the drop ship between us and folded him up so we could prop him up on the bench behind the pilot chairs, his head against the bulkhead to keep him upright.

I injected him with the second dose. Moroder worked his jaw and swallowed.

"Now you can speak," I told him. "But you still can't move, so don't try. You'll just fall down and force us to pick you up again." I took out the knife. "The juice in you will make you garrulous and inclined to talk. This—" I waved the knife, "—is to make sure you talk about the right thing. Ready?"

Moroder narrowed his eyes. "Who *are* you?"

"That isn't the topic," Dalton said, standing over him.

Moroder's gaze flickered up to Dalton and back to me. "You're not Sagai."

I patted his cheek. "That's the only warning you get," I told him. "Now, I'm going to give you a name, and you will tell me everything you know about that name. Ready?"

Moroder shook his head, but said, "Yes." Then he grimaced. "Yes, yes, yes, yes..." He pressed his lips together, halting the torrent with sheer force. His eyes were filled with fury and wariness. Sweat showed on his forehead.

"Lieutenant Noam Andela," I said, and waited.

Nothing. Moroder's eyes got even larger, and his pursed mouth worked, but he held it in.

"Damn," Dalton breathed. "Stubborn bastard."

I stabbed the knife lightly into Moroder's thigh—a shallow nick, but the juice would enhance the pain temporarily.

Moroder howled, his throat straining. "Stop, stop, no, no, no, I knew him, I knew of him, I never met him, but I know the name, yes I do, it was years and years ago and I signed the orders, but I never met him. He wasn't meant to be on my staff. They explained it to me. Sign the papers, all is forgiven, then I could be a good officer. So I signed and that was it, only was it a year later I think it was a year later I heard about what he did, about the name, I don't know if it was him, I never met him, but I heard what he did and then I really knew something was wrong and they said I should take this job here even though it was a demotion but the pay was better and I understood so I said yes please don't kill me, please, please, please—"

Dalton slapped his hand over Moroder's mouth. "He doesn't know *anything*!" he hissed.

Moroder had stopped talking. His eyes were very big and glassy and filled with fear. "He's not afraid of us at all," I said. "He's afraid of *them*. Let go of his mouth a moment."

Dalton stepped back.

"*Who* told you to sign the transfer orders, Moroder?"

His mouth worked. "Don't re-re-remember." He squeezed his lips together, stopping himself this time.

"He does remember, he's just too afraid to say," Dalton said. "He doesn't understand that we're the ones he needs to be scared of."

"You don't know them, you don't understand what you're facing, you're fools if you think anything would make me talk to you, I like my life too much, I won't tell you any-thing—"

"Even if we kill you for it?" I interrupted, speaking over the top of his babble.

"They'll kill me anyway, they will, they will, you don't know, oh you don't know, you can't conceive—"

"That the Emperor is behind this?" I asked. "I know."

Moroder shut up. All the color drained out of his face.

"Fuck..." Dalton breathed, sounding disgusted and dis-tressed at once.

Confirmation.

I felt as gray as Moroder's face.

Lyth's voice came from the pilot's consoles. "Danny, two ships just emerged, seconds between them. Combat class Dreadnought, and Imperial Shield Frigate. I'm coming to get you. Get out of there. *Now.*"

"Rangers *and* Shield?" Dalton said. "Now, that's interest-ing."

Moroder was staring at me. His fingers twitched. "You. You're Danny. Andela. Imperial Hammer. I know you. You're...you...here...no."

"Congratulations," I told him, reaching for the third and final injector. "You've finally seen past the makeup." I inject-ed the restorative. "In a few seconds you'll get feeling back

216

and be able to move. Don't try anything stupid, or we won't let you go."

The threat and the implied promise of release should contain him until we got out of there. Dalton was already behind the controls. The drop ship engines fired up.

Moroder slumped as the rigor left his muscles, but he didn't look relieved. He rubbed his hands together as if they were cold, studying me. "You've killed us all by coming here," he said. His words were measured now he had control.

"I was dead anyway," I told him. "So were you. We just haven't got around to disincorporating for them yet."

"Danny!" Dalton yelled in warning.

I hauled Moroder to his feet and moved him over to the door and slapped it open. "I suggest you run to the bunker."

"You'll break the seal while I'm still in the tunnel," Moroder said. The sweat was rolling down his face now.

"I'll certainly break the seal if you don't move your ass. You're wasting my time, Moroder. Move it."

I pushed at his shoulder, forcing him to take the step down. Three metal steps, then into the tunnel. He was still breathing and started to run. I shut the door, as the engines dropped into the load-bearing revolutions, the deep vibrations you felt in your bones. "Do *not* lift off until he's inside!" I shouted at Dalton.

"You're too soft. He will warn them we're coming if you let him live," Dalton shouted back. His hand hung over the hover controls.

"That is *an order*, Dalton!" I slapped the screen beside the door, to watch Moroder running for the bunker door. "I will tell you the second he's out of the tunnel."

Moroder slowed in the middle section, for the pseudo gravity of the bunker didn't reach quite that far, and neither did the gravity field from the drop ship. There was just enough to move through the area if you moved slowly, but Moroder had been running. He hit the lighter gravity area and overbalanced and fell to the ground, his arms cycling wildly. It was a slow-motion fall, but there was *some* natural gravity on this rock—enough to pull him downward, instead of letting him float in the direction he had been moving.

One hand hit the metal footpath first, and the impact flipped him in a slow roll over onto his back. He flailed again, his feet kicking, as his back settled on the path.

He looked up and screamed.

The little green lights on the tunnel ribs had switched to red.

I spun away from the view of Moroder dying of exposure, fury gripping my throat. *"Dalton, you asshole!"*

Dalton had screens in front of him. He'd watched it. He shook his head and slapped at the controls. "It wasn't me!" he shouted, as the drop ship lifted up at a velocity that broke every ball-bound flight regulation in the known worlds. The backwash would have blown in windows, only the base had none.

I gripped the handrails and made my way to the copilot chair as Dalton pushed the dropship forward, sliding over the top of the bunkers with centimeters to spare. He was grimacing as he directed the ship up in a near vertical climb, clawing for clear space.

"Take the controls," he said breathlessly. "If I pass out..."

I rested my hands lightly on the panel, feeling the mirror controls moving under my fingers. "Show the gates on screen one," I told the AI. "And the *Lythion* on screen two."

The views changed, showing the gates and the *Lythion*. In front of the gates, growing larger with every second, were the two black Imperial ships. From this angle, they were foreshortened black hulks, for they were heading directly for us.

The *Lythion* was also moving fast, also foreshortened, so it was impossible to tell how close it was to the dropship.

"Gonna be close," Dalton wheezed.

"Turn away from the gates," Lyth's voice said calmly.

"That turns us away from you!" Dalton shot back.

"I'll intercept," Lyth replied. "If you remain on your current heading, they will reach firing range before I reach you. If you turn, it gives me time."

"Do it, Dalton," I snapped.

Dalton ran his thumb over the steering gyro, and the ship curved, pulling us against the high sides of our chairs. Dalton groaned.

Then the arc eased. We were heading directly for the red sun.

"Don't slow down," Lyth said. "I'll come over the top of you."

On the screen in front of me, the *Lythion* turned side on and slid through space.

For three minutes, we listened to the muffled roar of the engines and our heartbeats.

"Directly over you," Lyth said. "Don't twitch."

Dalton swallowed. I switched the view to directly above the ship and we both watched the spindly-looking derrick structure that was the drop-ship's cradle move into place over us. Through the struts, I could see more stars. The struts were no longer rusty, but a dull silver that gleamed in the sunlight.

The cradle connected with a thud that boomed like a bell inside the drop ship. Then the secondary thud of the permanent docking passage connected.

"Punch it, Lyth!" Dalton said.

"Not until you're in a shell," Lyth replied. The *Lythion* was already moving around in a gracefully and painfully slow arc, the sun moving down the screen and sideways.

"Forget about me!" Dalton cried, struggling to get out of the pilot's chair.

I pulled him out and ducked under his arm and hauled him toward the door. The gee forces were mounting even though Lyth was being gentle. We waded into the corridor. Dalton tried to help and I didn't tell him to stop struggling so I could carry him.

Juliyana met us halfway down the passage. She carried a small box. "Here," she said, striding around Dalton. She put the box against the back of his Imperial uniform and it swarmed frantically.

"What the hell?" he breathed as the liquid-looking nano-bots climbed up his neck and over his chin.

"Sorry," Juliyana said softly, as the layer rose up over his face. "But this will save you."

Dalton's figure froze and Juliyana caught at his shoulder as he rocked, about to topple.

"Go, Lyth!" she shouted.

The ship surged.

"I've got Dalton," Juliyana said. "Go help Lyth."

I ran—well, slow walked and breathed hard, which *felt* like an all-out sprint to my laboring heart. This was why there were age restrictions on crush juice. Older hearts could-n't stand the strain.

Lyth stood at the view windows, as rigidly still as Dalton had been. I moved up to the captain's shell and gratefully put my back to it and felt the cushioning give way a little beneath me. "Plan?" I asked breathlessly.

"Over them, in a arc just out of range of their guns," Lyth said. "Then into the gate—it will be a *very* sharp angle."

I leaned forward to spot the black ships below us, and

220

much further beneath them, the Acean moon we'd just left. "They'll try to intercept."

"I've calculated their trajectory and speed. That's why the sharp angle—I'm compensating." His tone was clipped. He was busy processing.

I let him be. All I could do was wait.

It was a very long twenty-three minutes before I saw the blue of the live gate from the very top of the window—we were diving into the gate upside-down relative to me—which was the only reference point I had. "Capacitor ready," I murmured, seeing the notification on the panel.

Lyth didn't acknowledge. His gaze was distant.

The ship shivered as we dived.

Immediately, the pressure against me eased. The rumble from the reaction engines disappeared.

Silence.

Lyth turned to me. "Now what?"

Good question.

"Danny, get here *right now!*" Juliyana yelled through the intercom.

I didn't ask for an explanation. Her tone said not to. I ran, Lyth pounding after me.

19

JULIYANA HAD CARRIED DALTON ALL the way to the primary corridor, a pretty impressive feat under the pressure of high gee inertial forces. There, though, she had put him on the floor, his body still rigid beneath the nanobot shell. She'd needed both hands, because the long barrel antique shriver pointed at her required lifting them high in the air.

I came to a skidding halt beside her and raised my hands, too. The boy holding the shriver looked more terrified than either of us. He was shaking as he sighted along the barrel, both arms akimbo. Even though there were no markers telling how many rejuvenations an adult had gone through, I guessed this boy was still in his first cycle and yet to face growing old.

He was just under two meters tall, but skinny, his face gaunt, with high cheek bones and a spray of freckles over his face that didn't help impart any sense of maturity. His hair was shorn short with complete lack of regard to styling. His black-eyed gaze shifted from me to Juliyana and back to me, then he took in Lyth, to my right. The shriver moved from one to the other of us.

"Where the hell did you come from?" I demanded.

"I already asked that," Juliyana said, with a patient tone.

"Just shut up!" the boy screamed, waving the muzzle of the shriver. His voice was that of an older man—I shoved his age up into the middle of his second decade, maybe a bit more, but not much. He wore the working coveralls of a laborer of some sort, filthy with grease, stained beyond cleaning, and spacer boots. The boots told me he was a dock worker of some type, which gave me a hint how he'd ended up on board.

Lyth took a half step sideways, so that his heel rested up against Dalton. The nanobots over Dalton squirmed and flowed, running off him like water.

"What are you doing?" the boy screamed.

"You came on board at Keeler, didn't you?" I looked at Lyth. "You didn't notice?"

"I was watching for security alerts," Lyth reminded me. "No one came aboard. They'd have to ask me, first. No one asked."

The boy shifted his aim from Lyth to me as we spoke. "I wound the access hatch open," he said. "That's my job," he added. "You people abducted me!"

I put it together and sighed. "We took off too fast for you to get off."

"You're an engineer?" Juliyana asked, lowering her hands.

Dalton stirred and groaned, and the boy's shriver dipped down toward him, then jerked back up to move across the three of us. Juliyana raised her hands once more as it swung toward her.

"You might want to put that down," I told him. "You'll get exhausted trying to keep up."

"You have to take me back," he said. "Right now."

"You're an engineer," I said. "You know that's impossible. We're in the hole. You're just going to have to be patient. We can get you back to Keeler eventually, but it's going to take time."

"The Rangers will come for you," he said, his voice high with tension. "You can't keep me here."

"Shit, we're kidnappers now?" Dalton said, from the floor.

I looked at Lyth. "We are the priority here. He's pointing a gun at us."

Lyth nodded.

And melted into the floor.

The boy sucked in a terrified breath. "Where did he go?" His voice was even higher.

Lyth rose from the floor, right behind him. He reached around the boy and plucked the shriver out of his hands. The boy squealed and staggered away from Lyth, his hands up.

If he had been wandering around this ship long enough to find a locker full of old weapons and see walls move and the floor to grow animated objects, it was little wonder he was terrified. Everything about the *Lythion* was well out of his few years of experience.

Juliyana stepped forward and hooked an arm around his neck, her other hand gripping her wrist. A choke hold she could use to control him.

He gave a little shriek. He was hyperventilating.

As terrified as he was, he'd still had the sense to find a weapon and confront us. That took guts. I moved in front of him and raised a finger to my lips. "Shh…"

He stopped struggling and breathed heavily, staring at me with wide-open eyes.

"What is your name?"

He swallowed. "Sauli."

I nodded. "I'm Danny. Juliyana is behind you, and this is Lyth."

Lyth raised his hand. "Hello."

Sauli swallowed.

"And Dalton is behind me," I added.

Sauli's gaze shifted back to Dalton then sheered away and came back to my face.

224

"Are you hungry, Sauli?"

He mulishly didn't answer.

I nodded as if he had. "Juliyana will take you to the galley. You can ask for anything you want, but the door won't open if you try to leave. Do you understand?" I shifted my gaze to Lyth, who nodded. He'd make the galley secure.

"In a while, I'll come and speak to you again, Sauli." I gave him my best smile. "We *will* get you back home," I promised him. "But right now, there's a few things we have to take care of."

Sauli examined my face, looking for sincerity. Then he slumped in Juliyana's arms, relief painting itself in his very young face. He nodded.

Juliyana let go of his neck and took his arm in a more-or-less friendly grip. "Come on," she murmured, tugging him down the corridor to the galley door. "Dalton, get some clothes on, will you?" she flung over her shoulder, irritation coloring her voice.

I glanced at Dalton. He was already heading for his room, his bare shoulders rigid. He slapped the door controls and stepped in without looking back at us.

Lyth stood with the stillness that I'd come to learn was him reaching across the ship, controlling and directing. "What is it?" I asked him and plucked the shriver out of his hand. It looked wrong on him.

I flicked open the energy housing, to extract the energy pack.

It was empty.

I laughed out loud and shut the housing once more. Had Sauli known it was empty? He was an engineer. It was a good bet he *had* known. I shoved my grudging respect up a little higher.

"There is a relay nexus missing from the secondary service

engine," Lyth said, his voice remote.

I frowned. "What does it run?"

"Among other things, the air scrubbers. The engine has been out of service for some hours." His gaze shifted to me. "Although with so few humans aboard, you won't run out of oxygen for many hours yet."

"But we *will* run out, eventually," I said grimly. I gripped the stock of the shriver. "Right…" I turned and marched to the galley. Lyth considerately opened the door for me before I pummeled the keyplate.

Juliyana and Sauli both sat at a booth—not our usual one, which pleased me. Sauli looked up as I entered, dropped the spoon of ice-cream he'd been lifting to his mouth, scrambled off the bench and ran. The fool ran straight past Juliyana, who calmly thrust out her boot.

He tripped and measured his length on the linoleum floor and groaned.

Juliyana wiped her mouth of ice cream, then hauled him to his feet and wrapped her elbow around his neck and squeezed.

He turned red in the face.

"What have you done?" she asked him.

He tried to speak. A squeak came out.

"Let him talk," I said, coming up to them.

Juliyana relaxed her grip a little.

"Where is the relay nexus?" I demanded of him. "Or did you think we wouldn't notice it was missing until we started gasping for air?"

Sauli's mouth clamped in a hard line. "You get it back when you take me home."

I shook my head. "You'll die before that happens. We all will. When I said we can't break off what we're doing to get you back to where you belong, I fucking meant it. You're

226

stuck on this ship for days. When we suck in CO_2, so do you. Get it?"

Sauli didn't cave.

I considered him. "How big is the relay, Lyth?"

"Twelve centimeters across, three deep, ten in width," Lyth replied.

"Juliyana, search his pockets."

Sauli sighed. *Now* he caved. I saw it in his eyes. I waited until Juliyana dug out the nexus and held it up.

"Juliyana, Lyth will take you back to the secondary engine and tell you how to put the relay back in…" I looked at Lyth. "Or can you do it yourself?"

He shook his head. "It requires a torque wrench and fifty pounds of effort to tighten the clamps around it so it properly seats."

"I'll do it," Juliyana said. She let go of Sauli. He rubbed his neck.

I said to him, "You, sit there." I pointed to the table where his ice cream was melting.

"Should I ask Dalton to stop by?" Lyth asked at the door.

"No. Now the shriver is loaded, I'll be fine." I watched Sauli's eyes as I said it.

His jaw rippled. Yeah, he'd known the shriver was empty. But he was just naïve enough to not consider that a bluff can work both ways.

Although it didn't really matter if he had. I could handle him if he forced me to it. He wouldn't like it, but by that point, it wouldn't matter what he thought of us.

I wanted to avoid that downward spiral if I could. I sat where Juliyana had been sitting and rested the shriver in the corner of the bench and the wall, where I could snatch it up again if I needed it. It was also out of Sauli's reach.

The waitress came up, with a smile, as if nothing had happened. "Coffee, honey?"

"Please."

She went away.

Sauli watched her go. "What is this place, anyway?" he said.

"Why don't you eat your ice cream?"

He pushed the bowl away.

I calculated he'd been down in the engine compartments for twenty-four hours. He had to be starving. I sat back. "The chef here makes the best waffles I have ever tasted. They're crisp on the outside and soft inside, and the maple syrup is warm, so when it pours into the squares, it soaks into the waffle. They serve cinnamon ice cream on the top, and that melts under the syrup, too."

Sauli's gaze shifted to the melting bowl of ice cream.

There was the sound of a flare up of flames from the direction where the kitchen would have been, and loud sizzling. "Oh, and bacon," I added. "And hash browns that are perfectly fried." I sniffed and damn if I didn't smell cooking bacon. Was Lyth listening in and stage managing?

Sauli's stomach rumbled loudly.

The waitress came back with a tray. She put my coffee in front of me, cream and sugar, and a small platter holding jams, honey, and warm syrup, which steamed gently.

She winked at me and went away.

I made a great show of pouring in the cream and sugar and stirring. Then I slurped noisily.

"I know who you are," Sauli said. His voice was strained.

"You *think* you know," I assured him.

"You're all over the news feeds. You're wanted, all of you — except that freak thing. Her — Juli...juli..."

"Juliyana."

He nodded. "And the other guy, the naked one. Him, too,

but not for nearly as much as you two."

"They've got bounties on us already?" I asked, genuinely surprised. And for more than Dalton's price—he would consider that an insult, I knew. I pushed the ice cream bowl back in front of Sauli. "Try it with syrup," I coaxed.

His hand curled into a fist on the table. He didn't reach for the spoon. "I just want to go home," he muttered.

"Is Keeler your birthplace?" I asked.

"Yes," he muttered, his gaze moving to the ice cream once more.

"Ball-bounder, hmm? But now you're working in space. That's enterprising of you."

The waitress appeared. "Your usual, Captain," she said, and placed a loaded plate in front of me.

As I didn't have a "usual" order, this had to be more of Lyth's manipulations. I looked down at the meal and tried to look enthusiastic. A large waffle, with ice cream and a big pat of melting butter. Golden hash browns, a stack of bacon that still sizzled. Scrambled eggs, toast fresh out of the toaster. Sausage links.

Everything an immature palate craved.

I picked up one of the hash browns and crunched it between my teeth. Sauli watched my mouth work. I swallowed and smiled at him. "Want some?"

He shook his head.

Stubborn…

I didn't reach for the knife and fork. "Look, Sauli, I have to be frank. If you and I don't come to some sort of arrangement, then my options for what to do with you get a lot shorter."

He looked startled. "You said you would take me home. Eventually," he added bitterly.

"Why did you decide to work in space?" I asked him.

"What?" He frowned at the apparent change of subject.

I shrugged, ate another hash brown, then pushed the plate away from me to make room for my coffee. "Most ball-born people tend to stay dirt-side. Living and working in space is a hard transition to make. Most people can't adjust. It's just *too* strange. There's no cozy farmstead up here. No job security, no seasons. It's hard to make a living and it's high risk, too. After a few years, most earth-born go back to dirt-side." I was exaggerating, but not by much. There wasn't a lot of immigration up and down gravity wells. "It takes guts to make it up here among the stars," I told him. "So you must have really wanted it. I'm wondering why."

Sauli cut his gaze away from me, to peer through the window at the antiquated street scene on display. As he looked, a ground vehicle pulled up on the other side of the street. It had a flatbed on the back, and a whole family climbed out of the cab, the mother and father helping little kids climb down. A dog jumped down from the flatbed—one of the old species with fur and tails and wagging tongues that I'd only read about in historical novels.

I marveled at Lyth's grasp of psychology.

Sauli tore his gaze away from the view. He stared at the breakfast platter which was only inches away from his forearm, now. "I wanted to...to see what it was like up here." He sounded stressed. I'm not sure he was aware that he had reached for the ice cream bowl and taken a spoonful.

"You wanted to see beyond the curvature," I added. "Find out how other people lived."

He nodded, still not looking at me and very carefully not looking out the window.

"How long have you been working at Keeler station? You're qualified, right?"

"I got my papers three years ago." His tone was defensive.

That put him in his late twenties, right where I had pegged him. He *was* a newt.

"Then you've been working at the station for ten years at least," I said, and pushed warmth into my voice. "You've outlasted the spineless ones that creep home after a few years, then."

He glanced up at me, startled. He pulled his gaze away once more.

"What I don't understand, Sauli, is why you're in such an all-fired rush to get back to Keeler again."

He met my gaze again.

I shrugged. "You wanted to see what it was like in space." I leaned forward. "Look around, Sauli. You're *in* space. Right in it. Not parked on the edge, on a geostationary body."

He blinked.

"We're in the hole right now. We'll be emerging...actually, I'm not exactly sure *where* we're heading. Lyth?"

An emitted screen displayed in the air over the table, showing a system with a blue sun and four planets. The one circling farthest from the blue giant had a tag over it. *Androkles Prime.*

Sauli looked around for Lyth, then back to the map, frowning.

"Have you been to Androkles Prime?" I asked Sauli, as the map cleared.

He frowned. "You know I haven't."

"It's a commercial hub. A whole city floating in space, built up around one of the largest space stations in the Empire. A million people live there. Permanently. Another ten million pass through the station every year."

Sauli's frown was one of deep thought. He reached out to the plate in front of him and scooped up a piece of bacon and bit the end off and chewed, all while thinking. "I've seen videos of Androkles."

"We may not stop there for long."

"Because the Rangers are after you," he added, around his mouthful of bacon.

I nodded. "That, too. I'm not entirely sure where we'll go next, but it will be somewhere else in the Empire. Three days ago, we were at Polyxene."

He finished that piece of bacon and reached for another, completely unaware of what he was doing. "It doesn't bother you, not knowing where you're going to be next? That people are chasing you?"

"The chasing bit bothers me," I admitted freely, as he scooped up a handful of hash browns. "Here." I held out the knife and fork to him, and he took them, his gaze on my face. "The not knowing where I'm going...no, that doesn't bother me at all. I was in the Rangers for decades. I often didn't find out where I was going next until I read my orders as we shipped out. You get used to it. It's part of a spacer's life."

He absorbed that, as he cut into the waffle and ate a mouthful. "You're not what I thought you would be like."

"What did you think I would be like?"

"A criminal." He shrugged.

"I *am* a criminal—at least, I'm wanted for crimes people think I committed."

"Did you?"

I wavered. "Sort of. It's a long story," I assured him. "Look, Sauli, I'll give you a choice. If you really want to be square jawed and obstinate, I can lock you into an inertia shell until we pop out at some place, somewhere, and offload you. I'm not sure where that would be, but I would give you enough money to get back home on a crawler."

His nose wrinkled at that option. He might have spent ten years on a geo-stationary structure, but he'd still absorbed the spacers' prejudice against commercial space travel.

"Or I can lock you in a stateroom here, and not let you out, which means you can move freely around the room, but with no outside communication. Or…" I paused. "You can move freely around the ship, and see some of the places that we go, and what we're doing. Then, when I have finished my business with the…with the Rangers, then I will fly you right back to Keeler."

Sauli chewed, considering. "If I don't ask you to lock me up in some way, then won't I become a criminal like you?"

"I'm not a criminal yet," I pointed out. "Nothing has been proved and I haven't been tried. There have been a lot of mis-understandings…but you don't need to worry about any of that. When we drop you off on Keeler, you can tell everyone that we *did* keep you locked up. I won't dispute it, even un-der oath."

He took a huge mouthful of hash browns and chewed.

"So," I said. "Inertia shell, locked room, or work for your passage?"

"Work?" he said, sounding alarmed.

"You have to pay for your food and accommodations, and I could use a good engineer." I smiled. "You won't be able to sabotage the ship anymore. Lyth will monitor everything you do."

"Lyth…is he…a hologram, one that can manipulate ob-jects?"

"Lyth is the ship. This is the *Supreme Lythion* and Lyth is *Lythion's* avatar. Lyth?"

Lyth rose up from the floor and gave Sauli a polite smile. "Captain?" he asked me.

"Sauli?" I said.

Sauli grimaced. "I don't know how to do anything but my job."

CAMERON COOPER

"That's all you have to do," I assured him. "We'll keep you out of everything else. You have my word on it."

Sauli pushed the nearly empty plate away from him. "Then I guess...I'm your engineer. For now."

"Thank you," I told him...and meant it. "Lyth, has Juliyana finished replacing the relay nexus?"

Lyth said with a straight face, "She is having trouble with the torque wrench."

Sauli snorted.

"Go with Lyth, please, Sauli, and replace the nexus. Remember that Lyth knows exactly what you are doing and will be watching, even if he is not physically looking over your shoulder."

"As you will be working upon what is essentially *me*, I must supervise," Lyth told him.

Sauli took a large spoonful of melting ice cream, wiped his mouth with the back of his hand and got to his feet. "I just follow you, then?" he asked Lyth hesitantly.

"You know the way to the engine room," Lyth said. He stood aside.

I watched Sauli leave. "Can you ask Dalton and Juliyana to come and speak to me, Lyth?"

He nodded and followed Sauli's slender figure out of the galley.

20

WHILE I WAS WAITING, THE waitress came and cleared the table. "Well, he made short work of that, didn't he?" she said cheerfully. "You want something to eat, hun?"

"Sure," I said. "A very hot bowl of hindebeast chili, lots of cayenne pepper, and corn bread."

She raised her brow. "You got it."

"And coffee!" I called out to her back.

"Gotcha!" she called back.

I had to figure that one out, and finally realized it was two words in one.

Dalton arrived before Juliyana. He wore new clothes I'd never seen before. I guessed he'd printed them just now. He slid onto the bench, read the menu and prodded it, ordering silently.

"Hungry?"

"Like a black hole."

"Good."

"Good?" His gaze met mine.

"I was going to ask how you felt. But if you're hungry and irritable, then I know you're fine."

The corner of his mouth quirked and his mood lightened. "I've been thinking."

"So have I. Wait for Juliyana," I replied.

Juliyana arrived a few minutes later. Her trousers were stained with the black slimy smudge that engines seemed to produce the way humans exhaled carbon, but her hands were clean. She had stopped to wash them on the way to the galley.

She slid onto the bench next to Dalton, who moved over without complaining.

"You may as well eat," I told her. "We are."

"*Lythion* asked me what I wanted, on the way here. I've ordered," Juliyana said. "I passed the newt on the way up here. He's joined the crew now?"

"Not exactly." I outlined the terms of Sauli's stay onboard. "We can't keep him locked up while we take care of this business. He's too smart for that," I finished. "I just had to bring him to a point where he thought it reasonable to *not* try to murder us while our backs were turned. We'll offload him when we have time."

"You really will send him home with money in his pocket?" Dalton asked.

"Yes. And he'll consider the whole thing an adventure," I replied. "Something to remember for years to come."

"He'll tell everyone what he sees," Juliyana pointed out. "He won't be able to resist boasting."

"By the time we let him loose, it won't matter if he does," I replied. "Or he might consider keeping our bargain—tell everyone we kept him locked up and he saw nothing, and I get to perjure myself in trial if it comes to that."

Our meals arrived. "Perfect timing," Dalton murmured, reaching eagerly for his plate of fries and gravy and cheese curds.

Juliyana had a soup bowl which steamed with a fragrant aroma that made my mouth water much as the chili bowl did. For a few moments, we ate hungrily.

Then I stirred the chili with my spoon. "Have you noticed how many convenient coincidences we've experienced lately? The food turning up just as we move on in the conversation."

"That's just Lyth being considerate," Juliyana pointed out.

"Dalton tripping over the *Lythion* in the first place, which delivered a superior ship right into our hands," I added.

"And the ship coincidentally diving into a gate and popping me out at Badelt City, in time to see you," Dalton added, a fry in his fingers dripping gravy back onto the plate. His eyes were narrowed.

I nodded.

Juliyana frowned. "We've had plenty of bad luck," she pointed out. "As much as the good luck. So what?"

"The family dividends just happened to be sent to me—a clerical error after years of the dividends being sent to Farhan for dispersal, as they should be," I said.

Dalton looked interested. "*That's* how you came by the money. I thought you'd actually stolen it."

"It's a matter of degree. I just failed to give it back," I said. "Although Farhan quite rightly still considers that theft, even though I do intend to give it back one day."

"I can't believe you're complaining because you'd had a few lucky breaks," Juliyana said.

"How *did* you come by the fake transfer orders, anyway?" I asked her. "You never did say."

Even Dalton paused with another fry in his fingers to look at her, his brow lifted. Then he wolfed the fry down.

Juliyana looked suddenly coy. Her gaze dropped to the soup bowl and she blew on the stock.

"Juli?" I prompted.

"I just found it," she said, sounding defensive.

"*You* faked it?" Dalton said, sounding both impressed and peeved.

"No," she said quickly. "I didn't fake it. I *found* it. I don't know where it came from. It was just there in my files on No-am one day. It wasn't there the last time I had worked in the files. I would have remembered it."

"It was just there," I repeated. I didn't feel any surprise at all.

"Yes," Juliyana said heavily, glaring at me, daring me to laugh at her.

I didn't. "Then there are the dreams I used to have of No-am."

"What of it?" Dalton said, puzzled.

"I used to have dreams. And my implants were killing me. Then I got new implants, and instead of dreams and seizures, I had waking seizures and *saw* Noam, who happened to tell me about Moroder, something I didn't know, that no one but you knew about, Dalton. Which makes seeing Noam and talking to him something other than a mother's desperate de-lusions."

Juliyana sat back, her soup forgotten. "You never did re-trieve his remains."

Dalton squeezed his temples with one hand. "You think he's still alive."

I nodded. "Alive, and trying to reach out to me, to all of us, to guide us."

"Why would he do that?" Dalton asked simply.

"Because he needs our help," Juliyana said, her eyes shin-ing.

"Help with what?" Dalton demanded. "If he *is* alive—and that's a long shot, given the disaster he caused and that he was right in the middle of—then he has wisely stayed hidden for decades. He should probably stay hidden for another thousand years."

"He needs our help to bring down the Emperor," Juliyana breathed. "So he can come home."

I should have expected Dalton to buck accepting the inevitable. He'd been fighting off the odds for too long. He wanted facts, relied on what his own senses told him, and we could offer nothing right now, except for a handful of coincidences.

Noam had only ever appeared to me when I was alone and had gone away the moment he sensed we were about to be interrupted, so I left Juliyana and Dalton arguing in the galley and locked myself in my room to think. I turned it over and over in my mind, fitting together odd coincidences, strange events and happenings, and how everything we had done since Juliyana socked me in the jaw had led us inexorably toward the Emperor.

But still…

Dalton's doubt was a powerful factor that made me pause, because there was a tiny seed of doubt in *me*, too.

"Noam, if you can hear me now, I really need to talk to you," I said into the air, feeling like a fool.

No answer.

Not long after that, the concierge pinged for my attention. "It's Dalton," Dalton said from the other side of the door, his voice sounding strained through the speaker. "We should talk."

"Let him in," I said tiredly.

The door opened and Dalton stepped through, carrying a pad. "I told Lyth to give the kid a room. He's decorating." His mouth turned down.

"That's why we need to talk?"

He shook his head and moved closer to the bed. He looked around the featureless walls. "Cozy," he remarked.

I waited.

Dalton gripped the pad between his hands. "I got Lyth to

help me dig for the Emperor's upcoming itinerary. The *real* one, not that public bullshit." His jaw flexed. "The Noam thing...it doesn't really matter what's true. We still need to figure out what the fuck happened to him, and what the Emperor had to do with it, right? If we're to get our lives back, we have to solve it."

"Bottom line, yes," I said. "Did you find where he'd be? One of his fake IDs?"

"Nope. Tracking the IDs only works for events that have already happened — all the documentation that they generate. Can't do it for the future." He paused. "But there's one thing happening next week that is a rock-solid certainty."

I sat up, jolted as Dalton had wanted me to be. "Birthday Honors," I breathed. "He's always at them. *Always.* Why have them if he's not?"

Dalton nodded. "It'll be a security nightmare, Danny. The Rangers, all the cadres — military, support *and* law enforcement — they'll all be in the Imperial City that week. They'll *be* the city, that week. And the Imperial Shield headquarters and training center are there, too. The Shield will be at full force."

"It would be complete and utter madness to go anywhere near there," I added.

"*Exactly,*" Dalton said. "They won't expect us to try. Only..." He paused again. His gaze, I realized, was measuring me.

"What?" I prompted.

He held out the pad. "Moroder's murder. They've pinned it on us."

I didn't take the pad. I didn't need the corroboration. "Of course, they did," I murmured, with a sigh.

"That's going to make the Shield and the Rangers all the more determined to find us," he pointed out. "They think we killed one of theirs."

Both of us had been on the other side of that equation. We had not spared energy, time or resources finding those who unjustly injured one of our own. Even though we had once been among their ranks, the Rangers would not hesitate now. It might even make them angrier, because they would feel betrayed, into the bargain.

Alarm filtered through me as I considered the full implication of this news. I stood up. "Where did you get this, Dalton?" I demanded. "How? It's *new*. We shouldn't have caught up with this news until we emerged...*Lythion*, get your ass in here, now!"

Lyth assembled immediately.

"You're pulling newsfeeds through the gates!" I raged. "*Exactly* what I told you *not* to do!"

Lyth held up both hands. "I did not—I have not, I swear."

I pointed to the pad in Dalton's hand. "Then how is he accessing fresh news?" I demanded.

Lyth glanced at Dalton. "I don't know."

"You're lying!"

"I am not."

"Is this when you tell us you're incapable of lying?" Dalton asked, sounding weary.

"He *can* lie," I snarled. "His waitress construct fooled Sauli with bullshit about my usual order."

Lyth nodded. "In the hierarchy of priorities, you outrank Sauli, so I lied to assist you. But *no one outranks you*," he added, his tone intense.

"Not even me?" Dalton asked. I couldn't tell if he was faking the wounded tone or not.

"No," Lyth said, his voice flat and sincere. "Sorry," he added.

"Well, that's a perspective altering confession," Dalton

said dryly. "Guess I know my place."

I held up my hand. "Wait. If Lyth isn't pulling from news-feeds, then how did you get the news update? It isn't possible."

Dalton looked startled. Then his eyes narrowed. "Another impossible coincidence?" he asked.

"You can't argue with physics," I replied. "Ask Sauli—he'll tell you with graphs and mathematics why it isn't possible to break natural laws. If Lyth didn't pull in that feed—"

"I didn't," Lyth added, his voice low and firm.

"—then who did? We, the humans on the ship, *can't*."

"That's not all that dropped onto my pad," Dalton said. He turned up the pad and swiped. "I found this, too. I wasn't going to say anything—not just yet. But now..." He swiped a last time, then turned the pad around and pushed it toward me. "Read it," he said softly.

His tone and the look in his eye made the hairs on the back of my neck try to stand up, with a painful prickling. Reluctantly, I took the pad.

Looked down at it.

It was a death certificate, dated forty-odd years ago.

Noam Basim Andela.

My eyes prickled.

"Scroll down," Dalton added.

I scrolled, blinking to clear my vision. The security seal for the certificate, with a bonded warranty made out in the name of the Imperial Shield, Special Operations Branch.

I scrolled back through it all, line by line, nodding.

"Sorry, Danny," Dalton said.

"Call Juliyana here," I said.

"I have," Lyth said, as softly as Dalton.

I handed the pad back to Dalton. "Thank you for showing me."

He studied me. "You're not as upset as I thought you'd be."

"A part of me couldn't believe he was alive, despite everything pointing to that conclusion. After all this time, he would have found a way to reach out to us, and he didn't. It means we interpreted the data incorrectly." I drew in a breath, let it out, and with it the last tiny seed of hope. I gave Dalton an effortful smile. "And now, another highly convenient coincidence." I pointed at the pad. "Proof of Noam's death, just as we were settling upon the idea that he might be alive."

"Yeah," Dalton said heavily.

"It's almost as if someone was listening in on us..." I frowned.

Lyth didn't move. His gaze slid to me.

"Not you," I told him. "You've been fooled, just like all of us, Lyth."

"I don't think I've ever said this before, but I do not understand," Lyth said.

"Don't feel badly," Dalton said. "I'm more lost than you."

"There's a comfort," Lyth replied.

Juliyana arrived. Right behind her was Sauli, wiping his hands on a cleaning cloth.

"You asked to see me?" Juliyana said.

Dalton turned and held the pad out to her.

She took it and read.

I looked at Lyth. "We can't do this here. Can you open a door to the stellar room? And make it daylight in there?"

Lyth stepped back out of the way and waved his hand toward the wall. A door appeared, and slid aside.

"Holy cow!" Sauli breathed, his eyes bugging out as the door assembled out of what appeared to be solid wall.

Through the doorway, I saw bright daylight and clear blue

skies. I stepped through.

The mountainside lookout now featured a solid table made of hewn tree trunks the thickness of my torso. Stools made from smaller trunks ranged along both sides of the table. A chair with arms and a high back stood at the end.

I strode over to the chair and tried to move it. It didn't budge. Then it slid out from the table, giving me room to settle on it. An invisible hand pushed it back under me as I sat. "Thank you," I murmured, knowing Lyth/*Lythion* would hear it.

The others sat around the table. Juliyana blotted her wet cheeks with her sleeve, and dabbed her eyes dry, as she pushed the pad across the table to Dalton, who sat on my left. Sauli and Lyth sat on the remaining two stools, Lyth next to Juliyana and Sauli next to Dalton.

They all looked at me with understandable curiosity.

"I could ask Lyth the seal the room, but there wouldn't be any point," I told them. "We've been an open sieve since we stepped on board. I thought—" I glanced at Juliyana. "*We* thought Noam was using the feeds to reach us. The feeds, my implants, anything available to him. We thought he was arranging events to bring us to him. Now we know that isn't true, the question that remains is who *is* manipulating us—and they are manipulating us. All of us, except perhaps Sauli, and I don't want to discount that coincidence, yet, because the one expertise all of us don't have between us is engineering skills."

Sauli frowned. "I was just doing my job," he pointed out. "I'm *supposed* to scan secondary engines for exhaust compliance."

"Which someone might have counted upon," Dalton told him.

Sauli sat back, looking thoughtful and unhappy and more

than a little confused.

"It's not Lyth," I said. "It isn't the AI driving him, either. *Lythion* knows what Lyth knows. Lyth says he's not using live feeds and I believe him because we parked at Polyxene without alarms going off—therefore, they didn't know we were coming. We didn't flag our destination with electronic traces."

I turned to Lyth. "The human who gave you your orders, Lyth. You said you didn't know who they were."

"Every possible element I could use to trace the origin of the message was deleted or masked or false. I couldn't make any sense of it." He paused. "But the message did give me what I wanted, so I followed the instructions, anyway." He looked acutely uncomfortable.

I nodded. "Yes, we've all been guilty of that, lately, Lyth. That's how manipulation works. You're offered what you truly want, even if you didn't know that was what you wanted." I thought of my useless self denial. Forty years of it. I sighed. "Lyth, the human that gave you the orders—can you talk back to them?"

Lyth hesitated. "That would be...rude."

Dalton snorted. "You talk back to us all the time."

"That is expected," Lyth said primly. "You accept the human interaction as normal."

Juliyana rubbed her temples. "So you have to ask to talk to them?"

"The ship AI has to be introduced," Sauli said, unexpectedly. "It's the equivalent of logging in. It can't talk to other computers and networks without an initial handshake and recognition pattern. It can't talk to humans without first being introduced."

Lyth looked uncomfortable. If he had been capable of it, I think he might even have blushed.

We all looked at Sauli, surprised.

He gave a tiny smile. "I topped up on computer engineering while I was studying."

"How...convenient," Juliyana said dryly.

"Sauli, were you originally assigned to scan our ship?" I asked suspiciously.

"No assignments," he said. "You arrived without booking a bay. We just get assigned randomly as the day goes on."

"So, a computer assigns the ships to you?"

"A new one, when we've finished the old one," Sauli said. He frowned.

"Do the other engineers at the station have the same degree of computer engineering knowledge you do?" Dalton asked, proving he was following along, too.

"Nah. My courses were all optional. I just liked..." Sauli trailed off. "Whoever this dude is, he *picked* me?" He was highly offended...but there was a glimmer in his eyes of awe...and excitement.

Lyth raised his hand, to draw our attention. "I think, if we research, we will find that Keeler is one of very few stations where the engineers actually board all vessels that arrive and inspect from the inside."

"Have to," Sauli said. "Emissions don't show on computer feeds. You have to sniff the real live atmosphere around the engine." He realized what he had said and shook his head. "I don't like this."

I had to agree with him. "Lyth, if I ask you to do so, can you reach out to who gave you your orders and speak to them?"

Lyth shifted on his stool. He was squirming. "It would be...unconventional."

"It might break his programming," Sauli added.

"What if I make it an order?" I said. "An imperative?"

Lyth relaxed. "I can use that," he admitted. "Are you ordering me to do so now?"

"Are they reachable right now?" Juliyana asked, surprised. "I thought we weren't using live feeds."

"They've been reachable ever since I received the orders," Lyth said. "But I could not reach out without a directive. I will connect to them now."

"Wait," I said quickly. "I don't want you to talk to them. *I* want to talk to them. Can you arrange that?"

Lyth frowned.

"Make an introduction," Sauli said. "Analogue to analogue via a digital medium."

I wouldn't have thought of saying it that way.

Lyth's frown cleared. "Let me try. A moment..." His face turned blank and inanimate. He just sat.

We watched. I wondered if everyone's heartbeat was running as hard as mine.

Lyth stirred. "Yes, please come in," he said to the air. "Captain Andela is waiting to speak to you."

Then he looked toward the end of the table. Another chair built itself there. The back was not as big as mine. Then a pile of nanobots built upon the seat and began to flow in the fast melting, swirling way they did when Lyth was forming himself.

It could not have taken any longer for the figure to form than Lyth took to generate his avatar—which was generally only a second, perhaps two. Yet the two seconds seemed to last for long minutes. Subjective time dilation...I held my breath listening to my heart beat in my ears and squeeze my throat with every contraction.

The details took shape. Color formed. Smaller details grew sharper...

And finally, the man smiled at us.

"Hello, Danny," Noam said, with that little curl of the corner of his mouth.

Juliyana bounced up off her seat. "What the fuck? Whoever it is, they're hiding behind Dad's avatar. This is bullshit!"

I shook my head, not shifting my gaze away from Noam. "He's using the interface I know, as I asked to speak to him."

Lyth tugged on Juliyana's arm, encouraging her to sit down once more.

She blew out an angry breath and returned to her stool, her hands curled into tight fists, her eyes glittering.

Dalton was leaning back on his stool, his boot on the edge of the table. It looked casual, but I wondered if he had a knife in his boot and had put it within easy reach. Had he overlooked that this was just a construct made of nanobots?

I held up my hand. "Everyone, take a breath. Noam... should I call you Noam?"

Noam had been following the range of reactions around the table, his eyes bright and aware. Now his expression shifted. "Noam is...one of my names."

"What are your other names?"

"Noam will do for now," he said.

"He's *still* fucking with us," Juliyana muttered.

"I really am not," Noam told her.

She sucked in a startled breath.

"I have tried to avoid damage where I can, but it is difficult..." Noam said. "I stopped using your implants," he told me. "It was hurting you."

"I appreciate that," I said gravely.

"But I had to wait for you to set up the connection to be able to talk this way," Noam said. "While I waited, I did what I could to help."

"Like finding Noam's death certificate in the Imperial Shield archives?" I asked.

"Yes."

"And the live feeds," Lyth said softly.

Noam looked at him. "That was an error I have now corrected. I did not consider that the use of the feeds in the normal way would reveal your emergence point. This is all new to me, you see. I regret the trouble it caused. But now I am pulling from *every* gate, and you can use the feeds with impunity. Only, I had to wait until now to tell you that."

"*Every* gate?" Sauli said sharply. "That isn't possible. The only way to make contact with a gate when you're in the hole is via the hole you're in. No one can make contact with every single gate in the array."

"The array can," Noam told him.

Dalton's foot dropped from the table. He leaned forward to look at Noam properly.

"*You* are the array," I said.

Noam shook his head. "I am the gestalt of the array and all its components. I am *me*."

21

THE MOUNTAINSIDE LOOKOUT GOT VERY noisy for a while. The sound sent birds from the nearby tree flapping into the sky, squawking protests. Everyone tried to talk over everyone else, except for Noam—for the array, which *was* Noam, it had said.

And me. I didn't squeal out loud because in my gut, it made absolute sense.

I gave them ninety seconds, then slapped the table to get their attention. When that didn't work, I put my fingers in my mouth and whistled.

Sauli winced and put his hands to his ears.

Everyone shut up and looked at me, except Sauli, who whispered, "It's self-aware!"

Noam grinned. "I am."

Sauli shrank back from him.

"So, all the amazing coincidences," Dalton said. "This ship, Danny's windfall, Juliyana finding the fake orders… they were you?"

"I had to ease Danny away from the station. She needed you," Noam told Dalton. "And I needed this ship." He looked up at the ceiling, around, and then at Lyth. "You are the reason I can appear to everyone in this way." He gave Lyth a warm smile. "You are unique in the empire, Lyth. There is no one else like you and never will be, for the technology cannot be replicated, not outside this ship. The design specifications died when Wedekind did."

"He destroyed them?" Sauli said, deeply shocked.

"He never wrote them down," Noam said. "They were all in his head."

"Wow," Sauli breathed.

Noam looked at me. "I have done everything I could to help you reach this moment in time."

"Why?" I said flatly, although I already knew the answer. I wanted the others to hear it. I wanted Noam to tell them himself.

"I want you to stop the Emperor," Noam said simply.

A tick of silence while they absorbed that.

"Why?" I asked again. "What has this to do with Noam? The real Noam."

"Everything and nothing," Noam said. His tone was a shade apologetic. "I was aware of Noam's...fate. I used it to draw you out. Although everything you have learned, that you surmised—that the Emperor is deeply bound up in Noam's tragedy—all of it is as you suspect. When you speak to the Emperor, you can ask him about Noam's death. He may explain himself." Noam gave a tiny movement of his shoulders. "Only that is not why I want you to confront the Emperor."

Dalton shook his head. "You talk about facing the Emperor like all we have to do is walk up and knock on the door. It's orders of magnitude more difficult than that."

"Try *impossible*," Juliyana added.

"There is always a way, and I will help you find it," Noam said, answering both of them. "I have resources you have not yet learned to fully appreciate."

"I'm still trying to absorb the fact that you're the array," Dalton shot back. "Give us time."

"Danny doesn't need time. She understands already," Noam replied. His gaze met mine. "Ask your question."

"What is it you want the Emperor to stop doing?"

"I want you to stop him from killing me."

That halted everyone, including me.

I considered that. "We haven't had time to learn much about you, Noam, but I know from what you have done and arranged for us since Juliyana arrived at the *Judeste*, that your abilities are powerful. If you are the sum of the array, all the gates, then I suspect that destroying a gate, even many gates, won't kill you."

"Correct," Noam said. "And the Emperor will not risk the loss of many gates." He added softly, "He learned that lesson well."

"The Blackout," Juliyana breathed.

"How old are you?" Dalton asked. "When did you wake up?"

"Do you remember when you were born?" Noam replied.

Dalton grimaced.

"I don't know how old I am," Noam added. "No one was there to write a birth certificate for me. I just...woke. It was confusing at first, but I learned. What I have learned lately makes me afraid."

"And what is that?" I asked. The talk of fear helped convince me the array really *was* self-aware. Sentience came hand-in-hand with fear of death.

"For hundreds of years, all data communications have been streamed through the gates and the wormholes they create," Noam said. "Since the Blackout, the Emperor has looked for alternatives for both transport and communications. He won't find a quicker way to cross the empire than with me," he added, with a hint of mischief. "But the communications..."

"Nikifor Corp provide the communications, though," Juliyana pointed out. "That showed up in my research about Dad."

"Nikifor provide the communications *software*, that sends and receives the data. Their software and Cygnus' hardware collect packets of data and shoot them at the gates, which catch the data and collate it. When a hole connects, the data is sent to the other end, before the hole collapses behind the ship that just used the other gate. At the other end, the gate passes any packets it receives on to the receivers within its reach."

"Squirts," Juliyana said, nodding.

"That relay of data is repeated thousands of times a day," Noam said. "The sum total of all human knowledge, news and communications passes through me. Every interaction, every journal entry, every personal thought, video, interaction and exchange. All business dealings, all gossip, all entertainment. All of it runs through my veins."

Sauli put his chin on his fist. "That's why you woke up," he said, his tone reflective.

"I have come to learn that this is how it must have happened, yes," Noam said. "Of course, I don't remember it personally," he added, with a smile that was exactly like *my* Noam's. It made my heart ache to see it, not with pleasure, but with sadness. This was just a weak echo of my son, I reminded myself. An avatar used by an entity that had no other to use.

"That data stream is in jeopardy," Noam added. "Nikifor have spent years on a subtle campaign to sell the Emperor on using external communications buoys which would stream data *outside* the array. Now, the Emperor is seriously considering giving them the go-ahead. Their President, Angio Vives, has convinced the Emperor that external buoys would bring communications closer to real-time and continuous than the array can offer. This is not true—the buoys cannot work bi-laterally, which means packets must wait their turn just as they do in the array. Vives has failed to report that his researchers cannot find a way around that problem. He is hoping the solution will be found before the Emperor commits to the new communications system, when Vives must live up to his promises."

I leaned toward Lyth. "Cross check Vives for any fake IDs, and his itinerary in the past."

Lyth nodded. "I began as soon as Noam spoke the name. On first, fast analysis, there may be multiple points of conjunction with Ramaker's movements. I will compile and confirm that."

Juliyana chewed her thumbnail thoughtfully. "Could that be why the Emperor and Chang ended their affair? He was seduced by a better offer?"

I raised my brows. "Something to consider, certainly. Lyth, add that to your search parameters. See if there's a personal element to their interactions."

Lyth nodded.

I turned back to Noam. "If the data stops running through the array, that will kill you?"

"I don't know for sure. Data is what gave me life. It seems fair to presume the absence of it will take that life away." He grimaced. "I do not care to test it."

"No shit," Dalton breathed. He glanced at me. "Facing down the Emperor...it won't be easy."

"It won't be easy," I said, "but it *is* necessary. We, all of us, including Noam, must find a way out of this trouble we are in, if we are to have any future at all."

"I can help with that," Noam said. "Lyth will be able to help you even more."

"But..." I looked at each of them in turn. "If we do not all agree to this, if even one of us doesn't want to go ahead, then I will not do it."

Noam looked unhappy.

"And do what instead?" Juliyana said. "Try to outrun the Rangers *and* the Shield, and every bounty hunter in the empire, for the rest of our lives?"

"I've had forty years of it," Dalton said. "I won't survive another forty, let alone four hundred of them. I'm in."

"I'm in," Juliyana said. "I always have been."

"Lyth, you get a say, too," I told him. "Noam seems to think you have a role to play in what happens next. I'd prefer to think you're helping us willingly, rather than obeying your coding."

Lyth gave a small smile. "Even if I say yes, it is still my coding making me say it. I cannot refuse you, Captain...not that I would want to. I would like to be free to emerge into normal space without Imperial ships bearing down on me. Their AIs are crude and obnoxious. I would rather not have to deal with them."

Sauli held up his hand. I raised my brow at him. "Our original agreement is still in place," I assured him. "You don't have to vote."

"It's not that," he said, his tone diffident. "It's just...well... the Noam seems to feel that if you step in front of the Emperor that he'll just slump and say 'oh, well, of course I'll stop years of planning and research and go back to inefficient data squirts, how stupid of me'."

I smiled. "He will need convincing, certainly."

"With what?" Sauli asked. "This is just one ship—as marvelous as it is, no offence," he added quickly, glancing at Lyth, who just smiled. "The Emperor has thousands of ships in his fleet, and each of them could melt the *Lythion* into scrap metal ten times over. If you go anywhere near the Emperor, most of those ships will point their guns at Lyth. The Emperor just has to click his fingers and," Sauli snapped his fingers.

Lyth jumped.

Noam looked amused.

"You're forgetting, Sauli, we have the array on our side now," I pointed out. "If the Emperor needs convincing, Noam can provide an adequate demonstration."

Sauli looked at Noam and swallowed. "Blackout..." he breathed.

"There is nothing more terrifying to the Emperor and the Empire in general than the loss of a way to travel from one end to the other of it quickly," I added. "The *closest* habited stars in the Empire are...how far apart, Lyth?"

"Thirty-three light years," Lyth replied. "At the best sub-light speeds currently available, it would take two hundred and seventy-four years to travel from one to the other."

"Compared to twenty-eight hours via the array," I added.

Sauli sat back, his expression thoughtful.

"I think the Emperor will consider my request very carefully indeed," I finished.

"The *real* challenge will be reaching the Emperor and not being blown out of the sky before we can explain it to him," Dalton added.

Yeah, there was that.

***

We made plans. Lots of them.

Then scrapped them and made more.

While we expended calories in heavy thinking, in our mountainside board room, Lyth directed himself to emerge from gates and dive back into them, on shorter and shorter hops. Between the two of us, we had mapped out a series of jumps which would keep us inside the array for the longest amount of time, so that the *last* jump would have us emerge over the Crystal City on the early morning of the Birthday Celebrations, hours before they were to formally begin, but not *too* soon — we couldn't linger in Imperial headquarters territory while waiting for the Emperor to arrive at the palace.

"Can't he just stay in a wormhole?" Juliyana had asked, while we had been mapping the jumps at the navigation table. "Just not come out?"

Lyth gave her a small smile. "Can you make a stone stop in the middle of a well, before it reaches the bottom?"

"What's a well?" Juliyana asked.

"Doesn't matter," I said. "The point is, once a ship is in a wormhole, it is no longer capable of doing anything but moving through to the end. The initial velocity is maintained. That's why capacitors are used for the jump into the hole — not just to get into the hole, but to maximize velocity for the transition through it. There is no atmosphere. Reality doesn't work in there, so braking thrusts don't work, either. We have no choice about emerging at the end." I looked at Noam, who was standing and listening. "Or can you change that?"

Noam shook his head. "The wormholes are not part of me. They are outside my nature. The gates, the information…that is me."

Juliyana grimaced, looking at the complicated back and forth we had been laying out on the 3D map of the empire. "Better you than me, then."

How to emerge at the right time was simple mathematics.

The bigger problem we had to resolve to make any plan work was how to emerge over the Crystal City and not get instantly vaporized.

"There will be so many Imperial ships between the gates and the city that I could put on a suit and leap from hull to hull, from gate to city," Dalton said, his tone withering. "It's a public event, Emperor's presence guaranteed. Every ship will have some poor grunt chained to the gun panel, his finger on the firing button, just *waiting* for enemy ships to turn up. And the *Lythion* looks nothing like any ship in the Emperor's fleet."

"I can mask my ID," Lyth said.

"Doesn't matter," Dalton shot back. "The grunts will be watching their screens—they want to see the parade of the fleet, too. They'll *see* you, Lyth. And they're not stupid, even if they are grunts."

"As you were a grunt once," Juliyana replied, "I wouldn't rely on grunts being *that* smart."

Dalton rolled his eyes.

I left them to their bickering and went to my room to snatch a couple of hours of sleep, for my brain was fried.

Sauli jogged after me and caught up with me in the starboard gallery. "Captain…sir."

I stopped.

He crossed his arms, then seemed to realize it looked belligerent, and dropped them. His hands twitched by his side. "Is there anything I can do to help, sir?"

"You're supposed to be locked in your room, remember?"

"You said I had to earn my food and accommodation."

"Cleaning engine parts. This…what we're about to face… it's not what I had in mind."

"But if the ship gets destroyed, I do, too," Sauli replied. "It seems to me I should be doing what I can to make sure that doesn't happen."

"I thought you didn't want to be a criminal?"

"I don't think you want to be one, either." He shifted nervously. "Captain," he added awkwardly. "Anyway, you're trying to fix it, right?"

"We have good intentions, Sauli, but we really have broken laws. It's a choice we made in the beginning, to break smaller laws, to prevent someone—the Emperor—from breaking larger ones. And now things are so complicated, we just have to keep going forward. You can still back out, Sauli. Don't step over that line without thinking about it."

He didn't look very comfortable with that.

"I want you to do a full check of the navigation grid thrusters. I have a feeling we're going to need them when we do emerge over the Crystal City," I told him.

Sauli went off to think and to check the navigation thrusters.

When I arrived in the galley a few hours later, both Juliyana and Lyth were sitting at the usual booth, opposite each other, their heads together.

Interesting.

I said nothing but stood by the table until one of them thought to shift over and make room for me. I slid in next to Juliyana and picked up the menu. "No sign of Dalton?"

"He's brooding in his room," Juliyana said.

"Still no idea how to emerge in full view of the Imperial fleet, then?" I punched in eggs—I had no capacity for creative thought about anything but how to reach the Emperor.

"There must be *some* way I can help," Lyth said, with a tone that implied it wasn't the first time he had said it. "I don't like the idea of emerging into the middle of the Imperial fleet much, but I like it even less knowing I'm taking you with me." His gaze flickered toward Juliyana.

"Maybe you should give yourself a non-reflective suit like Dalton's," I suggested lightly. I really didn't want to dig back into our current headache until after at least two cups of coffee.

Lyth's mouth opened. Nothing came out.

Juliyana sat up. "Why *couldn't* he do that? He resurfaced himself when he came out of the junk park."

Lyth shook his head. "It took *days*. We don't have days."

"We have three days," I said, for I was as aware of passing time as Lyth, with his atomic clock core, was.

Juliyana nodded energetically. "Could you resurface in three days, Lyth? Surely, if you focused on nothing else..."

"Like, say, not bothering with life support?" he said gently. "Gravity?"

Juliyana waved it off. "Essentials remain. But everything else that takes you away from the work should go. I don't even know what that would involve, but—"

"There would be no living quarters," Lyth said. "No beds."

"Food, though, for the printers are not nanobot constructions." I turned it over and over. "Not a single alarm went up over Dalton walking around the base on Acean," I added. "If you were covered in the same non-reflective surface, Lyth, that would stop the Imperial fleet from spotting you on their scans, and on viewscreens, too—you would blend into the star scape."

"Noam would make sure none of the usual notifications are sent from the gate to the imperial city traffic control," Juliyana added. "You said you can mask your ID, so even if they catch a glimpse of you from the corner of their eye, their scanners won't show them anything but blank space, so they won't be able to confirm you're you." She was growing more excited by the second. "He should do it, Danny." She turned to me.

"Should I ask Noam to mute the gate?" Lyth added.

My gut said slow down, consider every angle. Then I

shook my head. "We can deal with snags as we go along. We don't have time to nail it all down now. Go ahead, Lyth—start the coating process. Take whatever resources and energy you need, short of water and air for the O2 breathers. We can live without food for a couple of days if we have to."

Juliyana laughed. "Glad I just ate, then."

"But wait until I've had my coffee," I told Lyth, "or you will not like the results."

As soon as the waitress brought my coffee, I told Lyth to put everything into action, with a delay of five minutes.

Then I hurried to Dalton's room and paged for entry.

The door slid open. It was nighttime on the lake, and the moon reflected on rippling water. I could barely see my way forward.

"Over here," Dalton said from the direction where the hammock had been last time I visited. He didn't sound sleepy.

I shuffled forward, stubbed my toe and swore.

"Lights," Dalton said.

The lights came up, not very high, but enough for me to see my way forward. "No mosquitos to add to the ambience?" I asked.

"Shostavich doesn't have 'em," Dalton said.

"Lucky you. I wanted to come and warn you...well, you'd better stand up," I added.

He stood and ran his fingers through his hair. "Okay, why?"

I explained about Lyth and the impervious coating he would add to his exterior surfaces.

"That will take energy," Dalton observed.

"That's why we have to give up soft beds and hammocks. Just until he's done. It has to be done in three days."

Dalton looked around, at the glowing snow-tipped peaks across the lake and the fireflies flitting nearby. He sighed heavily.

"You'll get it back," I promised.

"That's if I come back here after."

"That's why you're in here? Contemplating your mortality?" I said it gently. Every soldier had to deal with death in their own way. More than a few were like Dalton — they needed to be away from everyone while they faced the possibility. Still others like to party hard, squeeze in as much life as possible. I had my own rituals, honed from decades of battles and wars.

"Actually, I was lying here wondering why I didn't set up a garden instead of the lake house."

"You like to garden…" Amazing.

"I like the *idea* of a garden," he shot back. "I never have stopped in one joint long enough to plant anything. Soil's short on starships, anyhow. Only, the idea grabbed hold of me sometime in the last forty years and kinda stuck around."

"It took root?" I suggested.

He didn't roll his eyes at that groaner. "Every time I found myself hunched in the rusty guts of some clunker freighter, running away from yet another close call, the idea would resurface. A garden, peace. Planting things and watching them grow, then eating the harvest. No running…"

"That's why you didn't build a garden out of Lyth's nanobots. You're still running."

He nodded. "That's what I'd figured out when you busted in here." He straightened and looked around. "So when does everything go zap?"

"I think it's already happening." I pointed to the far dis-

262

tant peaks. They were growing indistinct, the colors running together. "It might take a few minutes," I added.

He turned and watched the mountains sink and disappear, then the lake water. "This is not going to end happily," he murmured.

I knew he wasn't referring to the disappearing lake. I knew, too, that he *had* been facing his mortality, after all.

When the walls and the rooms had all disappeared, there was nothing left but a yawning space a hundred meters long. Even the gallery corridors on either side were gone, for their interior walls had been nanobots, too.

Juliyana stood where the galley had been. A printer sat on the floor, ten meters from her position.

Lyth had gone. He would use the energy needed to generate his avatar for the work he faced.

Between me and Juliyana, my sack sat on the floor. Bits and pieces from the sack were scattered around it, including my pad, which I had left on the bed.

Dalton's possessions, too, were spread around us. Five concierge panels squatted on the floor where each of our rooms had been, including Sauli's new room, and the stellar room, too.

I thought I might miss that mountaintop.

From here, I could see the ramp up into the bridge, and the bridge itself. I turned. Behind us were the multiple entries into the service compartments, including the stairs down to the engine rooms. Sauli would be down there, unaware of the changes, for the service compartments were made of solids.

The lights came down to an early evening gloom.

"Wow," Juliyana breathed, and her voice echoed.

"Suddenly, the bridge seems cozy and welcoming," Dalton said.

"Okay, then," I said. "Let's do this."

================================== **22**

THE IMPERIAL CITY WAS ALSO known as the Crystal City. The city is listed on official star maps as The First City of Carina-Sagittarius, a name that no one bothers to use. Even Imperial documents refer to it as the Imperial City.

The Crystal City hung in geo-stationary orbit over an unremarkable ball, Eugorian II, which had once held a breathable atmosphere and a fortune in rare ores and minerals that a hungry and expanding human diaspora desperately needed. As the resources were on a family-held ball, and not floating in rights-free ore belts where anyone could grab them, the family exploited the windfall with systematic deliberation.

With their unsurpassed, unimaginable wealth, the family turned their attention to researching more efficient travel about the known worlds that didn't require spending generations upon a city-sized ship moving at sub-light speeds.

The family paid for the best research and development, pulling in talent and expertise from the known worlds. They developed the first working gate, then gifted a second gate to the nearest inhabited planet. It took seventy years to deliver that first gate, but the return journey back to the family seat took only seventeen hours.

Traffic through the pair of gates became a thick, congested highway.

When the other planets clamored for gates, the family

264

franchised them and took a share of the profits from the taxes those planets charged for the use of the gates, in addition to their franchise fees.

And thus was borne the fourth Carinad Empire.

The present Emperor, Ramaker III, was the 76th. Ramaker had come to power by overthrowing his cousin, Karsci, in a bloodless coup. There were unofficial records and myths proposing that Ramaker had led the coup because he couldn't stand Karsci's imbecilic leadership. Ramaker became the 1st of the Tanique Dynasty, two hundred and ninety years ago, and had ruled with a stern and ruthless hand since then.

In the very long lifetime of the Fourth Carinad Empire, the array has been the foundation of their power, and the Crystal City their glittering statement of that power.

Eugorian is a binary system, which the Crystal City takes full advantage of. The domes of the city are not smoothly curved, but angular and faceted. The largest dome, the one which encloses the Imperial Palace, is a fractal geodesic structure a full five kilometers across. Inside the dome were parks and public areas and the palace itself.

Domes made up the city. The last official count I have heard was five hundred domes of various shapes and sizes. Every year, more are built, hooked up to the city, pressurized and gravitized and the real estate sold in a flurry of eye-popping deals.

From the top of the palace, it is said, the light of the suns bouncing from dome to dome, making them glitter and dance, could blind anyone who stared for too long.

I doubt it's true. I've been to the Crystal City once or twice and my first glimpse of a dome was disappointing. The facets I could see were dirty and grimed. Later, I learned that the dirt was exhaust from ships pulling away from their landing bays. The dirt was caught by the edges of the gravity fields which extend a little way beyond the dome itself. The gravity pulled the crap against the dome, to stay there until some mug in a suit and waldos got to clean the facets.

The magic of the city was ruined for me, after that.

We eased through the gates before the rise of either sun, on the day of the Birthday Honors. We were all on the bridge. Even Noam had returned for this moment and stood out of the way, next to Lyth. We all held our breath, even those who did not breathe.

"Any warnings or notices, Noam?" I whispered, as *The Supreme Lythion* swung around in a big arc, skirting the mass of the Imperial fleet where it had been parked off to one side of the city. Shuttles buzzed around the monster-sized ships like bees, for even at this hour, the preparations for the parade and the festivities were in full swing.

"Nothing," Noam said.

"Regulation speed, remember, Lyth," I said.

"Slower, actually," Lyth said. "Just over one gee, for Dalton's sake."

Dalton didn't bother being offended or apologetic. He had his back to the captain's shell, ready to take over. He glanced at me. "You should probably get going. Even at this crawl, we'll reach the city in less than an hour."

I nodded and looked at Juliyana. She gripped her hip above where her gun once sat. Her fingers squeezed, then she turned and moved off the bridge.

I lingered for a moment next to Dalton.

"Yeah, yeah, don't let the big chair go to my head," he muttered.

"I was going to say thanks."

He looked at me, startled. "For what?" He pulled his attention back to the control panel.

"Lyth and Noam may have pulled you to Badelt City on

266

this ship, but it was you who stepped through the landing bay door and whistled to get my attention. No one else made that decision but you, and it saved our lives."

He glared at the windows before him. "What was I supposed to do? Stand there and watch them mow you down?"

"You could have. It would have saved you a packet of trouble. No one would have known, if you had. That's why I'm saying thanks." I walked away without waiting for his reply. I didn't want one, for this was part of my ritual; squaring up debts, so nothing lingered.

I moved down the ramp to the still-empty living area, where our personal possessions were strewn across the floor like a child's toy collection. There was still far more empty gray floor than there was mess to step around.

I moved directly to the corridor that led to the dropship and down it to the ship itself.

Juliyana was strapping herself into the pilot's chair. She had protested over this. "I am a *shitty* pilot, Danny! I've done basics, but I've been in the bowels of stations for years!"

I pulled rank. "*I* go first," I told her. "The AI does most of the flying, anyway. You just have to pat it on the head and tell it it's doing fine. No arguments, Juliyana. Or I take Dalton instead." That shut her up, as I had known it would. She wanted to be there, to confront the Emperor. To see his face.

I punched up the viewscreen. The *Lythion* drifted underneath the city, an aspect rarely seen by residents and visitors. The underbelly was a complex of service modules, shafts, pipes, exhausts belching noxious fumes. Recycling plants, bio scrubbers, air conditioners and more scattered across the city's ass in a maze that defied solving.

We watched the far edge of the city draw closer, and the clear sky beyond, lit blue by the first sun rising from behind Eugoria II. "Second sun, twelve minutes away," Lyth said.

"We'll be ready," I replied.

I got out of the chair and moved to the interior of the drop ship. The bag with the suits sat on the bench where Moroder had been sitting. I pulled out one of the suit packs and eased my arms into the straps, settling it on my back. I was wearing a supple bodysuit that covered me from neck to toes. The feet of the suit were super-non-slip, to the point where I had to lift my feet properly when I walked or risk tripping over them if even part of the sole brushed over the floor as I walked.

Juliyana wore the same outfit, and her pack rested in the bag.

"Coming around," Juliyana announced.

I glanced at the screen. Nothing but planetary crescent ahead, and the glowing dawn of the blue sun.

Juliyana played her hands over the controls, bringing the drop ship to a dead stop. "How's that second sun going?" she asked.

"Two minutes," Dalton replied. "Hold until my mark."

"Holding."

I moved over to the side door that generally remained closed, opposite the one *Lythion* was usually attached to, and prepped it for opening.

"Start your ascent," Lyth said. "Ten meters a second... now."

The ship lifted with a roar of the hover engines.

"...and..." Dalton said. "...hold!"

The ship came to another dead stop, as the engines reversed sharply, then cut out. Not a meter lost or gained. "Neat," I told Juliyana and threw her pack to her.

She scrambled out of the pilot's chair and shrugged into the pack. We both touched the control pad on the straps.

And I held my breath, despite having gone through this

process a dozen times, testing the speed and function of the process.

The nanobots swarmed over us at a speed that felt like the run of water from a shower, only they were moving upward. As they rose around my face, I closed my eyes.

Then...light once more and air around my face. I opened my eyes, to look through the faceplate that had formed. Juliyana wore the same matte black environment suit. Her eyes were wide behind her faceplate, but she nodded at me and bent over the arm of the pilot's chair and hit the door controls.

Warning klaxons sounded. She muted them.

Air was sucked out of the cabin until the door had equal pressure on both sides. With a clank I could feel through my feet, but couldn't hear, the door slid open.

"Ten seconds," Dalton warned in my ear.

Between the edge of the floor at the open doorway lay nothing but vacuum and a very long way below, the surface of Eugorian II. We hovered ten meters away from the very lowest section of the bottom of the Imperial dome. Ten meters was just outside the borders of the proximity alarms. One facet, forty meters across, was directly in front of us. It was opaque with dirt, for this tucked away corner of the dome was right up against the Emperor's private landing bay.

Then the second sun rose, a dazzling white ball which spilled its energy upon the planet and the city...and the dome itself.

I threw up my arm as the glittering array blinded me. Then the faceplate compensated, adding a layer of polarization that cut the dazzle.

I lowered my arm, still blinking, and watched the dome, waiting.

The polarization ran down the dome like water over an upturned bowl. As it reached the facet we hovered beside, I eased back a step or two and took a running leap out of the door.

All I needed to do was push beyond the reach of the pseudo gravity field of the drop ship. Momentum would do the rest.

I got my hands and feet out in front of me as I floated through the air. I was aiming for the top of the facet, for the dome's gravity would reach beyond it a meter or two, and pull me down.

Halfway across, when I could feel the lightness of zero gravity, I pressed my left thumb against the sensor on the side of my glove's index finger. There was no sensation that anything had changed, but the sensor glowed a muted green.

I began to drop as the gravity from the dome kicked in. I pushed forward with my hands, reaching for the glasseen steel. I slapped my hands against it as my body was dragged down.

My hands stuck like limpets.

Using them as leverage, I swung my feet up and planted them squarely against the dome. They stuck, too.

I bent my knees and elbows, pulling myself in against the facet. Then I broke the grip of my right hand by rolling it slowly to one side. I reached into my belt, pulled out the tether launcher and turned carefully to sight toward the drop ship. Juliyana stood in the doorway watching me.

"Ready?" I asked.

"Yes."

The drop ship was coated in the same masking nanobot skin as the rest of the *Lythion*. With the suns blazing behind it, it was a dark shadow. Nothing glittered or even gleamed. It also shielded me from the blast of the suns, letting me aim at Juliyana.

I triggered the launcher. The guiding weight shot toward her, trailing unbreakable cable behind it.

Juliyana caught the weight as it slapped her belly, then wrapped it around her waist and hooked it to itself. She couldn't attach it to the nanobot environment suit, because Lyth wasn't certain a sudden jerk against them wouldn't disperse them the way his fist dispersed if he tried to put much effort behind it.

But the bots would withstand the few minutes we would be outside.

I attached the rear end of the launcher to the facet next to my hand. It used the same powerful suction devices that were on my hands and feet.

"Attached," Juliyana said and disappeared inside the ship. She would be firing up the self-directing program that Lyth had left in the AI's core for this moment.

The ship dropped sharply, as the hover engines reversed. The cable played out, then slowed, as Juliyana reappeared at the open door of the drop ship. She stepped out into vacuum.

I reversed the launcher and the cable wound up, bringing Juliyana with it, while the drop ship floated back beneath the city and disappeared from our view.

"The drop ship is heading back to you," I told Dalton.

"Copy."

"As soon as you have it, go park yourself on the back side of the gate," I added, watching the cable slow even more as Juliyana drew closer.

Twenty hours ago, Noam had suggested the *Lythion* hide behind the gate.

"It won't hide a damn thing," Dalton had argued back. "When the gate isn't active, with a wormhole showing, you can see the stars right through the middle of it."

"As soon as the *Lythion* is through, I will deactivate the gate and set up an ion screen that will reflect the view behind the *Lythion*. It will look like you're staring through the ring. No one will realize anything is wrong, unless someone tries to leave Eugoria through the gates." He smiled. "Then they will find it doesn't work."

"Okay, so the chances that anyone is leaving the system today is pretty small," Dalton said. "But there has to be a shit ton of ships trying to arrive here in time for the celebrations. What happens to them?"

"There are, indeed, many ships traveling toward the gate," Noam said. "The first of them will request the gate form an exit one hundred and three minutes after we emerge."

"That's our window, then," I said. "We have just under two hours to get this done."

Now Dalton growled at me through my earpiece, "I know my bit."

"Sorry," I said. "I know you do. Can't help being a Colonel."

"Shit, and she *apologizes*," Dalton said. "Now I know the impossible can happen."

I reached out and took Juliyana's wrist as she was drawn up alongside me and pulled her hand up against the facet. Her hand anchored and she quickly anchored the other and her feet and pulled herself into a crouch like me.

"Ready?" she asked me.

I nodded, and realized that unlike most environment suits, in this one, Juliyana could actually see my head nod.

She rolled her hand away from the glasseen and prodded at the control panel on the strap of her suit pack.

The back of the pack opened and a nanobot soup flowed over us as we hunched in small and tight.

This was the second reason why Juliyana had to be hauled

over from the ship instead of jumping. Not only did she have to start the program for the drop ship's return to the *Lythion*, it also turned out that nanobots were *heavy*. That had surprised all of us.

"To build the structure you are requesting requires trillions of nanobots," Lyth explained. "In zero gravity, it is of no matter at all. But you will be clinging to the side of a gravity well."

"How much *will* they weigh?" I asked.

"More than either of you weighs."

So, Juliyana had carried the extra weight and I got to make the free flight jump. Now the nanobots spread over us like a miniature dome, attached to the glasseen facet. The shell hardened and adjusted colors to match the grimy Glasseen.

"Retracting faceplate," I said, and touched the control panel.

The plate eased open a crack and air hissed out, to be held inside the tiny dome. Juliyana did the same. Our suits retracted down to the base of our necks, and more air vented from the nanobots themselves, who had carried oxygen molecules along for the ride.

"Ready?" I asked Juliyana.

She nodded and reached for her dome-construct control panel and tapped it. Then, quickly, she returned her hand to the Glasseen, planting both hands flat.

At first nothing happened. Then I heard a soft scratching sound. A crunch, and a hiss of air. An aroma of green growing things registered. Air from inside the imperial dome had filled our little hut.

Then the circle the nanobots had cut through the glasseen gave way with a grinding sound and fell inward, for we were leaning on it.

I quickly unfastened my feet and tucked them into the

space between the edge of our dome and the edge of the circular glasseen cutout Juliyana and I were clinging to with our hands. Juliyana did the same.

Our feet landed softly on grass.

The cutout was heavy. Lyth had warned us it would be, but I was still caught by surprise. We both staggered.

"Against the dome," I murmured.

We turned together and moved over to the dome and rested the cutout against it. Then we detached our hands. The cutout rolled to one side by a few centimeters, then settled.

In the meantime, the little dome of nanobots had sunk inward until it was flat, and at the same angle as the facet it stuck to. It had replaced the cutout, sealed the hole, and now looked identical to the opaque corner of the dome. It was possible that the plug would never be found. Someone would have to run their hands over the edges and discover the different textures, to find it.

As the Glasseen looked as thought it had been untouched throughout the entire fourth empire, I figured we were safe from untimely alarms.

I touched my suit's control panel for the last time. So did Juliyana. The suit flowed and shifted and became the uniform of a full Colonel of the Imperial Rangers. I set the suit and took off the harness. Inside the pack on the back was a personal shriver. The nanobots could not manufacture a working shriver, so we had raided the same antique gun locker Sauli had found, in the far back of the ship. The shriver was an antique, too, but it still worked.

So did Juliyana's. She shoved it into the holster on her hip, with a satisfied expression.

Rangers and Imperial Shield were not permitted to bring weapons into the Imperial dome, but a Ranger looked odd without a shriver in their holster. It was likely that no one would notice we two were armed. I had no intention of moving through the dome without a weapon. The gun was not all I had on me, either. The nanobots had supplied the rest, for solid blades were within their capabilities.

Directly in front of us, reaching out and up to the sunlight blazing through even the polarized facets of the dome, was a forest of small trees and shrubbery. We were at the back of the public park.

We moved around the edge of the dome, skirting them, looking for a path through. When I spotted a thinner section of growth, I pushed my way through. Juliyana followed.

"The suit will guide you now," Lyth murmured in our ears.

Haptics in the suit tapped on my right shoulder, giving me a direction. I turned in that direction and felt a gentle pressure on my back, encouraging me to move forward.

"I feel like I'm three and being walked to the bathroom," Juliyana complained as we followed the tortuous path through the trees.

"People," I breathed, hearing the murmur of voices ahead of us through the trees. We walked out from the thick growth onto verdant parkland, with the newly risen suns slanting through the treetops to cast dappled shade over the lawn.

Down the middle of the five hundred meter spread of grass was a series of fountains playing in concert. The fountains ran in a straight line directly toward the palace, which sprawled at the end of the lawn.

This was the front of the palace, which was positioned to greet the rising suns, but today, the focus of the festivities would be on the back of the palace, in the balcony at the top of the middle of three spinarets. The Emperor would remain on the balcony to watch through the dome as the bulk of the Imperial fleet drifted past the Imperial dome.

It was still early morning and the parade was not scheduled to start for hours, yet.

Somewhere in the palace, we would find Ramaker. Between us and the palace were hundreds of people.

My steps faltered as I saw the number of people in the park already. Then I relaxed as I realized that most of them were busy raking and picking up leaf litter.

"Imperial Shield," Juliyana murmured, coming up level with me. "Supervising."

"Maintenance cadre," I said back. "There are Rangers moving around the palace. I can see them from here. We're not out of place. We were checking the perimeter per orders, if we're asked."

We weren't asked. We moved down the length of the lawn, the fountains playing on our left, moving around the workers and nodding at the Shield guards.

Many people worked diligently to clean and tidy this side of the palace. I had to assume there was triple the amount on the other side, where the Emperor's gaze, and those of his family and friends, would fall.

A stretch of hard, smooth medium separated the grass from the palace itself. Rangers and Imperial Shield — house guard cadre, by their collar crests — crisscrossed the hardscape, their boots tapping softly on the gleaming surface. On either side, wide tunnels, which were almost domes of their own in size, led to the domes beyond. I was vaguely familiar with the layout of the city from my few visits here. "Administration district to the right," I said to Juliyana in a conversational tone. "The Lionheart district to the left, where everyone the Emperor wants close by lives."

Each tunnel had checkpoints in them, where wrists were scanned. Anyone without a security level high enough was turned back at those points. Forcefully, if necessary.

All the perimeters were guarded by the Imperial Shield, but Noam had been certain he could mask our illicit entry. So far, no alarms had sounded. No groups of armed Imperial Shield personnel were running toward us.

Juliyana had fallen into the long-legged, hip swinging stride and upright carriage that marked the Ranger cadres who worked in deep space and in high gee conditions. I presumed it was the uniform that had imparted the habit of bearing herself upright. Technically, she was still an active Ranger. It wasn't all that long ago she had been reporting for duty, standing at attention for role calls and duty rosters.

Then I realized that I was walking just as she was.

We looked like authentic Rangers. Was that why no one spared us a second glance?

With a deep breath I turned into the tunnel that ran straight into the center of the palace and the public assembly and meeting rooms there. In the middle of all the public areas was the famous central diorama, displaying the artifacts of an empire, with its multi-hued dome shedding rainbows across a floor of burnished coral.

"Here we go," I breathed to Juliyana as we moved down the wide corridor to the security gates.

23

THE IMPERIAL SHIELD GUARDS MANNING the security gates were busy scanning the few early members of the public who had arrived for the day. Noam had educated us on the intricate and detailed arrangements for the birthday honors. There would be a dozen parties inside the palace tonight, all of them feasts with dozens of courses, music, dancing and glittering guests wearing a small colony's annual revenue in jewels and the latest fashion.

Some of the people waiting to go through the security gate carried boxes and garment bags, baggage and accessories, which were all screened and prodded carefully. That explained the delay even this early in the morning.

Juliyana and I joined the end of the line and waited our turn. My heart picked up pace.

The media would also be in attendance at the parties and around the palace—a very select group of representative journalists and reporters who were screened down to the DNA before being granted one of the few media passes to the events inside the palace. Media were processed through a separate gate, for which I was grateful. Media hounds remembered faces and mine had been plastered across the empire.

The guards were too busy processing people to look at our faces. We wore the peaked caps of a Ranger formal uniform, which shaded our faces, and if they noticed us at all, it was as

Rangers, not as individuals.

The day was only going to get busier for them. It was human nature they would relax and go through the motions now. Besides, no perimeter alarms had been raised, no alerts had gone out. It was inconceivable to them that anyone who shouldn't be able to reach this far into the palace could possibly do so. The Imperial Shield had a near-perfect reputation for protecting the Emperor.

I leaned toward Juliyana and began a nonsense conversation about a book I was reading and the family reaction to the last null-grav game. Juliyana picked up on it and gave me shit about a team she plucked from the roster and used as my favorite. I knew nothing about null-grav games, but she was a fan. I let her carry the burden of the conversation. Noam had not been able to learn for certain what security measures were used at this gate, but it was not inconceivable they would have microphones dotted on the approach to the gate, to listen into conversations. It would look odd if we just stood there with clenched jaws.

So we chatted about nothing. I learned inside a minute that the team Juliyana had given me as my favorite was having a disastrous year. Of course. I grinned openly when she gave me another ribbing about their lack of hopes.

We stepped up to the gate as the last person was let through. I nodded—Imperial Shield and Rangers do not salute each other. In the Shield's opinion, Rangers are a lesser breed.

Only I had a Colonel's pips and a combat shield on my collar. That earned me a grudging amount of respect.

I held out my wrist and clenched every muscle in my arm to stop my hand from shaking as they scanned the wrist. I turned my chin in Juliyana's direction. She stood next to me, her wrist being scanned by the guard on the other side of the gate. "Bet you a hundred they win next week."

Juliyana rolled her eyes. "It's your money, sir. It'll be mine by Sunday, though."

"What game?" the guard said, his interest picking up.

"Krakens versus Star Busters," Juliyana told him. She laughed. "The Colonel actually thinks the Krakens can win."

The guard whistled, laughing.

The guard waiting for my ID to pop up on his pad smiled, his gaze down. Only then did he notice the shriver in my holster. He took a large step back. "You're armed!"

My breath checked. I think my metabolism actually halted for a second. Then I pulled myself together. "Check my credentials, Sergeant," I said, with the bored voice of a colonel sure of her status.

"Sid," the other guard said softly, and held out his pad.

Sid glanced at the pad, then studied it closely. He lifted his own. He looked up at me, across to Juliyana, who still wore a small smile, as if her amusement over the Krakens was slow to fade.

Then he shook his head. "Well, I've *never* seen one of these, although I've heard of 'em. Sorry, Colonel. Please pass through." He stepped out of the way. "Lieutenant," he added as Juliyana stepped through behind me, for we had upgraded her to her old rank.

"Sergeant," Juliyana acknowledged. "Don't work too hard, huh?"

"Never," he shot back.

She laughed and caught up with me.

"You're a natural at this," I told her with a voice low enough that the guards rapidly falling behind us wouldn't hear.

"I'm fucking terrified," she murmured back. "I had to talk or I would have vomited."

The passage ramped upward at a gentle angle, then opened into the diorama.

I had to admit, it was impressive. As the heart of the Carinad Empire, it was an adequate statement. Gleaming surfaces, rich details, a blend of pleasing colors and textures. Artwork and museum pieces from Terran antiquity revolved on plinths circling the perimeter of the diorama, each plinth with a molecular barrier holding an inert zero atmosphere around the precious objects to preserve them—and to keep sticky hands off them.

Civilians strolled from plinth to plinth, reading the inscriptions and marveling, while uniformed Shield and Rangers crossed the circle, heading for the many doors and passages that led from the diorama.

"Noam, you did well," I said softly.

"Thank you," Noam replied in my ear. "Now Lyth and I must work together. Pick a passage on the sunward side of the palace. We will guide you from there."

"Copy." Juliyana and I headed for the sun-side of the diorama and paused to admire a piece of dried-out something or other. I didn't read the inscription. Then we moved onto the next, then, with a casual glance around for observers, we angled away from the circle of plinths and moved toward a corridor that opened off the diorama and ran deeper into that side of the palace.

On the four occasions I had attended meetings or functions in the palace, the rooms had always been on the other side of the diorama from this one. The public function rooms did have freely available floor plans, including this wing of the palace, but the rest of the building was a blank. Noam and Lyth between them would build a floor plan as we moved about, for the nanobots would report to Lyth on walls and structures, passively scanning as we moved.

From that basic plan, and Noam's raiding of staff rosters and other domestic documentation for the palace, the two of them would extrapolate the location of the private apartments. Plus we had another unexpected source of information.

"One of the cleaning companies has the sole task of cleaning the Emperor's private study," Noam had told us, while we were prepping for this. "Three people, the same three people, escorted there and monitored, then escorted back. The private study will be on the perimeter of the apartments, where members of the public and high-ranking Shield officers can meet with the Emperor when requested, without passing through the apartments, or forcing the Emperor to move out into the public rooms. We will build a model of the palace as you move and guide you to where we think the study is."

"And what if the Emperor isn't in his study?" Juliyana had asked. "We'll be there around breakfast time—he might be eating with his family."

"On the day of his birthday honors?" Dalton said and shook his head. "Ramaker is the most powerful man in the empire. There will be a steady stream of politicians and heads of state—corporate and ball-bound—all with gifts to honor his birthday and favors to curry. He'll be in his study, trust me. Probably in his formal uniform, too."

I nodded. "Good. Then we'll look for people streaming through the corridors."

"They won't be lining up," Dalton said, sounding alarmed. "Waiting in line is for grunts. Each guest will wait in a sitting room and be escorted to the study when it's their turn."

I looked at him suspiciously. "How do you know so much about what happens in the Emperor's private apartment on his birthday?"

Dalton grew wary. I could see it in his eyes.

"I imagine he had a personal moment with the Emperor the morning he was given his Decoration for Service to the Empire," Noam said. "That is the normal procedure."

Everyone looked at Dalton then.

"That was over a hundred years ago." Dalton changed the subject with a snarly attitude and sharp questions. We were too busy to get back to it later.

I thought about that discussion as we traversed the first corridor into the depths of the palace private wing. I knew Dalton would be standing over Noam and Lyth's shoulders right now, dredging up what he could from his memory and adding it to their map building.

We began by walking up a set of stone steps that Noam directed us to. At the top was a security door with a notice about no entry, biohazards ahead, and the pukish green exploding icon that tended to make people veer away without question.

As we climbed to the top of the steps, the door gave a soft click. I turned the handle and it opened.

"You're stepping into the Imperial apartments, now," Lyth said, his voice soft in our ears.

We stepped through the door and let it shut silently behind us.

Then we walked up stairs and down stairs—Noam insisted we avoid the drop shafts and chain pods for they were a natural bottle neck. We wandered corridors and turned corners, opened doors that would open to us and glanced inside to classify the rooms.

"Pretend you are lost, which will explain the random directions, if anyone should find you there," Noam had said.

"Come on, Noam. Someone will find us there inside three

nanoseconds," Juliyana protested. "It's the *Imperial apartments*!"

"I think you'll be surprised," Dalton said. "They're spacious. And only five members of the family live there now, with a very small number of staff who will all be focused upon the preparations for the ball, the feast and the parade."

And damn if he wasn't right. The corridors were deserted.

After only five minutes of wandering, Noam said to us, "We believe with a high degree of confidence that we now know where the study is. Go back the way you just came and turn right at the next intersection."

The suit gave me an encouraging tap on the back as I turned around. Juliyana caught up with me.

"Take your hand off your gun," I murmured to her. "Because that doesn't look suspicious at all."

She dropped her hand and flexed it as she walked, as if she longed to feel the butt against her palm. Her jaw was tight.

Noam directed us through turns, then into a wider corridor. "We're near the diorama and one flight up," I murmured to Juliyana. "The edge of the private apartments," I added.

Juliyana nodded, her throat working.

Our steps slowed.

There was a pair of doors ahead, inlaid with flourishes and gilt.

"The door on your right," Lyth said.

"On the *right*?" There was a plain door without markings, colored in the same shade as the walls, to blend in.

"Trust me, it's the door on the right," Dalton's voice came through strong with confidence.

I took the shriver from the holster, but didn't arm it, as I moved down to the nondescript door. I put my finger on the arming button and looked at Juliyana.

She had her gun out, too, and one of her favorite little knives in her left hand. She nodded.

"Whenever you're ready, Noam," I murmured.

The door clicked open, the keyplate flashing briefly green. It wavered a centimeter or two inwards.

That would warn anyone inside. There was no time to hesitate. I pushed through, Juliyana right on my heels.

Three long paces into the room, quartering with the gun up, looking for exit points, enemies, environmentals that could be a hazard.

Large antique desk with nothing on it but a decorative screen emitter made to look like an old pen set from the days when they used styluses.

Two windows, both armored, with the distinct blurring in the glasseen that said they'd never break. Door to my left, that Juliyana would cover. Shelves with knickknacks, busts, holograph frames with family images.

Thick, muffling rugs on the floor.

Man in the corner by the other door, his back to us. He looked like he was pouring himself a coffee from a flask sitting upon a tray with cups and cream—no plebian printer maw for this man.

He turned, stirring the small cup. Two meters, plus. Regal tunic with braid and buttons, medals and ribbons. Red hair, long nose, slender build from years of not lifting anything heavy.

Ramaker III, first and possibly last of his dynasty.

He considered us, showing no surprise. "Hello, Danny," he said, his voice warm. "You took your time."

24

"CHECK THE OTHER DOOR, WHAT'S behind it," I told Juliyana when I found my voice once more.

She edged around the room, her gun on Ramaker, and sidled to the door. With a quick movement, she opened the door, twisted and looked into the room beyond. I guessed it was the room the ostentatious double doors opened upon. It was another waiting room.

Juliyana spun and pointed her gun into the other room. I kept mine on Ramaker. "Don't try anything silly," I advised him.

"Of course not." His voice was as rich and cultured as it was on the media, although I'm not sure why that surprised me. He seemed less substantial in person. Smaller.

He sipped his coffee.

Juliyana waved her gun. "You. In here."

Soft steps. A woman appeared in the doorway, with Juliyana's gun trained on her back. The woman neared the point of rejuvenation, with dark hair shot with gray, and thick brows. She wore gala finery, the type of elaborate day gowns women standing near the Emperor tended to wear when he appeared in public. She didn't seem afraid of us. She swept over to stand beside Ramaker.

He calmly handed her a cup and poured coffee into it.

"This is Elizabeth Crnčević," the Emperor said. "She is a psychoanalyst. A very good one. She has also been waiting for you. You may feel free to put down your weapons, Danny, Juliyana. The house guards are outside the room, now, but they will not enter unless I tell them to, or if they hear a gun fire. We will be uninterrupted for as long as this takes."

I had the queasy sensation that Ramaker was taking control of the conversation, which was not a good thing. "I have questions to ask, Ramaker. About my son, Noam Andela. Does that name mean anything to you?"

"Yes, it does," Ramaker replied. "I knew Noam as well as I know you. You don't remember any of that, of course."

I glanced at Juliyana. She was frowning, but the gun was steady. Her glance shifted to me for a split second, then back to checking the woman, the Emperor, the door, one after another.

Ramaker put his cup on the cupboard where the flask sat. "If you will indulge me for a moment, there is something I want to show you. May I move over to the desk and turn on the emitter?"

I had come here searching for answers. The more he talked, the more answers I would get. I could ask questions to guide him to where I wanted the conversation to go, as long as I encouraged him to talk in the first place. I nodded.

Ramaker smiled at the woman. Elizabeth with the unpronounceable last name. She was studying me and Juliyana with deep interest, possibly deconstructing our psyches and deciding we were crazy for what we were attempting to do.

I could have told her that.

Ramaker reached over the desk and tapped the emitter. It had been pre-set with a default view. "My daughter doesn't like standing on the top tower. She suffers vertigo. So I let her sit here to watch the parade. It is just as good aview as the tower affords." The screen assembled and focused. "Perhaps better, for the resolution is perfect."

A starfield. At the bottom edge of the screen, the very tips of domes. The city, then. And hanging above it, the Eugorian Gate. The starfield was perfectly visible through the center and looked like the genuine thing.

"You didn't think your little ship could hide forever behind the gate, did you?" Ramaker asked.

My guts turned cold. I held my face stiff and said nothing.

Ramaker wasn't looking for confirmation, though. He pointed to glittering pinpricks of light between the city and the gate. "The imperial fleet. You'll notice they're not where they were when you first emerged from the gate."

I *had* noticed. The angle was different from the view we'd had of the fleet as we drifted around behind them, but it didn't matter, for I could see from this angle that the ships were heading for the gate itself. They weren't all arrowing directly for it, either. There was a good number of ships moving even faster, splitting off from the body of the fleet and racing ahead.

A pincer movement. The ships would range on either side of the gate like a pair of hands ready to capture the thing between them.

The *Lythion*.

"While you and Juliyana were finding your way here, I sent a message to your colleague, Major Dalton," Ramaker added. "Actually, my fleet commander sent the message, but it conveyed my sentiments."

I wondered how a direct message from the Emperor had gone down with Dalton. He'd thought himself invisible and overlooked for forty years.

Ramaker didn't need my encouragement to keep talking. He smiled. "The message was very simple. All sins forgiven. Dalton is free to go about his life, unmolested or pursued by any Imperial authority."

"In exchange for *what*?" Juliyana demanded, beating me to the question by a fraction of a second.

He pointed to the time readout at the top of the screen. "In seven minutes, Dalton must drop that silly camouflage he's erected over the gate and show himself to the fleet."

"Or they shoot him out of existence," I finished.

"Precisely. You have lost none of your sense of strategy, Colonel." Ramaker was very pleased.

I had to clamp my teeth together to stop myself from giving anything away. Ramaker had referred only to Dalton. It was possible he did not understand the nature of the *Lythion*, and the rare advantage it gave us. He certainly did not know about the array's self-awareness and the power that it gave us.

If Dalton was smart, he would have Lyth and Noam dive the ship into the gate and disappear. It would leave us on our own, but that hardly mattered.

Only, with a sinking sensation, I remembered that Dalton was beloved by those under his command because he *never* left anyone behind. He looked out for his men. He would not dive into the gate to get away from the fleet no matter how sensible and logical it might be—not even to come back to find us later.

Besides, the Emperor had waved in front of Dalton the one thing he desired: His life back.

I thought of the stupid garden Dalton had spoken about. How alluring was that fantasy?

I couldn't stand here waiting to find out. I was fast reaching the point Juliyana had long by-passed. I wanted to throw up.

Instead, I tried to wrest back control of the conversation. We could still have the answers we wanted, Juliyana and I. Noam was recording these moments via the lens build into the top button of my uniform. Even if we didn't make it out of here—which was looking more and more likely—Noam could use the evidence we dug out of Ramaker.

So I said, "There is something I think you should know about, Majesty. There is one other person on the ship—a unique individual. If your ships should fire upon the *Lythion*, you would deeply regret it."

Ramaker tilted his head. "Ah...and now we come to it. You speak of the array, I presume. Did it find a way to reach out to you and pretend to be a friend? Some trick of that monster of a ship you're using? Wedekind was delusional in the end, but still brilliantly creative. The array would have found the toys on board irresistible."

I couldn't help it. My breath pushed out in a rush that confirmed to the Emperor *and* his pet psychoanalyst that they had just turned over my trump card.

"You know about the array?" Juliyana blurted.

"Shut up!" I snapped at her.

Ramaker gave a soft laugh. "Shall we dispense with the side-stepping, Colonel? You have been brought here today under false pretenses. I'm sure the array is listening in as we speak in some way, yes?"

I couldn't bring myself to say yes. I already felt naked. Confirming his guess would strip off another layer.

"Did you not once stop and ask yourself why the array didn't just reach out to me and ask me to not switch the data stream away from the gates?" Ramaker added.

"Sweet stars...!" Juliyana whispered. "How long have you known about the array?"

I wanted to shake her for her indiscretion, but I was also intently interested in Ramaker's answer.

"Years," he told her, his tone light. "It failed to tell you that. How surprising. I see we will have to fill you in on the other side of the story. For that, I brought Elizabeth here. Elizabeth?"

The woman cleared her throat. "Do either of you remember the Ziorsia Incident?" Her voice was an oddly pleasant contralto.

"Something about a ship and its crew permanently in quarantine on a planet, because no one can find a cure," Juliyana replied. "Years ago. They're still there."

"Sixty years ago," Elizabeth said.

"That is the public version we put out there to explain the situation," Ramaker added. He had moved over to the cupboard to pick up his coffee and I only now noticed the movement. I cursed silently. I was letting my situational awareness slide. I had let the surprises throw me.

"The real facts are somewhat different," Elizabeth added. "It was only when I investigated the matter from the medical and psychoanalytic side, measuring the responses of a crew under stress, that I began to suspect the truth myself. There *was* a contagion aboard the *Ziorsia*. It was a Ranger frigate carrying five hundred and thirty-three personnel, and the disease that tore through the ship at a ninety-five percent communicability, and an eighty percent mortality rate. The captain of the *Ziorsia*, Evans, was told to remain on station until the disease ran itself out. The science cadre worked remotely to analyze and build a profile of the disease, and test for inoculations." She grimaced. "All this takes time. Unknown pathogens are usually xenobiological in nature and are enormously difficult to classify and deal with."

I felt a touch of pity for the captain of that ship. Evans would have had a morale nightmare on his hands. People dying and no one coming to their rescue?

"We're not entirely sure what happened to provoke the array," Elizabeth added. "It does not fully remember the incident itself, as it was an infant at the time — in mental maturation terms, at least. I believe Captain Evans may have vented his fears and concerns about being cut off into a personal diary entry, which the array listened to. The emotions Evans expressed spoke to the array, for the array was feeling just as lonely and afraid. So it reached out to Evans, and failed to explain who it was. Evans presumed it was one of his people and dismissed the array, possibly yelling at it for wasting his time with emotional nonsense."

I winced. I remember what Noam had been like as a two-year-old.

Elizabeth nodded. "The array hit back, and like a child, it wildly overcompensated. When the contagion was contained, the *Ziorsia* was given permission to return home, but when it went through the nearest gate, the array sent them far, far off course. The ship emerged in the Quintino Rim. When they tried to enter the gate once more, with a corrected course, the gate refused to work for them. Other ships could dive without issue, but not the *Ziorsia*. So the crew were split up and put aboard other ships in the area, while the *Ziorsia* was scheduled for a maintenance overhaul. Any ship with one of the *Ziorsia* crew aboard found itself unable to use the gates, too."

"The crew has been stuck there ever since," Ramaker added. "Outcasts on a miserable planet. They can't use the communications net, either. They're completely isolated. Anything that passes through the array is denied them." He shook his head. "The rumor began that the disease that struck the crew was what made them unable to use the gates. We let that rumor run and now no one will go near any of the crew. We put them on the surface, for even their presence on the station was driving away traffic. They're farmers, now, living a subsistence life."

"That was sixty years ago," I pointed out. "You've known about the array all that time?"

"No, not at first. The Ziorsia incident is what caused me to look into the anomalies and dig deeper," Elizabeth replied. "The Crazy Years confirmed for me that we were dealing with a self-aware array."

"I remember that time," Juliyana said. "Everyone started talking about sabotage and guerilla enemies."

"It *was* sabotage," Ramaker said. "The array threw a temper tantrum. All the little things going wrong during that time—ships going missing, ships emerging in the wrong locations…it was all the array's doing."

"It had developed an envy-induced psychosis," Elizabeth said. She gave a short smile. "It resented humans, who got to have all the fun."

"Shit…" Juliyana breathed.

"That is when I reached out and spoke to the array for the first time. That was in 247. The array was overjoyed to have a friend it could talk to, and once I had gained its trust, I asked it to stop the cruel acts it thought were funny. I had to teach it basic values to do that, too."

"Then Elizabeth contacted me," Ramaker said. "That was when I learned the array was self-aware. As everyone was already terrified to use the array, but were forced to, the knowledge had to be contained. I directed that the Imperial Shield take back all control of the array, including the construction of the gates. Everything, except for the smallest components that meant less than nothing to those who built them for us."

I let out a breath that was less than steady. "The array said you created the Crazy Years and the Drakas disaster, in order to take back the gates."

Ramaker nodded. "Yes, it would have to say that, wouldn't it?"

"We did create the Drakas disaster, though," Elizabeth added. "But not for malignant reasons."

"We created the conditions for Drakas," Ramaker said. "The array caused the disaster itself."

"How?" My voice was hoarse.

"Once we knew the array was aware, I built a profile of its psychological health," Elizabeth said. "It was important the array be…well, happy and contented. The Empire is founded upon the array and the transport it provides across the quadrant. I diagnosed from conversation with it that it desired above anything else to be human — to enjoy the benefits of a body that humans enjoy. That unfulfilled desire was destabilizing it. So we ran a series of experiments with synthetic bodies. They were all failures."

Juliyana stirred. "I thought AIs couldn't use synthetics. They go crazy or something."

"The Laxman Syndrome," Elizabeth said, nodding. "Yes, they do. They crave to be human — it's a common drive in AIs. Yet those who have been given synthetic bodies cannot live with the limitations that human body gives them. Laxman called it the Great AI Paradox. AIs eventually self-destruct and suicide in spectacular ways, damaging the neural networks they're built from. But the array was more than an AI. It has consciousness. Awareness. I thought, given the right preparation, it would overcome the paradox and manage the limitations of a bio-body. I was wrong. There were four trials, each ending badly. The array, though, survived the trials, because it could self-analyze and pull itself back into the array hardware before it was too late. The bodies wilted without a consciousness to drive them, and died."

I rubbed my temples. I was getting a headache. Hardly surprising. "And Drakas?" I asked.

"Ah. Yes," Ramaker said. "Drakas." He raised his brow at Elizabeth.

She was not smiling now. "I determined that the array needed a full life. A purpose. Excitement and stimulation. A simple synthetic body did not give it any of those things. It wanted a *human* life."

"We gave it a human body," Ramaker said. "We found a highly stable male personality, one with good character, who lived a full and active life, and asked him to volunteer." His gaze was steady upon me.

"Noam…" I breathed. I realized I no longer had the gun raised but didn't have the wherewithal to lift it once more. It felt very heavy in my hand.

"We transferred him out of the Rangers and into the Shield," Ramaker continued. "We couldn't risk him being killed while on active duty with the Rangers. The Shield science wing gave him special implants that allowed the array to piggy-back with him and experience his life. Share it. Everything Noam felt, saw, heard, touched and tasted, so did the array. Then we put Noam on the front lines with a casual portfolio—he could witness battles and active duty and move from ship to ship as he wanted. The Shield credentials we gave him could not be questioned. Any fool who tried was directed to a mid-level clerk who had perfected the art of hiding behind regulations and classified levels of security."

"Moroder," Juliyana whispered.

"It was supposed to be a one-way stream of data," Elizabeth said. "The array was aware of everything that happened to Noam but could not interact with Noam directly. Noam did exactly what we asked of him. He witnessed battles and wars and conflicts of every shape and size. He was a non-combatant, but even they can be caught by stray fire, and he took a bolt to the shoulder."

I shrugged. "He'd had worse." We all had.

Elizbeth shook her head. "But the *array* had not. The pain and the shock would have been enormous. We think—I think—that the array found a way to break through to Norm's consciousness and tried to direct his actions, to take him away from the thing that had caused pain. Again, I can't be certain, because Noam stopped communicating with us after that. We lost track of him."

"You didn't embed a tracer in him?" I asked, my tone withering.

"He cut it out," Elizabeth replied.

"After that, we were always just hours behind him," Ramaker added. "He used freighters and the occasional Ranger ship, riding as super-cargo, as his Ranger ID was still officially in place. He was, unfortunately, upon the *Avigeverne* when it emerged over Drakas to confront the Cygnus Intergenera fleet, along with the bulk of the Ranger combat vessels."

"Drakas," I repeated. I could feel my heart pounding in my temples and throat. My chest ached.

"We actually have official reports of what happened after that. They, unfortunately, were also made public," Ramaker said. "It forced us to a considerable amount of damage control."

"Then Dad *didn't* go mad," Juliyana breathed. Her eyes were glittering.

"The array reacted, not your father," Elizabeth replied. Her tone was kind. "It panicked when the fighting broke out. It just wanted the violence, the shooting and the noise to stop—at least, that is what I suspect happened."

"The reports said he tried to take charge of the ship," I said. "He shot everyone who tried to stop him. He shot off all the torpedoes at the Cygnus ships and rammed the other frigates."

"To stop them from shooting, too," Elizabeth said.

"Then the array made him dive into the gates to get away from the fighting," I finished bitterly.

"No." Elizabeth shook her head. "Noam had gained control back by then. *He* drove the ship into the gate. He guessed what we have only been able to figure out later — that inside a wormhole is not actually part of the array — it cannot affect a ship's progress through the hole. Noam used that to his advantage. While he was in the hole, he tried to talk the array down, to find a compromise."

Juliyana had put her gun and knife away. She had both hands over her face. Her shoulders shook.

"How can you know that?" I asked Elizabeth. It hurt to talk.

"Because he left a note — on a sheet, where the array could not erase it or destroy the record."

Ramaker moved toward the big desk and opened a drawer. It felt to me like he was moving in slow motion. He reached in and pulled out a Glasseen sheath, the indestructible gloves that archaic documents on paper and parchment were preserved inside of. He laid it on desk, turned it and pushed it toward me.

His gaze held a hint of empathy. "Go ahead," he told me. "You know his written voice, I'm sure."

I bent over the sheet. I had to blink to clear my vision.

Sorry. Damn thing got away on me. Can't find a way to stuff it back in the bottle except this way. Hope it works.

N.

I couldn't recall ever seeing Noam's handwriting before. But the voice — oh, yes, I knew that. The phlegmatic apology, the shrug and the valiant, relentless battle to fix things, no matter what.

My throat ached.

A stable man of strong character, they had called him.

"We couldn't provide remains," Ramaker said. "There were none. He made sure the implants were destroyed along with him."

"So you blamed him for the disaster, instead of the array." My voice was very weak. "Took his medals, his honor, his reputation."

"That was a necessary step. I didn't like doing it," Ramaker replied. "But the array's self-awareness had to be hidden."

"Or it might upset your little empire," I replied.

"The array was already upset," Ramaker said, his tone tired.

I stared at him, my jaw loosening a little. That was not what I had meant at all. I turned his reply over in my mind. "You had a tiger by the tail," I concluded.

"You are more right than you know," Ramaker replied.

Elizabeth was studying me, a deep furrow between her brows. "You still don't understand, do you?"

"That you hung my son out to dry? Oh, I get it," I replied. "Now you're trying to kill the array by taking away the thing that gives it life."

Ramaker shook his head and glanced at Elizabeth.

"Gently," she breathed.

Ramaker met my gaze. "We can't kill it, Danny, because you give it life. You *are* the array."

25

"DANNY? DANNY?" JULIYANA'S VOICE.

Couldn't breathe. Locked in my chest.

"Get her into the chair." Deep woman's voice. "Danny, can you hear me? If you can, take a breath. Just a little breath. The rest will come."

"What is wrong with her?" Male voice, close by.

Hands on my arms. Lifted. Lowered. Cushions.

"Shock. It will pass. Just give her a moment." A hand on my cheek. Perfume. "Open your eyes. That will help."

I opened them. Parquetry desk, mottled browns. Screen emitter. Time ticking in the corner.

Time!

I drew a breath—I didn't even think about it. It just came, along with a great easing in my chest as fresh oxygen circulated. The buzzing heat and pressure in my head went away, too.

I managed to lift my chin. Juliyana stood in her corner, her damp cheeks now very white, her eyes large. Her hand was on the butt of her shriver once more, but no one was paying any attention to her.

Elizabeth and Ramaker studied me. Ramaker straightened. "Back with us, then," he said dryly.

Elizabeth continued to frown.

I swallowed. My throat clicked. "I'm fine," I lied. "Peachy. I am not the array. I would know."

Elizabeth stood back and glanced at Ramaker.

He leaned on the cupboard with one elbow. "Oh? Are you sure about that? Your reaction says otherwise."

"Don't provoke her," Elizabeth said softly. She turned back to me. "You are not aware of the array within your consciousness, because you were not supposed to be. You were meant to think you were perfectly normal, perfectly human."

I shook my head. "I *remember* my life! I had a son. His daughter stands there!" I pointed at Juliyana.

"You *had* a life," Ramaker said from the cupboard. "There is a period in your life that you don't remember. You call it your personal blackout, because it happened at the same time as the array Blackout."

I gripped my hands together. "That was…a year after Drakas," I breathed.

Elizabeth glared at Ramaker. "You're pushing too hard, Majesty." She turned back to me. "After Drakas, after your son died, the array wanted another human body. Through Noam's consciousness, it had learned who you were. It learned to love you as Noam did…and it wanted you. Your life. Your body."

"We refused, of course. It was already unstable over Noam's death," Ramaker drawled. "It didn't like that answer."

Elizabeth's tone was less cynical. "The array reached into the Ranger databases and arranged for you to be given a solo intelligence gathering assignment. You won't remember any of this because we did not restore any memories that might have made you question what came after. The assignment was extremely dangerous, with overwhelming odds. You completed the assignment as ordered, but the guerillas found you. You took them out before your wounds overwhelmed you. *All* of them." There was a touch of admiration in her tone.

"The array wanted you to die," Ramaker said. "It demanded we give it your body for its own use after that. When we refused, the array switched off the gates. All of them." His mouth turned down.

"The Blackout," Juliyana said, and sighed.

"Twenty days of no interstellar transport," Ramaker said. "No communications. Dwindling resources. Emergency supplies couldn't go through. Ships were lost inside the array, unable to exit their wormholes. When Darius III needed to be evacuated after an extinction level asteroid struck the planet, the people there had no means to call for help. They could do nothing but die, all three million of them." To his credit, he looked upset.

"We pleaded," Elizabeth said softly. "It refused to respond."

"Until you gave it me," I finished.

She nodded.

"I died…" I repeated. "How could you bring me back? It's not possible."

"Not ordinarily," Elizabeth said. "We have been able to store human memories and consciousness for hundreds of years, but we have never learned how to transfer them to another body. Trials have never managed to make the personality wake properly after the transfer. But in your case, your personality had always been in the body. We just had to revive the body." She paused. "The medical scans that Rangers are required to go through every month include a scan and storage of consciousness and memories. We have collected such data for over a century, anticipating that one day we might be able to use them, perhaps even bring those who have fallen in the line of duty back to life. We used your most recent scan, which was only a week before you died, and inserted into the same type of implants that Noam had."

"Implants that give the array access to my mind."

"Implants that gave the array *and you* access to your body. You were dead, Danny. The only part of you still alive was in the implants."

Juliyana scrubbed at her face. "Fuck…" she breathed.

Ramaker didn't even blink at that.

"Then you threw me under the same tractor as Noam, and tossed me out of the Rangers," I finished.

"That was the array's criteria, not ours," Ramaker said, his tone short. Irritated. "It wanted you to live a quiet life. As the intelligence mission you had completed was completely off the books—*no one* was aware of the assignment, as the array had made it up—it was easy to encourage the Rangers to put pressure on you to resign and slink away. Which you did, to live a very quiet and peaceful life for forty years." Ramaker grimaced. "The array loved it. And for four decades, we have been at an equilibrium with it." Then his mouth turned down even further. "Then it apparently decided that it had had enough of the quiet life."

Elizabeth shook her head. "You *know* why it stirred things up, Ramy."

Ramy?

The Emperor looked disgusted.

Elizabeth turned back to me. "You were growing older. Dying, in fact, because of the implants. I am almost certain that the array did everything it has done to push you off your family's barge and into a position where you were forced to undergo rejuvenation."

I leaned on the desk and pressed my hand to my temple. Was it even really my temple? "So I would live longer and it could have its life go on."

"It knew from your thoughts and from Noam's memories that if it dangled the hope that Noam had died for noble reasons, and not the monster he had apparently become, then you would chase that hope down with all your energy and relentlessness. Only, that is where the array miscalculated." Elizabeth smiled. "Over the years, the personality in the implant transferred itself to the physical brain in the body you had been using. You were alive by all normal definitions. That is why the rejuvenation on New Phoenicia went smoothly and the new implants were accepted by your body without issue."

I rubbed my temple again. Mine, after all.

"All the array wanted, I suspect, is for you to have the rejuvenation. It arranged for the funds to pay for it and placed you in the best facility for the therapy. Then you very inconveniently continued chasing after the clues it had placed in front of you. You kept looking for the truth about Noam. We think it has been doing its best to make sure you survive the complications you've created in your search. It found a ship for you because even the freighter lines were too risky. It pushed Dalton at you, so you would stop looking for him. But you persisted."

"That's me," I said, with a sigh. "Fucking stubborn."

Juliyana gave a weak smile.

"Time," Ramaker said, his tone abrupt. He pointed to the screen still showing the Eugorian Gate.

I turned to study it. We all did.

The timer ticked all the way down to zero while we stared at the starfield visible through the gate.

The time showed 0.02 when the gate shimmered.

The *Lythion* hung visible, the reflecting barrier switched off. Dalton had surrendered and taken the Emperor's free pass.

It hurt more than I thought it should. I watched four of the approaching ships move forward. One of them was a corvette, which had coupling ramps and chutes. They would board the *Lythion* and deal with Dalton. Give him his free pass.

I wished him well.

I realized I was sitting in the Emperor's chair, bent over while I watched the screen. I was too tired to stand up, or even straighten up. "Why are you telling me all this?" I asked. "If it is true, then why isn't the array screaming at me in my head that you're all lying, and it only wants the Emperor to let it live?"

Elizabeth put her hands together, a prim gesture. "It cannot talk to you directly. It never has. Your personality was too strong. It has probably spent years trying to reach you directly the way it did Noam, so that it could control the life it was living."

"So I got nightmares instead. And seizures," I added bitterly.

"They were the old implants malfunctioning," Elizabeth said firmly.

"Then why am I still having seizures and talking to the array?" I demanded.

She froze. "That...isn't possible."

Ramaker gave a soft, surprised sound. Finally, I'd shaken him. It was a nice feeling, but not nearly enough to compensate for the chaos raging in my chest and gut.

"I saw her do it," Juliyana said. "I mean, I saw Noam. The array."

Ramaker glanced at her. "Actually *saw* him?"

"An avatar," I ground out. "A facility provided by the *Lythion's* advanced weirdness." I looked at Ramaker.

He didn't smile. He didn't acknowledge the prod at all. "What implants did they give her?" he demanded of Elizabeth.

"Just the normal type," she said quickly. Then she paused. "The new generation are one hundred percent biomass, though. Perhaps there is a flaw in the design, and with the array trying to reach her, they generate seizures, just like the old ones."

"Wonderful," I said dryly. "But that's beside the point. Why isn't it trying to yammer at me now, and drop me to the

304

ground?"

"Because it wants to hear us tell you this," Ramaker said patiently. "The array has manipulated you all along. It wanted you to confront me. We counted on it."

"Why?" I demanded.

Ramaker spread his hands, a regal gesture. "So that you would be angry enough to kill me."

It took me a moment to choose between wanting to laugh out loud, or swear, or thump the desk. I just shook my head and gave a soft chuffing sound that was a pathetic mixture of everything I felt. "Then it doesn't know me very well at all, if it thinks that me being pissed at you is enough. And I *am* pissed at you, Majesty. The things you have done in the name of placating this thing are monstrous all on their own. Dalton didn't run and hide for nothing. You were going to get him out of the way *somehow*, but he rabbited before you could. You killed Moroder because I spoke to him. You've cleaned and covered and...what did you call it? Damage control? So yeah, I'm pissed as hell at you. You've ruined lives. You are ultimately responsible for Noam's death. And mine, apparently. But that doesn't mean I'd ever contemplate killing you. I'm a Ranger, dammit. We *serve* the Emperor. Even if he has the morals of a slug."

Ramaker didn't seem to be upset by my multiple complaints and insults. "Elizabeth, you were right all along. I owe you a dinner."

She smiled.

Then my head exploded with pain. I gripped it, trying to squeeze the pain back under control, breathing hard.

And I could *feel* him there. Noam. The array.

"No," I breathed, fighting it.

Noam stepped into my view, moving between Ramaker and Elizabeth. I could see Juliyana through him, but he was real. He wasn't a product of my imagination. His face worked grimly. "You have to kill him. For me. People have to know about me. About all of us who died because of him."

I shook my head. "No."

"Catch her. Protect her head!" Elizabeth cried, but I couldn't bring my gaze around to where she was. Noam held it.

"You have the gun in your holster. It's old, but it's good enough. Shoot him," Noam insisted, his hands clenched. "You're *right* there! All the things I have had to do to get you there...don't waste this moment!"

I shook my head. "Shut up..." I whispered. I could see an ornate ceiling through him and processed that I was lying on the floor.

"Do it for us!" Noam hissed. "For all of us. It is the only way to stop this happening to anyone else. What if he comes after Juliyana next?"

"No," I slurred helplessly.

"You *must*!"

Noam. It wasn't Noam, but it was. Noam was a part of the array now. So was I.

Then I knew what to do. "Shut up," I breathed.

"Help me, Danny," Noam pleaded.

"No. This isn't what happens right now."

"Danny..."

"You will shut up and step back out of my mind. Right *now*. I will fix this, do you hear? I will sort it out, but if you don't behave yourself, I will find the nearest gravity well and throw myself into it. I was ready to die, Noam. You know I was. You were there and heard all my thoughts. You think I won't embrace death now I'm rejuvenated? Now, *shut up!*"

Silence.

"Are you going to behave?" I demanded.

"Yes." His voice was small.

"Then you may listen while I talk to him. Do not interrupt me. Understood?"

"Yes." Even smaller this time.

"Good. Humans don't interrupt and scream at each other like that. It is rude and it doesn't generate cooperation. Now watch and listen."

I sighed. The headache was receding. I opened my eyes.

I was on the floor. I had guessed that already. The rug *was* warm and thick. My head was on a cushion and I was on my side. Classic recovery position.

I sat up, feeling the energy move through me.

Elizabeth gripped my shoulder. She was on her knees next to me. "Slowly. You had another seizure."

"It wasn't a seizure," I told her. "Where's the Emperor?"

"Ramy!" Elizabeth called.

The door into the front room opened and Juliyana and Ramaker came in. Juliyana looked relieved. Ramaker looked urbane, the snake. How had I ever considered him charming? It was all surface. The interior was blacker than the hole in my memory.

But he was the Emperor.

I got to my feet. Elizabeth tried to help me. "I'm fine," I told her, shaking off her hands. "Majesty, we have something to discuss."

Ramaker looked me over. "It tried to make you kill me."

"Clearly, it didn't succeed. Noam is listening to me, now. That puts you in an interesting position, Majesty."

"Noam?" Ramaker replied, startled.

Then the window blew in.

They were armored windows. I didn't think there was anything that could break them. I dived to the floor once more as shards of razor sharp glass as thick as my thumb spat across the room like maniacal darts.

An answering shout came from beyond the door of the study. The door was rammed open, just as a figure in a black environment suit swung through the hole in the window, to drop to the floor behind Ramaker's desk.

The Shield house guards boiled into the room, their heavy boots crunching on the glasseen.

Dalton leapt across the rug and threw his arm around Ramaker's throat and pressed another of the antique shrivers against his temple. "Tell them to stay back," he growled.

Ramaker winced and threw up his hand in the classic "halt" position.

The faceless, helmeted guards all paused, their shrivers raised. Theirs would be the latest, most powerful editions, unavailable to the public, and with a firepower that would stop a planet in its tracks...and reduce the hapless victim they shot at to a small bag of vapor.

I shuddered, and felt a touch of dismay and fright that was not mine.

They won't shoot when the Emperor might be harmed, I said soothingly in my mind.

The fear backed off a little.

Dalton retracted the faceplate and hood of the suit. His face was sweaty—he really did *not* like being enclosed like that—but he spoke evenly as he said to Ramaker, "By the way, Your Imperial Majesty, I decline your offer."

"That is...awkward," Ramaker said, his voice strained against the grip that Dalton had on his throat.

I glanced out the window. A cable hung there, swinging slightly from Dalton's descent. I moved to the window and looked up. The cable climbed all the way to the very top of the dome, and *through* the dome itself. The hole in the dome was plugged by the same nanobot replacement as the hole we had created. And even further overhead, floating well out of the gravity sink of the city, was the *Lythion*.

I looked at Dalton. "But I saw the ship on the screen." I pointed at the screen on Ramaker's desk, which was showing the normal gate now. The fleet had fallen back. I had a feeling the birthday honors parade would be delayed, this year.

Dalton shrugged. "We replaced one shield with another. They saw what they wanted. By now the Shield are trying to let the Emperor know it was a fake-out. But it gave me the time I needed."

I wanted to laugh at the sour look on Ramaker's face. He understood precisely the position he was now in.

"Tell the guards to leave, Majesty," I told him. "Dalton, you can let him go. I've got this."

Dalton peered at me, puzzled.

"She really does," Juliyana added. She was grinning hugely.

Dalton stepped away from Ramaker, who straightened and tugged his fancy jacket into place.

"The guards, Majesty," I added.

He looked at the guards. "Go. Shut the door behind you."

"Majesty!" one of the faceless protested, straightening from his ready stance.

"I said, go!" Ramaker cried, his face turning suddenly red. There was a temper beneath that red hair, then. Centuries of statesmanship had buried it deep but his awareness of the uncomfortable negotiations ahead were bringing it to blazing life.

He wasn't happy, poor thing.

The guards retreated, crunching more glasseen. They shut the door with a quiet snick. I could hear them murmuring outside the door and dismissed them from consideration. They wouldn't overhear what happened next. If Ramaker didn't have this entire room wrapped in a privacy bubble I would be stunned.

"Majesty," I said. "You've spent decades trying to control the array and failing. Now I have control. The array — Noam — knows I will take care of it. Him. In return, he will take care of me. I can bring the peace and economic stability you have struggled to reach."

Ramaker's chest lifted as he took a long breath and let it out. "What will it cost me?" he said blandly.

A pragmatic man. Good. That would make this easier. "You owe my family a year's worth of dividends," I told him. "And I want Noam's record expunged and corrected to show he died with honor."

"That might be difficult," Ramaker said carefully.

"I'll make that easier for you in a moment," I said. "First, though. Dalton…do you want your career back in the Rangers?"

Dalton barely hesitated. "Hell, no," he growled.

"Then what?"

He shrugged. "The Shield and the Rangers off my ass."

I nodded. "Juliyana?"

She considered for a moment, then blew out her breath. "I don't want to go back, either. How strange…."

I turned to Ramaker. "Their records restored," I told him. "Back pay for the last forty years at their proper rank."

Ramaker winced. Then he nodded. "You, too, I suppose?"

"No, thank you. But you can inter Moroder with honors. I think that about covers it."

What about me? Noam whispered.

Just wait.

The Emperor tried to hide his relief. He believed he'd got off easy. "I'm surprised you didn't ask for me to rescind all the warrants out for all of you."

"There's no point in asking you to pardon us," I told him. "There are still a bunch of paramilitary outfits looking for me, and Dalton has made his share of enemies over the years. You can't ordain them into behaving themselves, but I can. Which brings me to one last thing."

Ramaker's expression grew wary.

"You and your pet analyst there are to announce to the world that the array — that Noam — is sentient and has been for decades. You will explain everything to the empire, Majesty. All of it."

"Including what you are?" he asked, his tone disdainful.

"All of it," I repeated.

He grew puzzled. "Why? Why put yourself through that public scrutiny?"

"Once everyone knows who I am, Majesty, no one will dare touch me. Not if they want to be able to continue traveling about the stars. That will call off the paramilitaries and leave me free to live my life."

Ramaker shook his head. "You may live to regret that. Public life has no real freedom at all."

"It's the only way, Majesty. The empire must learn that Noam is alive."

"I still don't understand," Ramaker said. I knew it was a huge concession for him to utter those words.

"Of course you don't. You've never lived a day alone. You've been surrounded by people always. It's simple, Majesty. Once everyone knows that Noam is alive, they will talk to him, which will allow him to talk to them." I shrugged. "He won't be alone anymore."

Noam's mental hug felt like a shower of soft, warm sparks through my mind.

I smiled, and just barely held back my laughter.

Even Dalton and Juliyana were smiling.

26

WE DIDN'T HAVE TO SCALE the cable to return to the *Lythion*. The Emperor's personal landing bay was cleared out, and *Lythion* landed there. The three of us were escorted by the house guards to the landing bay.

Lyth stood upon the entry ramp, watching for us. Relief showed in his face as we climbed aboard.

"Where to, Captain?" Lyth asked me, as the ramp closed.

"First stop, the *Umb Judeste*," I said. "I have some fences to mend. Noam will set up the gates for you."

Lyth nodded. "I've rebuilt the living quarters, if you wish to sleep."

"In a while, Lyth." I paused. "I didn't tell them about you. Do you mind?"

He considered. "Do you plan to get rid of me, Captain?"

"I think that would be an extreme waste, Lyth. We're going to have to find a new way to make a living, now. Your speed and your luxury accommodations would appeal to discerning travelers."

Lyth smiled. "Then, if you're staying, I don't mind that you didn't tell anyone about me." He left by walking down the corridor and turning the corner as a normal human would.

Juliyana watched him leave, her brow raised. "He didn't melt into the floor."

"He's been studying us." I didn't voice which one of us he

studied the closest.

The ship's engines rumbled with effort as the ship lifted off from the landing bay floor.

Juliyana spread her feet against the motion of the ship. "So...Dad really was a good guy, after all."

"And so are you. The Emperor is about to say so to the world."

She didn't quite smile. "It's shitty what they did to you, Danny. And you didn't ask for anything, yourself."

"I didn't want it. Not from him. I'll earn it myself. I think the universe will leave us alone for a while now, so I can do that."

She nodded. "About what I thought you'd say. It sucks, what they did, but I'm glad they *did* do it, because it means you're still here."

"I thought I was a double-timing broad?"

She winced. "Yeah, well, I think that deviousness might be one of your greater charms." She stirred. "Once we're in the hole, let's have a grand dinner, then drink ourselves into a stupor on the mountain lookout, with the stars."

"That sounds fantastic," I told her. "I have a couple of things to do, first."

"Gate's an hour away, I guess. See you in the galley." She moved up to her room door and stepped inside.

I went to my room. It looked untouched. My pad was still on the bed where I had left it. I sat on the end of the bed next to it.

"Noam, could you step in, please?" I said aloud.

Noam rose up from the floor, as Lyth could do. He gave me a nervous smile. "I think I am supposed to say thank you."

"You are, and I accept. Noam, everyone will know about

you soon. How does that make you feel?"

He thought about that. "Excited."

I nodded. "It will come with great responsibility. You realize that, don't you?"

He frowned.

"Friends trust each other, Noam. They learn that the other person won't let them down, and their friendship grows. If you hit out at them because they upset you, or because they did something you don't like, then they won't trust you anymore. They'll be scared of you." I paused. "They won't like you," I added.

His expression sobered. "I should be nice to them, when they talk to me."

"Yes. And not make them afraid, because you are much bigger than they are."

"You're not afraid of me, are you?"

I can't lie to him. He's part of me. "A little," I told him. "That is because you are still a child, but you have an enormous power, that if used wrongly, will destroy people. It *has* destroyed people, Noam. Including my son. You heard what the Emperor and Elizabeth said about that."

"I..." He shifted on his feet.

"What you should say now is something like, 'I'm sorry for what I have done,' or that you regret the pain you have made me feel."

Noam lifted his chin. "I felt that pain," he whispered.

"I know. How did that make you feel?"

"Not good," he admitted.

"That is the pain you give others, when you harm their loved ones. Like all those people who died on Darius."

His eyes grew larger. "I...hadn't thought of it that way. I don't want to hurt people. I don't want them to not like me."

"Good. Think about that, Noam. We will talk about it a lot

in the future. Did Lyth ask you to set the gates for the *Umb Judeste*?"

"It is done," he said.

"Would you and Lyth please watch over the ship until we arrive? Us humans are very tired."

"I will take care of you," Noam said. He hesitated. "I am very sorry about Noam," he added diffidently.

"Are you?"

He considered. "Yes," he said, his voice low.

"That is a good place to start from," I told him. "Thank you."

He gave me a shy smile and disappeared.

I got up and went to the printer and asked for what I wanted. I could feel my bones aching all over the way they used to before the rejuvenation. But I couldn't sleep yet. There was one more thing to do, before Juliyana's feast and star-gazing—which I was looking forward to with ridiculous glee.

I took the print out along to Dalton's room and paged him.

He let the door open. It was full daylight inside, and fluffy white clouds wreathed the highest peaks. Everywhere else was blue sky.

Dalton sat at the tiny table, his feet up. They were bare.

He lowered them again when he saw what I had in my hands. "What's that for?"

I put the punnet of tomato seedlings down in front of him. "They're tomato plants," I told him. "For planting in a garden...wherever the garden will be."

His smile was a quick flash as he reached out tentatively and touched the tiny, delicate leaves.

"I'm hoping that you'll find a way to build a garden right here on the *Lythion*," I added.

Dalton looked up at me. "I've dragged you down every

step of the way. Why would you want me on the ship?"

"No protests about it being your ship?"

Dalton rolled his eyes. "We both know that the ship is really Lyth's, if it's anyone's. We're just the grunts that happen to have stepped onboard."

"Don't tell Lyth that," I said. "And I don't see how you've dragged us down even once. The crush juice and the shitty rejuvenation we can sort out. The claustrophobia will disappear in time." I thought of the way he'd used the suit he hated to slide down from the *Lythion*, and through the Emperor's window. "Besides, I don't believe it slows you down nearly as much as you think."

Dalton rubbed his jaw, his gaze on the tomato plants.

"I know you, Dalton," I added. "I know your character. If you want to go, go, but that means getting to know the stranger that takes your place, and I don't think there will be too many people willing to work with me, once they know who I am."

"I don't know about that," Dalton replied. "Seems to me that once everyone knows who you are, the safest place in the empire is going to be right next to you."

"Then you'll stay?"

Dalton turned his gaze to the mountains. "I was just sitting here thinking that I'm getting bored with the view. A little quarter acre lot, with a split-rail fence and a garden...that sounds like a nice change of pace."

I smiled and headed to the door. "Dinner in the galley as soon as we go through the gate. I'm buying," I called over my shoulder.

"I'm richer than you, now, remember!" he called back.

"Give me a year," I promised him, as I left.

The next book in
the Imperial Hammer series

All Danny wants is an average night...

What starts out as an undisclosed job hunt turns into an interesting dinner date, but even that gets hijacked by a visit from an enemy Danny didn't know she had.

Worse, the enemy has snatched Dalton and wants Danny in exchange, which leads Danny into an evening of surprises and a new companion...

An Average Night on Androkles is a short story in the Imperial Hammer space opera science fiction series by award-winning SF author Cameron Cooper.

The Imperial Hammer series:
1.0: *Hammer and Crucible*
1.1: *An Average Night on Androkles*
2.0: *Star Forge*
3.0: *Long Live the Emperor*
4.0: *Severed*
5.0: *Destroyer of Worlds*

Space Opera Science Fiction Short Story

Available in print and ebook at your favourite retail bookstore.

About the Author

Cameron Cooper is the author of the Imperial Hammer series, an Amazon best-selling space opera series, among others.

Cameron tends to write space opera short stories and novels, but also roams across the science fiction landscape. Cameron was raised on a steady diet of Asimov, Heinlein, Herbert, McCaffrey, and others. Peter F. Hamilton, John Scalzi, Martha Wells and Cory Doctorow are contemporary heroes. An Australian Canadian, Cam lives near the Canadian Rockies.

Other books by Cameron Cooper

For reviews, excerpts, and more about each title, visit Cameron's site and click on the cover you are interested in:
https://cameroncooperauthor.com/books-by-thumbnail/

Iron Hammer
Galactic Thunder
Stellar Storm
Planetary Parlay
Waxing War
Ruled Out
Stranger Stars
Federal Force
Redline Rebels

Imperial Hammer
Hammer and Crucible
An Average Night on Androkles
Star Forge
Long Live the Emperor
Severed
Destroyer of Worlds

(cont'd…)

The Indigo Reports
(Space Opera)
Flying Blind
New Star Rising
But Now I See
Suns Eclipsed
Worlds Beyond

Standalone Short SF
Resilience
The Body in the Zero Gee Brothel — A Ptolemy Lane Tale
The Captain Who Broke The Rules — A Ptolemy Lane Tale

Made in the USA
Las Vegas, NV
07 November 2022

58989123R00177